Also by Jenny Zhang

Dear Jenny, We Are All Find

Sour Heart

Sour Heart

Stories

Jenny Zhang

LENNY

NEW YORK

2018 Lenny Trade Paperback Edition

Published in the United States by Lenny, an imprint of Random House, a division of Penguin Random House LLC, New York.

LENNY and the colophon are trademarks of Penguin Random House LLC.

Originally published in hardcover by Lenny, an imprint of Random House, a division of Penguin Random House LLC, New York, in 2017.

The following stories have been previously published in different form: "The Empty the Empty the Empty" in *Diagram*, "We Love You Crispina" in *Glimmer Train*, "You Fell into the River and I Saved You!" in *The Iowa Review*, and "The Evolution of My Brother" in *Rookie*.

LIBRARY OF CONGRESS CATALOGING-IN-PUBLICATION DATA
Names: Zhang, Jenny, author.
Title: Sour heart: stories / Jenny Zhang.
Description: New York: Lenny, [2017]
Identifiers: LCCN 2016058411 | ISBN 9780399589409 (pbk.) |
ISBN 9780399589393 (ebook)
Subjects: | BISAC: FICTION / Literary. | FICTION / Short Stories (single author). |
FICTION / Coming of Age. | GSAFD: Bildungsromans.
Classification: LCC PS3626.H36 A6 2017 | DDC 813/.6—dc23
LC record available at https://lccn.loc.gov/2016058411

Printed in the United States of America on acid-free paper

randomhousebooks.com

246897531

Book design by Diane Hobbing

For my mother and my father

Contents

Sour Heart

We Love You Crispina

Back when my parents and I lived in Bushwick in a building sandwiched between a drug house and another drug house, the only difference being that the dealers in the one drug house were also the users and so more unpredictable, and in the other the dealers were never the users and so more shrewd—back in those days, we lived in a one-bedroom apartment so subpar that we woke up with flattened cockroaches in our bedsheets, sometimes three or four stuck on our elbows, and once I found fourteen of them pressed to my calves, and there was no beauty in shaking them off, though we strove for grace, swinging our arms in the air as if we were ballerinas. Back then, if one of us had to take a big dump, we would try to hold it in and run across the street to the bathroom in the Amoco station, which was often slippery from the neighborhood hoodlums who used it and sprayed their pee everywhere, and if more than one of us felt the stirrings of a major shit declaring its intention to see the world beyond our buttholes, then we were in trouble because it meant someone had to use our perpetually clogged toilet, which wasn't capable of handling anything more than mice pellets, and we would have to dip into our supply of old toothbrushes and chopsticks to mash our king-sized shits into smaller pieces since we were too poor and too irresponsible back then to afford even a toilet plunger and though my mom and dad had put it on their list of "things we need to buy immediately or else we've just lost all human dignity," somehow at the end of every month we'd be a hundred dollars short and couldn't pay the gas bill in full, or we'd owe twenty dollars to a friend here and ten to a friend there and so on, until it all got so messy that I felt there was no way to really account for our woes, though secretly I blamed myself for instigating all our downward spirals, like the time I asked my father if he would buy me an ice-cream cone with sprinkles, which made him realize I had been waiting all month to ask and he felt so sorry for me that he decided to buy me not only an ice cream with sprinkles but a real rhinestone anklet that sure as hell was not on the list of "things we need to buy immediately or else we've just lost all human dignity," and that was the sort of rhythm my family fell into—disastrous and depressing in our inability to get ahead—and that was why we were never able to afford a toilet plunger and why our butts were punished so severely in those years when it wasn't as simple as, Hey, I'm going to take a crap now, see you in thirty seconds, it was more like, I'm going to take a crap now, where's my coat and my shoes and also that shorter scarf that won't dangle its way into the toilet and where's the extra toilet paper in case the Indian guy forgot to stock the bathroom again (he always forgot), and later, when we finally moved, when we finally got the hell out of there, it still wasn't simple either, but at least we could take shits at our own convenience, and that was nothing to forget about or diminish.

Before Bushwick, we lived in East Flatbush (my parents and I called it E Flat because we loved the sound of E Flat on the piano and we liked recasting our world in a more beautiful, melodious light) for a year and a half on a short little street with lots of stoops that needed fixing. We knew everyone on our street, not by name or by way of actually talking to them, but we knew their faces and we knew to nod and mouth, "hi, hi, hi," or sometimes just "hi, hi," or "hi!" but always something.

Our neighbors were island people from Martinique and Trinidad and Tobago. A couple of them confronted my father one evening to set the record straight that they weren't Dominicans. We're West Indians, they said. Tell your kids that. My father came home confused by the entire interaction, but later my mom and I figured they must have been referring to those asshole Korean kids who lived a little ways down from us and hung around outside their apartments wearing baseball caps with the bill unbent and pants that sagged around their knees, calling out whatever pitiful insults they could think of. Once, when I was walking home from the bus stop, they yelled, "Yo, it's the rape of Nanking! It's really the rape of Nanking!" as if yelling out the name of a terrible war crime had the ability to scare me when I was nine and had been loved my entire life by parents who vowed daily to spend their whole lives protecting me, and though in 1992 it was true that I was a small, unexceptional thing, one thing I never was was scared. Those Korean kids were goons who were going to end up dead or incarcerated or dead one day, and my parents and I loathed them and loathed being confused or associated with them just because to everyone else in our neighborhood, we were the same.

The Martinicans and the Trinidadians were the kind of people who acted like their homeland would always form a small, missing, and necessary bone in their bodies that caused them ghostly aches for as long as they were alive and away from home, and it bothered me how they clung to their pasts and acted like bygone times were better than what was happening in the here and now. They were always having cookouts in the summer and dressing in bright colors as if our streets were lined with coconut-bearing palm trees and not trash and cigarette butts and spilled food. Eventually though, I came to admire them greatly, especially the women because they had such enviable asses, which caused their belts to dip into a stretched-out V right at the spot where their cheeks met, and I used to follow that V with my eyes and so did the men, who apparently never got bored of seeing it either.

My mom had no such ass, but commanded attention anyway. The men on our block liked to stare at my mom whenever she walked past—fixed, long, concentrated gazes. Maybe it was because her hair was so straight and long and fell down her back like heavy curtains and she had skin so white that it reminded me of vanilla ice cream. That was why I drew little cones all over her arms, which she let me do because my mom let me do anything as long as it made me happy.

"What makes you happy makes Mommy happy," she would always say to me, sometimes in Chinese, which I wasn't so good at, but I tried for her and for my father, and when I couldn't, I would answer them in English, which I also wasn't so good at, but it was understood that while I could still improve in either language, my parents could not, they were on a road to nowhere, the wall was right up against them, so it was up to me to get really good, it was up to me to shine and that scared me because I wanted to stay behind with them, I didn't want to go any further than they could go.

Sometimes, I would forget what I was supposed to say after she said something like that and I would say the wrong thing, like, "And what makes me happy is eating ice cream. Mrs. Lancaster can go suck it. Who cares if I don't show the work? I still got all the right answers. She's a tool, Mom."

"Sour girl," my mom said. "If your teacher asks you to show work, then show the work. Can't you speak anymore without using ugly words? And I take it that what makes your mommy happy doesn't make you happy? Am I right, sours?"

"No," I said. "I'm sorry, I meant what makes you happy makes me happy too. I just forgot to say it." It embarrassed me whenever my mom or my dad trumped me (although it was never on purpose) with how thoughtful they were, and by comparison, how thoughtless and selfish I had been in only thinking of myself when it seemed like every second of every day my parents were planning to undergo yet another sacrifice to make our lives that much better, and no matter how diligently I tried to keep up, there was always so much that was indiscernible. It was so hard to keep track of every detail, like how my parents shared the same pair of dress shoes, alternating their schedules so my father could wear them during the day and my mother at night even though they were four sizes too big for her and that was why she tripped so often and had so many scrapes on her body.

There were so many days when I came home to an empty house with nothing at all to distract me except an oozy desire to come up with all the ways I could possibly sacrifice enough to catch up to my parents, who were always sacrificing. But I didn't know how I could compete with my mom, who got fired from her job baking donuts after spending a night scavenging for a desk so that I wouldn't have to do my homework on the floor or the bed or standing up with my workbook pressed against the wall, and how she found me a beautiful desk that was perfect except someone had sprayed FUCK YA MOMMA on the side of the desk, and how she dragged it down twenty-something blocks on her own and was too exhausted to wake up in time for work, and that was why she was fired and why she couldn't ever keep a job because she was so tired all the time from taking care of me. Or how was I supposed to compete with my father, who was so good about not wasting a single thing, like how when I was four, I used to always throw up my food and no one was able to figure out why except maybe it had something to do with how the previous year, my parents and I left the only country we had ever known to come to this one, or maybe it had to do with the time I caught severe pneumonia after my mom put me in a beautiful blue tiered-lace dress for my first birthday in the United States in the middle of a snowstorm in December without a proper coat or tights, and I had to spend a month recovering in a hospital even though we couldn't afford more than a night, and the bills from that were part of the reason why, for so long, my parents had to work three jobs at a time and even then, still couldn't seem to get a leg up on their various loans—official and unofficial. After my bout of pneumonia, I was terrible at keeping food down and there were times when my dad would spoon the food I had vomited up directly into his own mouth so that not a single morsel of food went wasted because back then we had strict daily portions of what we could afford and the only way to replace the food I had vomited up was for my father to give me his portion of breakfast or lunch or dinner while he had my regurgitated rice and vegetables and pork—*that* was how much he was willing to sacrifice for us.

When I got home from school (if I went to school that day),

I would sometimes wait, slumped against the wall, for my parents to come home with a box of donuts at one in the morning, or leftover mei fun at eleven at night, or a pair of earrings with the paint peeling off from when my mom worked as a seamstress for a woman named Donna who gave my mom treats to give to me because she liked how I wore my bangs so high and pouffed and how I thanked her a million times whenever I went with my mom to work, and as I waited those six or seven hours alone in the apartment, I wondered what I could do to show my mom and dad that I, too, was part of this amazing, intricate machine that saved us from the kind of utter and complete desperation that coincides with everything falling the fuck apart.

Even though my mother was the sum total of everything you could ever ask for in a person, my dad was born with a wandering eye and would die with his eyeballs lolling around, still frantically on the lookout for attractive women, or at least that was what my mom told me. Shortly after we were kicked out of our Flatbush apartment and found the class A steaming heap of dung apartment in Bushwick, my dad started dating a woman he met through one of his waitering jobs, at the Chinese noodle house where he worked the late-night shift on weekends and holidays.

Her name was Lisa and she was from Taiwan. She wasn't beautiful, not like my mom who had eyes that reflected the moon, even in the daytime, and not like my mom who had thin arms and wore dresses all the time, even in the winter, and not like my mom who had a long high neck that made her look unapproachable; my dad's girlfriend was short, like a broken tree trunk, and she had big breasts but that was all she had going for her. She wore heavy perfume that made her smell like the unwashed armpit of someone who, after running a half-marathon, had foolishly thought rubbing a bunch of flowers into their pits would mask the stink, but it was like my mother always said, "You can't wash a turd with soap and expect it to smell nice."

The first time she came over to our apartment, I couldn't stop sneezing because her perfume was so strong and I was allergic to artificial scents and bitchy dopeheads who had no business spending time with my dad. My dad introduced her to me as, "Your auntie Lisa."

"She's not my auntie, Dad." I looked at Lisa; her big stupid knockers hung down very low and I wanted to kick them back toward her face. "I'll call her nothing, thank you very much."

After that, she would come over every now and then, always when my mom wasn't there, although my mom knew and it wasn't a secret, it was just one of those arrangements where one person got what she wanted at everyone else's expense. Of course, Lisa didn't give a rat about me or my mom and probably not my dad either, she was just a desperately lonely person who needed to be part of someone else's world. She pretended to be nice to me when she came over, sometimes offering me sandwiches or once, she brought over a blender and asked me if I wanted a milkshake, and I told her I was picky about my food, and she asked me what I meant, and I said, I mean I only like the food my mom makes and I only hate the food that people I hate make, and she said, Oh, suit yourself, and I said, Your perfume makes me sneeze, did you know that? and she said, I'm sorry, but I can't do anything about that.

Yes, you can, you cunt, I mumbled.

What was that? she said and after that, there was just silence.

I prayed nightly for her to be attacked and maimed on her

way to our apartment in Bushwick, but she always made it intact, ruining my afternoon when I got home from school and found her already in our house, waiting for my dad to show up, sitting on the couch cushion that we pretended was a regular couch and not just a bunch of cushions on our floor, flipping through TV shows and making it seem like she wanted me to choose which program to watch, but the minute I got up for a snack, she'd immediately change the channel, and when I returned, she'd say, "Oh, I thought you didn't want to watch that show anymore, so I switched over."

I told my father that I hated seeing Lisa in the apartment, but what I really meant was that I hated Lisa, period, and he told me to try for him and I said, But why shouldn't Lisa try for me? Why do I have to try for her? and my father said, Not for her, for me, and she did try, sour gummy. She brought you that bicycle, didn't she?

It was a boy's bicycle and it used to belong to her kid who was all grown up and probably hated her for giving away his bike. I never used it even though I wanted a bicycle so bad for so long because I wanted things to happen for the right reasons.

My mom didn't complain about my dad's girlfriend. He always had one, it turned out, I just never knew about the others because I never knew all the things that went on between my mom and my dad, but my mom knew and she accepted them and she told me not to sweat things like that because we still had each other, he still came home to us, he still loved us more than anyone else, we were still his number-one girls.

My dad's girlfriend entered our lives at the worst possible time: I was finishing up third grade and we were dead broke after my dad's school was shut down and my dad decided he would never teach again and my mom lost her receptionist job on top of us having to move to Bushwick because we had lost our deposit on the apartment in East Flatbush due to our landlord being crooked and punishing us unfairly for not paying three months' rent because my mom's mom in China was dying of cancer and my mom had spent three months' salary on flying back to see her mother at the end of her days.

On the day we moved out, our landlord was watching us from his window (he lived on the third floor, right above us) the whole time, and I stuck my middle finger up at him and yelled, "Have some compassion, you shriveled-up cock. Haven't you ever known someone who's died?" while my parents were securing our two mattresses to the top of our maroon Oldsmobile.

"Leave that old dried-up worm alone," my mom told me, patting down my hair and pulling my fingers out of their clenched positions.

"I hate him."

"Us too, my sour apple. Us too. But what's done is done, sourheart. Don't you see? Everything happens for a reason. Everything happens for a good reason and we have to be patient if we want to find out what that good reason is. Do you see?"

I saw. I didn't know how my parents felt about moving so often. Sometimes we lived in four or five places in the span of a few months. Our possessions were whatever we could fit into our car and strap onto the roof, but all the same, I couldn't help but feel a surge of excitement every time we left a place, like it was the first day of school and there was still a chance for me to not be so much of a fuckup and that chance only existed in the window between when I sat down at my new desk for the first time and when my teacher introduced herself and gave out the first homework of the year—it was like that each time we loaded up our car and started driving to the next place and the next place and the next, and in a way it wasn't so bad, it just meant there was no such thing as failure, only starting over a million times and then some.

Then there was one year, the year when I had to repeat first grade because I hadn't done any assignments and failed all of my tests because the most effort I ever put forth was toward drawing trees that looked like broccoli on all of my exams, when we lived in Williamsburg, and it was a good year because my dad found a room with a shared kitchen and a private bathroom for $200 a month, and in that room, I slept between my parents every night and often woke up with long scratch marks up and down my legs and arms because I was born itchy as all hell and I would die itchy as all hell unless a crafty genius somewhere decided to invent a miracle drug that would save me from this long and itchy life.

    The worst of it was when I was five and we lived in Washington Heights in a shared room that was all mattress and no floor and my skin itched like there were little tiny ants carrying sticks of fire and doing somersaults and cartwheels all over my body. Everyone said it was normal to go through hell your first year in America, but no one prepped us for our second. I had placed out of ESL after the first few weeks of kindergarten, but when I changed schools in January after my parents heard about a room in Washington Heights that was so cheap it was practically illegal (and many years later, at a dinner party, a young housing rights lawyer, who had been avidly listening to my father tell the story of our first years in America, interrupted him to say, "You know that living situation actually *was* illegal"), the administrators of my new school insisted I needed more ESL. "Her grasp of English is not firm," the principal said. So I was stupid again, even though I was sure that I wasn't. My itching came back with a

vengeance—it hadn't been that bad since the six months before my family immigrated to New York.

At night, my skin burned in that cramped room with five
mattresses on the floor all pushed up against each other, my
mom and dad and me on one mattress, and my mom's childhood friend Shao Guoqiang and his wife and kid occupying
the two mattresses next to us. They had grown up together in
the same longtang and he had been instrumental in advising
us through the whole visa process since he was one of the first
to immigrate to the U.S. and everyone had been impressed
until we heard that he had abandoned his studies in painting
and sculpture and was barely supporting himself, buying
umbrellas at wholesale prices from Chinese exporters and
selling them on the street when it rained. He had been the
one to tell us about this room in Washington Heights, which
had been previously occupied by several Chinese graduate
students in the Columbia visual arts program who fled the
country suddenly because of some shady situation with expired visas. His wife, Li Huiling, supposedly made an avant-
garde film about "the poetics of imperialism" back in
Shanghai but had given up her dreams of smashing Western
imperialism with art since becoming the mother to a very
hyper five-year-old boy, and if that wasn't enough to stop
her, being five months pregnant was probably gonna do it
("Can you name her Annie if she's a girl?" I asked, after
watching Annie in a Nobody Beats the Wiz store while sitting
in a shopping cart that my parents left in front of an aisle of
TVs so they could go and do this scam where they noncha-
lantly grabbed small items like Discmans and batteries and
then walked right up to the cash register to return them for
credit, which they then used to buy something expensive,
which they then returned for cash). On the third mattress
from us was my dad's friend Zhang Jianjun, who was an ESL

schoolteacher taking night classes in business management and accounting, and his wife, Lu Shiyu, who came from a family of diplomats and professors and poets who turned up their noses at the thought of their daughter being married to a wannabe mercenary, and they were a somber couple because they had left their daughter behind with her grandparents when she was only two while they saved up money to bring her to the U.S. and it had been several years and they still couldn't afford to send for her. And on the fourth and farthest mattress away from us were Wang Tao and his wife, Liu Xiaohong, whose mother was apparently a very high-up Communist leader during the Cultural Revolution and had been directly responsible for many people's deaths, at least that was what I gathered from sleeping between my mom and my dad who whispered through me like I was air, like I was their phone cord, like I was what carried their voices to each other, especially when I pretended to lie there still and sleeping—that was when they would say everything to each other and even though they didn't know it, I was part of it too. That was the year when my skin itched the most, and my parents wondered if it was because we were sleeping ten to a room that should have had two, and whenever I scratched or whined or made an annoying sound like, "Ahhh-grrrrrrrrrraaaaaaaad, I hate itchiiiiiiiiiiiiiing," the daughter of diplomats and the ESL schoolteacher and the avant-garde filmmaker and the painter and the husband of the woman whose mother supposedly tortured and killed hundreds of "intellectuals and bourgeois effetes" would scold me and my parents, "Haven't you learned to control her yet? Can't you see we're trying desperately to sleep in the middle of the night?" and it put pressure on my parents, who at the time had no choice but to live like that, and on me, who had no choice but to be so itchy that I had to cry out in the middle of the night.

We lasted eight months before moving to a shared room in Chinatown with a broken window we covered with duct tape. It became unbearably cold once winter hit so we packed up and crashed on the floor of my mom's friend's apartment in Woodside for five weeks before we were found out by her landlord who threatened to evict all of us, which severed my mom's friendship with her friend who hadn't really wanted us to stay with her in the first place. After Woodside we moved to another floor, this time in my mom's cousin's friend's sister's apartment in Ocean Hill that would have been perfect except for the nights when rats ran over our faces while we were sleeping and even on the nights they didn't, we were still being charged twice the cost of a shitty motel just to stay there and when my father said to our host, I get the feeling you don't want us here, our host said, I get the feeling you aren't very grateful, so we got out of there and then tried to live in my mom's cousin's house while my mom's cousin was in Shaoxing visiting relatives, which was all right except that it was right next to the Cypress Hills Cemetery, which spooked my mom and me, and then finally at the end of first grade, right after I found out I was being left back, my dad found a really nice room for rent in Williamsburg. A deity must have been watching over us then, because not only was it the best room we'd ever lived in but the landlord also threw in a free microwave and a queen-sized bed that had bedbugs we were responsible for getting rid of if we wanted it (of course we did) and on the day we moved in my mom declared as we walked into our shared kitchen, "We need to buy a toy for our little sour grape. I say a stuffed teddy bear that's taller than me."

"And I say we fill this half of the freezer with vanilla-bean ice cream," my dad said.

"Both!" I cried out. We ended up getting one carton of

vanilla-bean ice cream and a teddy bear that came up to my forehead when I placed him on the ground.

The year we spent in Williamsburg was my least itchy year, and also the best for all the other ailments that I was afflicted with: my allergies to dust, cats, dogs, pollen, all types of nuts, perfume, anything that had a strong odor, the air after it rained, the air when it hadn't rained for a long time, anything that was warm and necessary for winter like sweaters or wool coats or stockings or mittens or socks. Everything got calmer. I was doing well in school for the first time, turning in most of my homework, and I even got a 95 on a math test, which had never happened before, and we all joked that it was a blessing for me to have been left back because it was better to do something right the second time around than to get away with doing it wrong the first time, although it wasn't a joke, it was just the truth and the truth was also that we were happy to have our own place again and not worry so much about where we were going to sleep.

At night, if I was itchy, my mom would scratch my left leg and my dad would scratch my right leg while I slept with double protection—I wore oven mitts on both my hands, and on top of that, my parents tied a plastic bag around my wrists with a rubber band so that I wouldn't scratch myself bloody in my sleep. In the mornings, my parents woke up with blood underneath their fingernails, dried and dark as a scab even though I was the one who had been wounded. Sometimes, I looked like the victim, long lines of blood scratched up and down my legs and back and arms and chest. Once I asked my mom to scratch my nipple until it split open and I lay there in bed cradling my own tit to sleep. The next day in school I failed a test because it was hard to concentrate when my undershirt was sticking to my pussed-over nipple. Then there were the nights when my parents would fall asleep before they had sufficiently scratched me and I would have dreams of being so itchy that I rolled down entire jagged mountains to flay off my own skin. I would wake up in the morning with skin missing from my legs and arms, the pain finally superseding the itch. It was like that back then, the weird union of what was possible with what was just reverie conspired against me, turned my thoughts into blah blah blahs and my words into yadda yadda yaddas and it was why I was left back and why I liked sleeping between my parents so much—I needed to be bound by their flesh before I could materialize.

Our apartment building in Williamsburg was razed to the ground after a year. We got four thousand dollars to move out, which at the time seemed no different from a million dollars, but later we realized how paltry a sum that was and how little we had been valued. We spent the money on a one-bedroom apartment in East Flatbush. My father quit most of his part-time jobs when we moved because he finally passed his exams on the third time around and got his teaching license.

I didn't like my new school. On the first day, my teacher sent me back to ESL even though I had passed out of ESL two separate times and was referred to as "a little genius" by my first ESL teacher and as having "incredible language acquisition" by my second. It was Washington Heights all over again and though I wanted to tell my new teacher that I knew English better than her sweaty thin-lipped veiny flaccid face did, I kind of just lost the will to keep saying the same thing over and over again, so I dutifully attended ESL while everyone else was in art and music, and was forced to participate in activities so humiliating that I understood why the kids in special ed acted out all the time.

We had to do things like write out the word "chair" and

then draw a picture of a chair underneath the word, only I drew pictures of women with huge breasts, and dongs so big and fat that they went off the page because I wasn't going to let the administrators of P.S. 233 bully me just because my parents weren't present on the first day of school to tell the ladies in the main office that I was as close to a native speaker as someone who wasn't born in America could be and I had only been left back because I sucked at school in general, not at speaking English.

I hated school so much that by the time third grade rolled around I was only going to school two or three days a week. My parents let me skip whenever I wanted and they thought all of my reasons were valid, just like they thought it was okay for me to get C's and D's because they knew they weren't always there at night when I was supposed to be eating dinner with my family and they weren't there when I needed them to check over my homework and they weren't there to read me bedtime stories so I would love reading and usually they were gone before I woke up in the morning for school.

At the time, my dad was making a pretty decent salary teaching language arts at a declining middle school in East New York that was under constant threat of being shut down. It was so terrible that apparently the social studies teacher had been jumped after school by four seventh graders who shattered his knee and broke his nose, and before that, two consecutive principals resigned in the same year, and then there was a terrible rumor that one of the female teachers had been raped by a couple of eighth graders late one night in the parking lot.

The only reason I knew any of this was because my dad brought me to hang out in his classroom when I asked him to, and I knew not to ask him too many times but there was something about Thursdays that made me feel like I was born without a brain and that I would die without a brain if I had to go to school, and so there were a few Thursdays when he would take me with him to work, which was the best day of all because it was Computer Day, otherwise known as Fuck Off Day. We spent the whole day in the computer lab and all of his students, even the ones who carried knives and guns to school and tried to sell pot laced with harder stuff to fifth graders, would print out pictures of puppies snuggling with each other or outrageously cute unicorns for me because they thought I was so much smaller than most kids my age and they liked pretending I was the class baby.

"You're our pet, Christina. Pet Christina!" they said. "Get it? It's like a noun and a verb. See, Mr. Zhang? Don't be saying we never learned anything from you."

In my father's third period class there was a black girl named Darling, whose name was pronounced "Dah-ling" as if she were a character from *Gone with the Wind,* another movie I watched in The Wiz while my parents were off scamming and when they were done and came back to get me, my father remarked to my mother, "These people will never let go of the past, will they?" and I didn't know if he meant the white people in the movie or the black people, but I knew we were not "these people" and to my parents that was a good thing, but I wasn't so sure. Darling wore her hair differently every time I saw her, sometimes it was cornrows and sometimes it was big and everywhere and other times it was half cornrows, half big and everywhere, and sometimes it was straight and stiff and oily like the sheen on a cast-iron pan that had never been washed with soap. "Can I touch it?" I asked her once and she let me but added, "Don't go around asking other girls that. It's not polite."

Darling had been left back twice and was almost as tall as my mom. The first day she saw me, she grabbed my hand and told me that she was my older sister and I could ask her any-thing and if I wanted to go to the bathroom she would escort me. She was usually the first one in the computer lab and would squeal when she saw me sitting in the far right corner with my dad, playing that typing game where words fell furi-ously from the sky and you had to correctly type each one to prevent the Manhattan skyline from being destroyed by words like "rat" and "philosophy" and "torrent."

"Christina's here," she would announce and then everyone would run in and pull their seats close to me and the girls would start braiding my hair and the guys would pool together their quarters to buy me a soda (which sometimes my father allowed and sometimes didn't) and my father would shout at us to settle down at a computer station, and then finally Dar-ling would stand up and put two fingers in her mouth and whistle and say, "Everyone leave Christina alone. I'm helping her with her homework and unless you people think you know third-grade math, you better leave us alone. I know none of you know shit about math."

"Dah-ling," my father said.

"Sorry, Mr. Zhang, I didn't mean to cuss, but it's the fuckin' truth."

My dad tried to enforce the three sheets per student rule, but everything went out the window when Darling discovered how to print banners that used up thirty-plus pages. One time Darling and all the other students were huddled in a corner, whispering and being perfect students to the point where my father couldn't help but ask, "What's the occasion? Up to no good? Is that why you're all so quiet?"

They ignored me the whole class period and I was so con-fused that I almost cried and had to unpouf my bangs and let them down to cover my eyes and I was about to tell my dad that I never wanted to go to work with him again but right as the bell rang, the class presented me with a banner long enough to go around all four walls of the room, and it just said, WE LOVE YOU CRISPINA over and over again. My name was misspelled because Darling and Chadster were fighting over the keyboard and Darling pushed Chadster when he was trying to type out my name because she wanted to be the one to do it and then everyone liked the way it sounded so they just kept it that way. Darling wanted to put the banner up on the wall, but my dad refused. "Are you crazy? Get out of here. Go to your next period and stop wasting paper in my classroom."

"Sorry, Mr. Zhang," Darling said, "but this isn't your classroom anyway. It belongs to the taxpayers." Darling helped me fold up the banner in sheets of four. "Here you go, Crispy," she whispered into my ear.

"What?"

"Crispy, short for Crispina," she said, brushing her fingers gently across my bangs. "But only I get to call you that, okay?"

I threw my arms around Darling's waist, something I used to do all the time with my mom when I was really little. We'd walk around our apartment in Shanghai like that, me swinging from her waist like a monkey. You're a tree and I'm the sour fruit! I would shout in Chinese. You're the ear and I'm the earring!

"Aw," said Darling, "my pet Crispy." I glowed through the rest of the day, carrying the folded-up banner in my hands with noble attention and care, like it was a gift for the queen. My father told me to just dump it in the trash on the way to the car, but I told him I wanted to hang it up in my room.

"You want typos all over your room?"

"I like it."

"It's just so typical of these kids." He shook his head. "They don't care about doing things right. They have no standards. Where do you think they're headed?"

"Home?" I guessed.

"Nowhere. They're headed nowhere. Their lives are going nowhere."

"Oh yeah," I said, even as something soured inside me (and not in the delicious way) like it always did whenever my dad talked like that, as if he was so sure. Didn't it bother him that he was teaching his students poetry when he was certain it wouldn't make a difference in how their lives turned out? Didn't it bother him to be so sure that it was futile to even try? And what about us? What standards did we have? Weren't our fates sealed as well? What was I ever going to become? What stopped other people from looking at us and pitying us, how we didn't see the pointlessness in working so many jobs, moving from one shit place to another and scrimping on pennies, how we couldn't face the reality of our situation: that none of this was leading up to anywhere that was any different from where we had just been.

When my third-grade teacher, Mrs. Lancaster, sent my mom the FOURTH AND FINAL notice that her presence was required pronto for a parent-teacher conference or else I was in danger of being left back again, my mom tore up the notice and said, "I'm worried we aren't letting you grow up. Are we stifling your development, baby girl?"

"Let me worry about that, Mom."

"Let you worry about that? You can hardly be the one worrying about yourself."

"Why not? I know what's bad and what's good."

"Wrong," my mom said. "That's exactly what you don't know."

"How?" I asked.

"How what, my stone-tough peach?" my dad said, coming in through the front door on his day off with two bags of groceries in each hand.

"What took you so long?" I asked, running up to him. I took a bag from him and carried it to the kitchen. "Mom thinks I should sleep by myself tonight."

"You know I agree, tartberry," my dad said, unpacking the groceries, which were all nonperishables because our refrigerator wasn't working well and all the food we had bought the week before had soured.

The only good things about sleeping by myself in my own bed were, firstly, it was just a smaller mattress on the floor next to my parents' bed and, secondly, I was still close enough to hear them whispering to each other in the mornings when they thought I was still asleep. Sometimes, my fraudulent sleep lasted for what felt like hours, but there was not enough time in the world to help me understand what they were saying or what my dad was doing to make my mom slap him in that way that sounded as tender as when she stroked my hair away from my face and scratched the parts of my cheek that had gotten itchy from my loose hair, and I gave up at some point on trying to figure out their whisperings and would instead bolt straight upright and start to get dressed, knowing my mom would ask me to stop what I was doing and slide in between her and my dad just like I used to when I was itchy all the time, and I would say, "How come you don't need me to be independent now?" and she would say, "I want you to be the hot dog and your dad and I will be the bun," and I would jump in between them and my dad would say, "Or what if our lovely daughter is the turkey and you're the cheese, my lovely wife, and I'm the lettuce?"

"Then who's the bread? And who's the mayonnaise and who's the mustard?" And the work of parceling out who was who and what made each type of sandwich or burger or hot dog or any sort of meat-between-bread thing so delicious was a project that we devoted ourselves to until the morning sun became the afternoon sun and our arms were cramped from holding each other, and I knew somehow that I wasn't supposed to like this, that I was supposed to want to go over to my friend's house and I was supposed to want to paint my nails and play tag and jump rope and do the things that kids my age did, but the truth was I only ever wanted to be sandwiched between my parents, I only ever wanted them to need me and I only ever thought about them and all the ways in which I could please them or, better yet, impress them with how much I wanted to remain their daughter and how much I wanted them to remain my parents.

"You know," my mom said, "one day, you'll be a parent and you won't feel so much like our daughter."

"But you'll always be our daughter," my dad said. "And you'll still know you're our daughter."

"Of course you'll feel like our daughter. That much won't change. But you won't feel like the only thing you are in this world is our daughter."

"That's right," my father said. "Because one day you'll also feel like a mother. And the feeling of being a mother can be so much more extraordinary than the feeling of being a daughter."

"And your own daughter won't ever look at you and think that you must also be a daughter. You know what we mean, sour candy?"

"I think so," I said.

"That's why I wish you could stay this age forever," my mom said. "What if I could always be thirty-six and you could always be nine and your father could always be thirty-seven? What if, sour honeybee?"

"I'll do that," I said right away. "I'll stay nine. I don't want to be someone else's mom."

"Oh, sours, you say that now," my dad said. "You say that now, but you will not want to miss being ten and you won't want to miss being eleven and twelve and thirteen, and you won't want to miss dating boys and learning how to drive and having your first cigarette—"

"Zhang Heping," my mother said.

"Sorry." he said. "And you'll want to be twenty and you'll want to fall in love for the first time and the second time and the third and the fourth—"

"Heping," my mother said again. "So, how many times have you fallen in love? Over a hundred?"

"Just the one," my father said, drawing my mother and me closer to him.

My mother rolled her eyes. "You can't give up the rest of your life to stay this way."

"I want to. I like the idea of staying here."

"Oh, sours."

"I really do, Mom. This is what I want. To stay like this for-ever."

"Let's ask the gods for help," my father suggested.

"Okay," my mother said, and we got out of bed and into a circle, the three of us, and we stomped our feet and shouted, "Let us stay, let us stay, let us stay, let us stay," until our voices got hoarse and the next day mine was squeaky and my mom's was sultry and my dad liked the way she sounded and I saw them holding hands and my mom fixing my dad's shirt collar in the morning and I felt like this was the reason why I never wanted to get older, because why move forward when it was so brilliant to just remain as we were?

* * *

When we moved to Bushwick we all slept on the same mattress again because there wasn't room for my smaller mattress and because the hoods on our block stole it before we even had a chance to drag it up the stairs to our new apartment. They also stole my dad's car radio every few weeks and then sold it back to him on the street corner by the Jewish deli.

"It's a hundred."

"What? A hundred? I got it for ten last week."

"Times have changed, brother."

One time, the three of us came out of the subway and saw that the kids who routinely jacked our possessions were having a garage sale with stuff from our apartment.

"We can't buy everything back," my mom said, looking at our pillows and our sheets and our bowls and her winter coat and our TV (which we had found broken outside on the street on garbage day, but my dad, whose survival skills were so amazing he could learn anything just by closing his eyes and visualizing the steps, had fixed it in a week's time) and our VCR that had been given to us by my dad's restaurant boss who liked to give him things every now and then to remind my dad who was in the position of giving and who was in the position of taking.

"I'll cut a deal with them," my dad said and closed his eyes briefly to visualize his strategy and walked over to talk to the main thug, who had the whitest sneakers out of all three of them and the longest T-shirt—it went down past his shorts when he stooped. "A hundred for everything."

"Fuck you. Five hundred or get out of my face."

"Look, you've run us dry. You think we have the money?"

"You're richer than us," I yelled out and then hid behind my mom.

"So she talks," he said. "Five hundred or get out of my face.

That's the last time I'll say it. The next time, I won't be saying it."

"Look, I'll give you a hundred. That's more than you can get for this stuff."

"I don't care if I get twenty and I buy myself a shitty steak dinner, but I'm only selling this shit to you for five hundred and I told you not to ask me to say it again."

"Please," my father said.

The white-sneakers hood turned to his friends and shouted, "We in for a steak dinner. Drinks on you, shit talkers."

"Yeah, yeah, yeah," they all shouted.

"There are a couple of ways that people will always know you are my daughter," my mom used to say to me.

"What's one way?" I asked.

"One way is that we both love eating sour things."

"Okay, what's another?"

"Now, wait. Don't just brush that off. You and I love eating sour things. Sour grapes, sour plums, sour peaches, sour apples, sour cherries, sour strawberries, sour blueberries, sour nectarines, sour candies, sour soups, sour sauces, sour sour sour everything. Most people like sweet grapes and sweet peaches and sweet apples and sweet berries."

"I guess that's true," I said.

"It's remarkable, don't you see? And we also like really hard fruits."

"Yeah. True. We hate soft peaches. We hate soft, sweet peaches and we love hard, sour plums."

"That's right," my mother said. "We're two of a kind. Remember yesterday? The man outside of the subway was selling grapes. Remember that?"

"Yeah, he kept saying, Sweetest grapes you'll ever find in Brooklyn. He was like, Dontcha wanta try a sweet grape, you two sweet things?"

"So we went to look at his grapes and I said, You say they're sweet?"

"And he said, Yes, so sweet."

"And I said, You're sure they're sweet? Very, very sweet? You aren't lying to me?"

"And he said, Put it this way, there isn't a single sour grape in the lot."

"And I shook my head at him, and said, Well, you just lost our business then, because my daughter and I only like sour fruits."

"And the man started yelling after us going like, Hey hey hey EY you, EY, EY you two. Check this out, these grapes are sweet and tarty. Oh look, I'm sucking in my cheeks, it's so tart."

We laughed at our own cleverness, the little signs that proved we were running our own lives, that, in fact, what had made that day profound was that we had outsmarted the hey EY guy, and *not* that it was the day my mom lost her job working as a receptionist for a local apparel company, and *not* that it happened in the same month that my father's school finally shut down and he quit teaching because he was tired of breaking up fights and having his car broken into while he was at work and feeling like a social worker when he wasn't even fond of humanity to begin with, coming home defeated every evening and vomiting in the morning sometimes from pure anxiety for the day ahead. That this day was significant *not* because it was also the very night when my father didn't come home for dinner because he was with his girlfriend, which meant my mom and I had nothing to eat because my dad had all the cash we had left and he was supposed to come back with food for us. The two of us went hungry that evening, our stomachs aching at first from hunger, then from laughing, then again from hunger, and then later when we went to sleep we heard each other sniffling but it was the sort of night when neither of us could be moved to console the other and that was when the great depressed hollow opened up between us and remained for the duration of the night and only closed up a tiny bit when we woke up to my father standing over us, asking if he could be the top bun and if my mom could be the bottom bun and if I could be the cheese and the pickles and the burger and the ketchup and the mustard and the onions and all the things that make a cheeseburger the most astounding food in the entire world.

We left Bushwick not because we finally saved up enough money but because our apartment in Bushwick collapsed when no one was in it and the reason why no one sued or anything like that was because we were living in this house that had been divided up into four apartment units and the slumlord who owned the apartment only rented to desperate people like the Cambodian family of eight who lived above us and didn't have proper documentation, or the Cantonese ladies below us who ran a shady massage and hairstyling parlor in their living room, which my dad went to a few times for a shave and a trim, and once when he came back with a botched haircut, my mom cried and said, "You're the reason why we suffer. You're the reason we live like this and I can't do it anymore."

The only good thing about our apartment collapsing was that after we loaded up our maroon Oldsmobile to drive to my dad's former co-worker's brother-in-law's house out on Long Island (where everything was clean and there were no sidewalks, just big wide empty streets that curved into dead-ends and long-ass driveways and perfectly manicured lawns that led to massive houses that seemed haunted and unapproachable, where we had an open invitation to stay until we found another place to live) but before we got into the car, the three of us picked up the broken rubble from the street and hurled the pieces at the windows of buildings where we thought the hoods lived, the ones who assaulted our neighbor Mrs. Lili and were the reason why she moved back to Taiwan, and the reason why we were never moving out of New York, and even if we did move, it would be because we felt like it and not because we had to. I don't know if we knew that then but we must have because why else did we stay? Why else didn't we move down to North Carolina where my aunt and uncle lived in a new house at the top of a beautiful rolling hill, where they took long walks at night and never felt afraid or watched and kept their front door unlocked during the day and left valuables in their car? Why else didn't we pack up and drive down there to live the good life with them unless we were trying to stand our ground, trying to prove that we belonged here?

That must have been why we hurled the rubble at the apartment buildings where the hoods lived, the ones who stole from us and beat up our friends, the ones who smashed in our car window and bent our steering wheel all the way until the top and the bottom of the wheel touched each other like a pair of lips, and that must have been why my dad yelled out, "Why don't you wipe your assholes somewhere else because no one lives here anymore?" and my mom said, "Go eat a couple of dicks for breakfast, you assmunchers," and I said, "And wash it down with some of your own liquefied shit, you specks of crap," as if we were reading from a script. No one bothered to ask where the others had learned to talk like that.

It was obvious and we knew that one day we would forget those words and only know words like, "Would you pass the caviar?" or "Could I have another bottle of that $200 wine and yes, it's okay to waste," only it would be more refined, more natural, a manner of speaking we had not yet conceived of and so could only crudely imagine.

We jumped into the car, wild and scared. My father gunned it and we sped past yellow lights turning red and before any of us even had a chance to catch our breath, we were on the highway and the construction on both sides felt to me like the old way rebuilding itself, even though I knew nothing would ever emerge, that ten years from now, we would be on this highway again and I would see the orange vests and the safety cones and the men deep down in the ditches calling out to each other and the same old lanes, still dangerously narrow, and the traces of the faded white safety lines that we were as dependent on for marking the passage of time as scientists were dependent on the whorls in the trunks of trees to reveal the long history of what had been and what would now be.

My father wrote to his father and mother for help six weeks after our apartment in Bushwick collapsed. We took too long to find another place to live and had to leave Long Island because it was too far and too expensive to get from there to the various places in Manhattan and Queens and Brooklyn where my parents were going to get better jobs, so we took our things to Flushing and camped out in the living room of my dad's friend Xiang Bo and his wife, who said we could stay with them if we paid a third of the rent, chipped in for groceries, and did all the cleaning. Ten days later, we received an invitation from my grandparents for me to come live with them in Shanghai for a year while my parents got back on their feet.

"A child is a great expense," they wrote, "and it's unnatural for a child's paternal grandparents to die without seeing their grandchildren grow. A child should go to a good school and gain high marks, and a child should come home to adults who have already prepared a warm snack, and a child should have dinner at six-thirty sharp every evening, and a child should be put to bed by adults who love her before nine-thirty every night, and a child should wake up to a family who will all still be in the house when she leaves for school, and a child should have many beautiful and healthy friends." My mother read the letter out loud in Chinese and my father translated the parts I could not understand, although who knew what he was making up and what he was leaving out and what he himself did not have the words for.

"No," I said. "No, no, no, no, no, no, no, no, no, no, no, no, no, no, no, no, no, no, no, no, no, no, no, no, no, no, no, no," I said to my parents, banging my fist on the floor. "No, no, no, no, no, no, no, no, no, no, no, no, no, no, no, no, no, no, no," I said, throwing the stuffed bear my parents bought for me in Williamsburg at Xiang Bo's window, "no, no, no, no, no, no, no, no, no, no, no, no, no," I said as my mother explained to me the benefits of going away for a year, maybe less, "no, no, no, no, no, no, no, no, no, no, no, no," I said as my father called me all of the sweet names of sour things that I loved so much, "no, no, no, no, no, no, no, no, no, no, no," I said as my parents promised that I could skip the next full week of school if I would just calm down a little right now, "no, no, no, no, no, no, no," I said as my mother begged me to stop hitting myself, "no, no, no, no, no, no," I said as my parents each grabbed ahold of my wrists and held them down by my sides, "no, no, no, no, no," I said as my father got down on his knees and prostrated himself in front of me and begged me to stop crying because I was breaking his heart, "no, no, no, no, no," I said, crying myself into a terrible weakness as my father picked me up in his arms and carried me past the kitchen to the living room, "no, no, no, no, no, no, no, no," I said as my mother held my hand while my father carried me, telling me that nothing was set in stone yet, there was still a lot of hard thinking ahead and we would only do what was best for us as a family, "no, no, no, no, no, no, no," I said as my father spread a blanket on the floor, "no, no, no, no, no, no," I said when he went into the bathroom while my mother undressed me, "no, no, no, no, no," I said as my mother put my pajamas on me and my father came back and lay down next to us.

"No, no, no, no—"

"Good night," my mother said.

"No, no, no—"

"Good night," my father said.

I tried to steady my breathing in the dark. We whispered our love you's and the next morning, I woke up thinking I was born sad.

My parents promised they would involve me in every decision, they promised that there would be time to figure out other ways, they promised me a yellow room with painted flowers and a living room filled with green plants for my mom and an all-white office with wooden floors and a single desk and chair for my father, but we were broke and eating food we found in dumpsters outside of Chinese bakeries—the mayo and the dried pork gave my stomach seizures, and once, I ate a fish sandwich that my dad found in its original packaging and broke out in hives. My mom stopped getting her period because she was so stressed. I saw her sitting on the toilet, clutching her stomach. "There's something in here that wants to come out but it won't."

"Sorry, Mom."

"It's okay, my tart."

My mom applied to twenty jobs and my dad applied to twelve. There was one day when he came back with his hands in the air, telling us that there were no jobs in the newspaper today but we knew he was seeing his Taiwanese slutmaster and my mom slapped him across the cheek in front of Xiang Bo and his wife, who later told us that we ought to find a new place to stay as soon as possible because the house was too small and her children—a self-absorbed, acne-ridden boy named Eddie who never spoke except once to yell, "Get your perv ass out of here," the time I accidentally walked in on him when he was peeing, and his hyperactive little sister, Lucy, who didn't seem to understand "no" was a word that meant something and would spend whole afternoons prancing around, saying, "Aren't I just so beautiful"—were easily frightened, and besides, Xiang Bo's wife said, Things aren't exactly Versailles around here. Her husband had to work two jobs to support the family and one of them involved biking through rain and snow to deliver Chinese food to rich white people who hated us but loved our food and that was why we needed to go.

My mom was always on the lookout for ways to make some extra cash. She caught wind of this new thing where a bunch of old Chinese geezers with nothing to do would spend the whole day taking the bus to Atlantic City and back. Apparently, a few of the bus companies paid passengers to make the trip, and as long as you didn't squander the money gambling, you were looking at a solid net profit of twenty bucks per round-trip. My parents and I planned on going together so that we could be three-fifths of the way to a Ben Franklin. My mom crimped my hair and I begged her to let me smoke so my voice could be all husky like the gambling women in the black-and-white movies I sometimes saw my parents watching late at night on TV but she said I had to wait until I was eighteen and I asked her if she had waited until she was eighteen and she said, No, but that was in China, and I said, Well, another reason why you shouldn't be sending me back to that hellhole of a place, and my parents looked at each other and my dad told me to drop it and my mom held my hand very tightly.

It turned out that the twenty dollars was a raw deal because the bus only ran once in the morning and once in the evening. We were dropped off super early and every time we sat down somewhere on the casino grounds to rest our feet, one of the security guards would come over and tell us that we were in a No Loitering zone and my dad said, "How is a little girl sitting down loitering?" and the guard said, "This is Atlantic City, right? If you aren't gambling, you're loitering," and then when twelve o'clock rolled around I started to get so hungry that I felt pins in my stomach and by twelve-thirty, those pins had become knives, and by one, those knives had become detonated bombs, and by two, I had fifty exploding land mines in my stomach, and finally my mom took me to the food court where all the food was overpriced and expensive and we spent twelve dollars on a sandwich and soda and then my mom started to get hungry so we spent another seven, and after we ate, my mom said her ankles were hurting and my dad said, You should have worn sneakers, and my mom said, You should have supported the family with any job you could get.

By the time the bus came back to pick us up, my mother was in tears and we had already spent twenty-seven of our forty-dollar profit. (The bus company didn't pay me a cent because I wasn't old enough to gamble.)

"It'll always be like this," my mom said, pressing her head against the seat in front of her. "We'll always try to be ahead but we'll always be behind. We'll be like this forever."

"That's not true," I said. "We're thirteen dollars ahead."

"You see how awful we are to our own daughter?" my mom said to my dad. "You see what a shithead you really are? All of your games and all of your jokes and all of your smiles and all the things you do to make yourself seem like a good father are just shit. You're just a piece of shit covered in vomit sitting in a pool of shit that everyone vomits on and it makes me sick. You're such a piece of shit that I could vomit on you right now."

The guy in front of us turned around and told my mom to stop pushing his seat. "And can you shut the hell up while you're at it?"

My mom lost it and ran up to the front to tell the driver to stop the bus immediately and throw out the creep in the back who was sick and twisted and trying to harm her and her daughter. At first my father and I thought she meant the guy sitting in front of us but when we heard my mom shouting, "His name is Zhang Heping and I'm going to throw myself off this bus if you don't stop driving it right now," we realized we were all going to have to get off the bus and maybe that constituted hitting rock bottom. Maybe we were beyond repair, standing on the shoulder of the New Jersey Turnpike, not speaking to each other until my father made the joke of unbuttoning his shirt to get the attention of one of the cars whizzing past us and when my mom ignored it completely, he started to unzip his pants, and when my mom said, "No one wants to see that and you're not helping," my dad undressed down to his underwear, and the semis and the sedans and the pickup trucks and the clunkers with the scraped-up side doors, and the convertibles with perfect paint, and the cars with too many bumper stickers, all of them beeped their horns at my family, and I wondered then how magic was distributed in the world and when and if my family would receive our fair share because I was no longer worried about how we were going to travel the seventy-something miles to get home without spending the last of our thirteen dollars, I just needed my mother to turn around and look at my father and laugh at how skinny his two legs looked, sticking out from under his protruding stomach that we once joked was a home for the world's roundest watermelon—that was the kind of magic I was after.

This was how I pictured it happening: we would pay off our debts, my parents' friends would forgive us for all that we had asked of them and were forever unable to repay. My father would re-enroll in school, start teaching again, and he would tell his girlfriend to go take a hike. My mother would find a job where she could better her English skills and be as good as me and my dad. As for me, I would go to school four or even five days a week, and we would rid ourselves of the toxins that surrounded us.

"Push harder," my mom said, putting her hands over mine as we leaned our weight against the car. Earlier that evening, our maroon Oldsmobile broke down while we were on Harlem River Drive. We knew it was going to happen one day and we were surprised our car lasted as long as it did. It was the middle of the night, the closing hour of midsummer, and five days before I had to go back to Shanghai. We had no idea where we were going, we just wanted to spend time together as a family, away from everyone else.

We pushed the car off the road, all the way down to the riverbank. My dad took off the plates and decided we had to dump it in the river and run. We didn't have the money to tow it to a junkyard.

"It's not even moving," my mom said.

"It's moving. I can feel it moving," my dad said. It was in the moment when we felt the car starting to move away from us, when we realized we could let go now, that I suddenly couldn't bear to leave it floating alone in the Harlem River with all the junk and debris and foam and the smell of urine and garbage and shit and decaying stuff. I flung myself into the water, climbing onto the car and shaking my head no when my dad said he was going to bring me back to shore.

"I told you I didn't feel like driving out tonight."

"Oh, tartberry, you said you wanted to spend every night this week together. You said you wanted to see the city at night," my mom said.

"Don't make me swim," I said before jumping back into the water and swimming away from the sinking car. I looked back at my father who was swimming after me. "Don't make me swim away from you."

"I won't, my sourest apple," my dad said. "I won't make you do anything you don't want to."

"Don't make me go," I said as my dad pulled me onto his back.

"Just hold on very tightly to me, sour grape," my father said, swimming us back toward my mom.

"Don't make me go, Dad. Don't make me go," I said, once on solid ground, looking at my mother, who was crying and holding her arms out to me. I let her pick me up even though I was too big and she was too skinny because I knew how brief these moments had always been and always would be, and if there was still a chance to be in my mother's arms, I was going to take it, I would always take it.

"It's temporary," she said, stroking my wet hair. "It's only temporary, it was always only temporary."

"It's not temporary," I said. "You said we'd always stick together. You said you'd never give me up."

"We aren't, my sourest grape," my father said. "You will always be our darling. Our Christina."

"That's not enough," I said. "I want to stay here. It's not enough. Don't give me away."

"We haven't given you up," my mother said. "It's only temporary. It's going to be as short as possible. It was only ever going to be the smallest amount of time."

I felt her shivering, and I felt myself fading out, feeling like it was remarkable that on this night, of all nights, my mom and my dad and I were huddled together promising each other things that could never be.

"Take care of us," I said, shaking my fist up at the sky where a plane was flying overhead. "Watch over us," I said to the people in the plane, who must have seen me because everything went white for a moment and when the colors of the world came back to me, I was on my father's back again, my mother a few feet behind, and when she caught up to us, I told my father to put me down and let me just stand there for a minute. We stood there and did not move. What I would have given to know exactly what they were thinking then, the graveness of our thoughts suddenly becoming petty when we realized the car had risen back up again, floating on the Harlem like a monster of our own creation, and we knew it would take nothing short of a gargantuan effort to push it back down to the bottom of the river.

The Empty the Empty the Empty

Even though Jason was the second shortest boy I knew and his nickname was Shrimpy Boy or sometimes Shrimpson, I still wanted him to be my boyfriend, and it was the easiest thing in the world to do. All it took on my part was nothing because I lived, breathed, and exuded mind-boggling, head-spinning, neck-craning, heart-pounding, ravishing beauty. I was the best-looking girl in fourth grade. I had straight, long black hair that never tangled. In the mornings before our teacher, Mrs. Silver, yelled at us to sit down at our assigned desks, the other girls, who were taller and fuller and already developing tits and asses, cooed and aahed at me and ran their fingers through my hair and told me they wished they could be me, they wished they could have my hair, have slender arms and legs like me, and sometimes, out of sympathy, I told them that I wouldn't mind knowing what it was like to have tangly, messy hair, and sort of thick arms and legs.

My clothes came from clearance sales for grown adult

women who rummaged through the one- and five-dollar bins. My sweet, resourceful mother spent hours sewing and hemming the dresses and skirts to my size, and that was how I was not only naturally the most gifted in the realm of physical beauty but also how I became the most well-dressed fourth grader in all of history. I never played tag unless it was to give the boys in my school a good look at my rump whenever my skirt flew up, which always happened when I ran because, according to my classmates, I ran like a "demented psycho," with my butt all stuck out in the air and my hands flying everywhere.

I ran all the time and had to tell boys to stop chasing me especially during recess when everyone who was anyone played the game of Boys Chasing Girls, which was a game where boys chased girls, and the rules were simple: a boy who liked you had to chase and insult you, and then you had to insult him back, and if the boy really, really liked you and wasn't afraid to show it, then he would do something really outrageous like spit on a spot you were going to sit on and say, "You should really sit there," and if you did, he would explode in laughter and say, "I can't believe you sat there," and when that happened, you essentially won the game because that was the most real indication there was that he wanted your ass and you were going to give it to him.

By February of fourth grade, Jason was my boyfriend. He pushed me during a game of Boys Chasing Girls.

I said to him, "You can't push me around."

And he said, "Well, I just did."

And then I said, "Hey, what's that on your shirt?"

He was supposed to look down and then I was supposed to slap him from his chin up to his nose, but he didn't fall for it so I had to say, "Um, I just told you there's something weird on your shirt, don't you want to look at it?"

And that was when he blurted out, "Do you want to be my date for the dance?"

We went to the winter Snow Is Everywhere dance together, and I danced like a woman who was about to have her legs hacked off the next morning so tonight was all there was for showing everyone what these legs could do, and this boy Qixiang came up to me and said, "Wow, how do you get your feet to move so fast?" and I said, "It's genetic!" The class gossip Minhee Kim saw Qixiang acting head-over-heels obsessed with me and went and blabbed to Jason.

"Hey, Qixiang is trying to step on your girl. You guys should fight."

Jason came up to me and said, "I thought you were my girlfriend. Now everyone thinks I have to fight Qixiang."

And I said, "Well, I didn't see you raise your hand when Mrs. Silver said, Raise your hand if you're a pacifist, so . . ."

So in fourth grade, by Valentine's Day, Jason was my boyfriend of one week and already he was willing to fight for me. Honestly, I wouldn't have been surprised if he was also willing to kill, maybe go to outer space to fetch a burning star and bring it to me to win my heart; anything was possible when a boy loved you that much. My best friend, Francine, who could throw a curveball like a pro, told me that Yun Hee Song and Lata Pargal had been telling everyone in our class that Jason already had his first wet dream.

"You know what that means," she said, batting her eyelashes at me, like the sick perverted puppy dog that she was fated to—and in some ways, had already—become.

"No. What?"

"Now we just have to wait for you to get your period and he can totally get you pregnant!"

Great, I thought, as visions of daytime television talk shows flashed through my brain. I had spent the summer before fourth grade with my brother Eddie and our cousin Frangie, who was close enough to being Francine in name but not in spirit, and actually wasn't even my cousin, but I had to call her that because my mother said it was the only polite thing to do for a nine-year-old girl whose own father had murdered her own mother less than a year ago with his deathly stinginess, and it was literally deathly, my mother said on the phone every day to anyone who wasn't sick of hearing about it, because he refused to pay for an operation that would have removed the cancerous lump in her uterus in time to save her. He had essentially put her and Frangie in lockdown for all of last year, no one went into their house, and God knows how that woman must have suffered in that awful, shut-in place where no one was allowed to reach her, my mother repeated over and over again in conversation, shuddering and shaking her head as if the person she was telling this to on the phone could see her, could see how visibly shaken up and guilty she felt over this whole thing, how her compassion allowed her to feel so much for other people.

And it did, she took in strays all the time: our house was never just our house, it was a place that people in need passed through. We were running the world's first zero-dollar-a-night hotel and let all kinds of randos in. Sometimes it was a young family recently emigrated from a small village in Hunan, who all smelled so bad I had to stick cotton balls up my nostrils just so I wouldn't faint in my own house, and when they took their once-a-month bath they always left a ring of rat scum around our tub. Or else it was a young Taiwanese woman my mother met in the supermarket, who had all kinds of weird facial tics we weren't allowed to even react to because my mother said this woman had lived a traumatic life beyond anything you could ever imagine, and I said, Well, I can imagine anything so that doesn't count, and my mother said, Oh, but you can't imagine this, no one can, and I said, Then how can it be true if no one can even *imagine* it? and my mother said, This conversation is over and don't let me catch you staring.

Before we took in Frangie the worst was when my father's old classmate from Shanghai brought his wife and his daughter, Christina, who had a face so gloomy and teary that she made me think being ten was going to be the most sorrowful year of my life. They stayed for nearly six months until my mother finally said it was not appropriate to bring women over to our house when there were young, impressionable children in the home, and Eddie had laughed at that and said to me, What does she think we see out there every day? and I asked him, Where? and he said, There, gesturing outside where, at that exact moment, our neighbor Sally was showing off her pet rattlesnake to her boyfriend, who, a week earlier, had slapped her on the mouth so hard that she stumbled backward and fell on her ass in the middle of the street. She sat there dazed while her boyfriend got in their car and drove away. I saw the whole thing from my living room window and counted to fifty in my head before going outside to help her up, trying not to stare at the blood between her teeth when she smiled and thanked me for giving her a hand.

But in conclusion, my mother told me, there was only one polite thing for a family as lucky as us, a family who loves each other as much as we do, and that was to take Frangie in as one of our own, which was why I had to call her my cousin, sometimes even my sister, and why she ate dinners with us and slept over at our house a lot, forcing me off my own bed and onto the floor so that she could have a "warm and happy home life." I wanted to wring my mother's neck and say, HELLO, what about your *real* daughter? What about her warmth and happiness and home life which you've so callously denied her and given to a total stranger who has a really weird name? I was supposed to feel sorry for Frangie just because her mother died (so what) and her father spent three months in a mental institution (who cared), where I imagined him to look like the costume I came up with for the Monsters' Ball bash in third grade when I got my mom and Eddie to wrap me in a big roll of gauze from CVS. As usual, I was dancing on turbo-charge when all the gauze unraveled and suddenly, I was standing there in my underwear and my little nubby breasts, and everyone was staring openmouthed at me.

Just kidding, that only happened in my dreams the night before the dance, and in real life the gauze flapped around my arms and legs gloriously, the lights in the gymna-sium followed me everywhere I went, and surely I was the shining, burning asteroid-comet-sun-galaxy-universe-rings-of-Saturn-ninth-wonder-of-the-world-never-gonna-burn-out star of the dance. The next day though in school Minhee and Yun Hee were talking about who was dancing with who and who had their butt all poking up against whose thingie thing, and I coughed loudly as I walked past them and said, "All I know is this butt is tiiiiiired," and Minhee looked at me with that bored expression that made me feel like I had never been interesting in my whole life and Yun Hee asked, "Why? You didn't even go," and that's when I realized for all the lights and for all the moves I had in me, for all that I natu-rally dazzled and sparkled, I still had to work harder to be no-ticed, and so I said to them, "That's because I was at my stupid crazy-rich cousin's house trying on pearls from the sea, you pinwheel," and Minhee was like, "Whoa, what's your prob-lem?" and I was, "Whoa, what's your problem?" which was the first sign of defeat, when all you could do was repeat someone else's words.

And anyway I didn't have blood cousins in America and

had never touched a real pearl to my neck, though my mom kept plenty of fake ones in her jewelry box and said this was all for me someday, but it was much more likely she would end up giving away all her jewelry to people she barely knew—Frangie-types who she felt more sorry for than she felt for her own kids, which was maybe why she was always trying to get me to call Frangie my cousin, but I came up with something even more generous, which was to give her a thousand of my father's dollars so she could stop bothering my family, and it wasn't like my father didn't have it to spare, because my mother never seemed to worry much about money, and neither did I, and she said once, "Our family is so rich," and technically the rest of that sentence was "with love for each other," but still.

My mother said I needed to stop thinking materialistically, and I said, I don't even know what you're talking about, and she said, Stop talking back to your MO-ther, and I said, You stop talking back to your DAUGH-ter, and she said, I'myourmotheryougotthat? all in one rushed breath, like she was blowing on a dandelion, fully aware of how little it took to destroy one. She kept saying, I'm your mother, you got that? I'm your mother, you got that? not letting me get a word in and putting her hands over her ears to show me she couldn't hear me even if I could get my thoughts together fast enough, and finally, because I felt like my head was going to explode, I screamed as loud as I could:

STTTTTTTTTTTTTTTTTAAAAAAAAAAAAAAAAAAAAA AAAAAAAAPPPPPPPPPPPPPPPPPPPPPPPPPPPPPP!

My mother looked at me with disgust and said, Are you crazy? Did you become crazy? What possessed you to scream like that? You know what, Lucy? I'm your mother and you're my daughter, so you do whatever I say, and if I say you have to be nice to your cousin Frangie, then you are going to be nice, and if you mention the thousand dollars again, I'll cut your hair as short as your brother's and I'll shave off the long hairs on the back of your neck and it'll take five years for your hair to grow back and if you try to resist me, I'll tie up your hands and shave your head bald.

It was during the long summer before fourth grade started when Frangie was my "cousin" and when my brother boiled frozen dumplings that my parents kept in the freezer for lunch, or else microwaved frozen pizzas for us, or sometimes, if he was in a great mood, he would fry up an omelette or make ramen and crack an egg on top when the broth boiled, that Frangie and I watched shows where every other word was "you beep little beep beep beep, I'm going to beep beep on your beep-ing beep-hole, you deserve a beep-ing so beep-ing hard that I might just beep you right the beep now, and don't you beep-ing try to beep-ing stop me from beep-ing the beep-ing crap out of your beep-ing beep-beep-beep-beep-beep worthless brain. So beep you, and suck my beep like you beep-ing should have in the beep-ing first place, you beep-ing, beep-ed out slutbag."

We watched them all day long on the couch, or sometimes slumped halfway down to the floor, sometimes on the floor completely, sometimes lying on each other like we were forming the letter *T* or the letter *L* or the letter *V* or the letter *A* without the middle line or the letter *O*, except Frangie was as inflexible as a tree trunk and I had vertebrae like a fish and could bend myself into a sine wave if I wanted to.

The first thing I said to Francine, my best friend in the whole world, when school started up again for fourth grade was, "Hey beep, beep beep beep beep beep-ing beep beep you."

"What's that?" she asked me.

"Cursing!" I said, proud to finally know something before Francine did.

"Beep is not a curse."

"You mean *is*. Is a curse."

"You're fucking crazy!" Francine said. "See? That's cursing."

I didn't get how Francine already knew how to curse, and I was still imitating the sound that covered up curses. I wanted to know what TV shows she was watching that I wasn't getting on my cable box. It put me in a bad mood, and on the walk home with Frangie, I told her that she might not want to come over to my house today because I might feel like slipping some crushed-up poison into her soda when she wasn't looking and she better not tempt fate and just go back to her real home and not be such a little wimpy piece of hangers-on in my home, my one and only home that because of her felt like it wasn't even mine, and because of her, I felt like an awkward intruder in my own house, so go away already.

Frangie stared at me with her deep-set, unblinking raccoon eyes, looking like she had been scarred even though she was the same as me, and if she was scarred, then I was scarred, and no one had the right to look more scarred than anyone else because the sympathy that a scarred person who looked scarred could elicit was so much more than a scarred person who didn't look scarred could get, and that wasn't fair at all. I stopped in the middle of the street, crossed my arms, and said to Frangie, "You know, not everyone feels sorry for you." She smiled a little but it looked really painful, and then she ran in the direction of her father's house where she almost never lived because he was so irresponsible and out of it that once Frangie told me her dad let her drink beer and she got super tired and fell asleep on the floor. I waited until I couldn't see her overalls and purple backpack to continue walking home.

When I got home, I started a fight with Eddie, telling him that I needed to draw a picture of his butt on his bedroom wall for my science class because we had to come up with a hypothesis that could be tested out, and I wanted to test out my hypothesis that if I drew a picture of my brother's butt on his wall then his real butt would disappear. Eddie got really mad at me every time I charged toward his wall with a marker and at one point he pushed me back so hard that I thought he had dislocated my shoulder. Of course, he didn't care that he was six years older than me, because he wasn't the type to budge an inch for his little sister who only had nine years of practice fighting with other people against his fifteen years of hard-earned training. He pushed me down on the carpet and grabbed my ears tight and said he wouldn't let go unless I said, "I'm sorry for being a little twat, I'll never bother you again," which made me so angry, I hacked up a big glob of spit and sent it flying into his face. It landed right between his eyes, and as he was wiping it off, I wriggled out of his grasp, sprinted into my room, and locked the door.

When my mom came home from work, she asked me how my first day of school was and I told her it was okay except that Eddie made me cry and now I was going to have to go to school with puffy eyes, which wouldn't at all match the pink cotton skirt I had picked out and lacy anklet socks with patent-leather Mary Janes that I had been wearing around the house all summer in preparation for wearing them outside all autumn.

"Honey, you shouldn't fight with your brother. He's very stressed these days. There's a lot of homework for high schoolers. You should let him do his work and you should do your own homework and help Frangie with hers when you finish yours."

"How can I do my homework when Eddie's bothering me? And anyway, Frangie's always here and she never leaves, and I don't like it when she invades my privacy."

"This is Frangie's home too. She needs to be here until her dad gets better and you shouldn't be making her feel unwelcome. When did her dad pick her up?"

"He didn't. She just ran home by herself."

"Lucy."

"What? If you gave me your car, I could drive her home," I said, pretending to paw at my mom's arm like I was a kitten, and smiling with no teeth, the way I had practiced thousands of millions of times in front of the mirror when I was alone.

"Lucy."

"Mom, why can't Dad order the good cable? Francine gets like a hundred more shows than us. It's not fair."

"Everything's not fair to you, little complaining girl."

"Well, it's not."

"Lucy, you know your daddy is very busy right now. He's studying for his exams so he can get a better job so we can move into a bigger house, remember? Do you ever see him sleeping? No, you don't, because he has to stay out all night delivering food so that we can keep this house and have good things to eat."

"So?"

"*So?*" my mother said, and I immediately regretted asking. She had this way of looking at me that made me feel like I had to apologize for being her daughter, that it wasn't fair she had to love me no matter how obstinately stupid I was, or how I constantly frustrated her with my inability to comprehend what was beyond obvious. I'm sorry, I said to her in my head, all the time, but never in real life, just like my mother, who never said I'm sorry to me in real life either, only I had no idea if she also apologized in her head, and if she realized that she had the power to hurt me, to disappoint me as much as I disappointed her, to make me feel so alone that sometimes I couldn't recognize myself in front of mirrors or in pictures.

"So would you like to stay up all night biking all over the city? Would you like to come back from school and go to another school and then come back from that school and go to yet another school?" I nodded my head at my mother, forgetting I was supposed to be shaking it side to side, the whole time apologizing furiously in my head, Sorry, Mom, sorry, sorry, sorry, sorry, sorry, sorry, sorry, sorry, sorry, sorry, sorrysorrysorry, sorry again, sorry again, I'm sorry, I'm so sorry, I'm sorry again, now I'm sorry again, I'm sorry, so sorry, I'm sorry, really sorry, really sorry about this, I'm sorry, I feel so sorry, I'm sorry, Mom, I'm sorry, I'm sorry Mom, I'm sorry, I'm sorry, I'll never stop being sorry, I'm sorry forever, I'm always sorry, I'm sorry for everything.

"Of course. Of course you'd say yes. You think it's funny, but your father is killing himself for us and all you can do is complain. Lucy. Lucy! Are you listening to me?" In my head I said, And sorry on top of the first sorry, sorry for this, and also sorry for before this. "Forget it. I can't be bothered with you right now."

That was the way fourth grade went. I tried to soar through the air like an eagle, tried to cut through the wide expanse of sky to reach some realm of infinite possibility, infinite compassion and understanding, but it was impossible—I kept crashing into things and receiving head injuries. My mother made me feel clumsy when I thought I was graceful, she made me think my faults were incorrigible, her sudden bouts of impatience made me feel small and slow as a turtle, like the time I dreamed I was a giant who poked out the windows of skyscrapers with my fingers and then suddenly Elmer Fudd showed up and shot me in the knee, and I started shrinking until I was no bigger than a turtle the size of a thimble, and then I was a turtle the size of a pebble, and then I was a turtle the size of a period and when I woke up, I couldn't help but see turtles everywhere, in the small brown birthmark on my brother's upper lip, in the pierced holes in my mother's earlobes before she put her prized pearl earrings through them (the ones that looked the most real even though they were plastic just like all her other earrings), in the tip of the ballpoint pen my father used to sign my field-trip slip so I could go with my class to see the dinosaur bones in the American Museum of Natural History—my day was infested with turtles.

Thankfully, I wasn't a turtle, not even close, and though I wasn't exactly an eagle either, I still stretched out my arms and looked to the sky. Surely there was someplace where it was safe, where who you thought you were matched up with how others treated you, where there was forgiveness in great abundance, never to be depleted, and as far as I knew, the first step to getting there was to have a boy who loved you and only you. For the first two weeks, Jason was the perfect boyfriend. When our teacher, Mrs. Silver, asked us to describe what we liked in the opposite sex, Jason raised his hand and said, "I just like it when they're pretty," and everyone turned to look at me, the pretty one. Yeah, I was lucky. I was chosen. There was just one problem—the whole wet-dream thing made me wish I knew how to drive a bus so I could ram it into Jason, ideally disabling his penis but leaving him alive, although a dead boyfriend would probably give my mother a reason to stay home from work and spend a few days with me. How, I wondered, did Francine know about his wet dream and how did she know that was what it took for a boy to get a girl pregnant? There was no way in hell she learned it from the mandatory pre–sex education sex education we started having in the second half of the year, something that was supposed to be a punishment but we all took as an honor. After all, we had never heard of any other fourth graders getting to take pre–sex education sex education and most of our parents, when they found out, revealed to us that they had *never* learned a *single* thing about sex when they were in school.

The day it was announced that boys and girls would be separated for an hour each week to learn about S-E-X, we lost our freaking minds. Minhee gathered all the girls around at recess and spun her finger at all of us, "Who here has done *it*?" Francine jokingly wiggled her hand in the air and I smacked it back down.

"Stop lying," I said. She smiled at me the same way she'd smiled when I cursed wrong on the first day of school, which bugged me.

I was actually looking forward to learning something, but all we ended up doing on the first day was sit around in a circle looking at diagrams of girls' bodies at various stages of development from no boobs to tiny nubs to big fat round globes, and then somehow got into a long conversation about what sort of touch was appropriate and what was inappropriate. The whole thing was as foreign to me as a house free of Frangie. I mean, all touch was wonderful and the small amount I had experienced in my life was too precious to split off into categories of "wanted" and "unwanted." And what if we wanted more touch? I felt like asking but never did.

Typically fourth grade was too young for even *pre*–sex education sex education, but a woman with spiky blond tips and big pins all over her blazer informed us at a mandatory assembly that we had been targeted as a high-risk school and measures had to be taken to ensure for the future. She spoke to us spitefully, as if we were awful, terrible children, and used the words "at risk" several times without going into detail. What were we at risk for?

After I told my mother about the assembly, she started to fret that there were too few white kids in my school. Am I at risk? I asked her. It's a sign, she said and then trailed off to make a phone call to someone who must have needed her to finish her thoughts more than I did. Over half the kids in our school were black or Spanish, although every time I called them that at home Eddie would correct me, "It's not Spanish. It's Hispanic. And that isn't even an adequate term because they comprise a lot of different cultures from different countries."

"Well, you're His-stupid."

"Forget it," Eddie said. "There's no point in explaining anything to you," but later, I went to his room and knocked on his door very softly and opened it a crack and stuck my head in and asked, "So what's Francine then if her dad's His-panic and her mom's black?"

"You could just say she's mixed."

"Oh, okay," I said. "Is that high risk?"

"Get out," he said, and for once I didn't make a whole show of banging on his door after he had locked it behind me. Still, I didn't know what the risk was—was it just obesity and junk food? Nearly everyone in my grade, except me and this really mousy, quiet girl Mande who I kept forgetting even existed, had more tits and more ass than my own mother. It's the hormones, my father said, that they inject into the chips and the Cheetos.

My God, my mother exclaimed. It's in the Cheetos?

Sometimes, when school let out, men walked past and hooted at groups of us standing around outside. "Nice ass, mami," a construction worker once shouted at Francine when her back was turned to him and I pointed at him and said, "You talking to me?" and he said, "No, your friend with the nice ass," and I said to Francine, "How rude can some people get?" but Francine just shrugged. "They're all like that," she said.

"Yeah," I said, pretending to know.

During our weekly hour of pre—sex education sex education, Mr. Kosecki took the boys into the gymnasium and showed them who knows what while we stayed in the classroom with Mrs. Silver. She had us hold hands at the start of each lesson and say in unison, "What happens in this room stays in this room."

Then she'd bring out the question box she had decorated in glitter and gold stars to start off the hour. We were supposed to drop anonymous questions that we had about sex and being a woman/girl into the box, and at first no one did, but after the third class, the questions started coming in. Someone wanted to know why her one tit was bigger than the other and we all immediately turned around and looked at Fanpin Hsieh. Another girl wanted to know if it was possible to get addicted to the smell of your own vagina the way kids in first grade got addicted to eating their own boogers. Someone else wanted to know why she humped the couch after watching a VHS of *Lady Chatterley's Lover* that her parents had left lying around. The week after that, someone else said she also went and saw her parents' copy of *Lady Chatterley's Lover* and humped her couch, but also what was "humping"? The week after that, four more girls in our class watched *Lady Chatterley's Lover* and dry-humped their couches, and Mrs. Silver grabbed the question box and made a motion like she was going to throw it out the window but then set it back down on her desk. "If you aren't going to take this seriously, we can spend the hour copying vocabulary words instead."

Francine and I had renamed it "tame education" from the very first diagram of a vagina that looked like a deluxe Polly Pocket opened on its side, and anyway, if we wanted to see a vagina couldn't we just look at our own? Francine looked at mine and I looked at hers all the time. She was already starting to grow hair on hers—little curly black hairs all lined up around the center.

Francine came over my house once or twice a week without telling her mom or dad, neither of whom cared anyway. They let her do anything and didn't care when she came home, didn't care if she walked home blindfolded or with her laces tied together: as long as they didn't have to come pick her up, they were happy. I envied Francine and she knew it. Whenever she came over, we'd shut ourselves up in my room and tape a sign to our door that read, IF YOU LOOK LIKE A HAIRY APE, OR IF YOUR NAME RHYMES WITH SDKGLADEIGTONACBHDZZANGIE, DON'T COME IN HERE. The ape thing was Francine's idea, and Sdkgladeigtonacbhdzzangie was mine.

I liked opening and closing her vagina lips, pretending it was a regular mustached lip turned on its side.

"Good morning, class," I said in my ventriloquism-of-a-vagina voice, as I maneuvered her vagina lips to look like talking lips. "Today, we are going to talk about periods."

Francine loved my jokes and I loved hers. I didn't have a single hair on my vagina, but in fourth grade it started to secrete fluid once or twice a day.

"I thought I peed my pants again," I told Francine.

"Ew," she said. "Don't you know how to hold it in?"

"But look, it's not pee." I showed Francine my underwear, the hardened crust of yellow discharge, and we both smelled it and pretended to faint. Sometimes, Francine stuck her index finger into my vagina, screaming the entire time she was sticking her finger in.

"Oh my God," she screamed. "Oh my God, oh my God, oh my God, oh my God, oh my God, oh my fucking God."

"Stop screaming, Francine."

"There's swampland in there," she told me.

"So? You have a frozen tundra in yours."

The whole point of Francine sticking her finger in my vagina was so she could taunt me later when I had forgotten that we had spent an entire afternoon digging around in each other's vaginas, and when I least expected it, she would suddenly put her fingers up to my nose.

"Smell it," she said, "smell it, smell it, smell it."

I always told her no way. "Not unless you smell your own." Sometimes, I'd stick my finger into her vagina, and she'd stick hers in mine, and we'd cautiously smell our sticky fingers and then we'd cross our arms over each other to give the other person a good, long whiff. I thought my vagina smelled a little bit like my feet in the summer when I wore sandals, but also like these fried anchovies my parents ate on top of porridge in the mornings for breakfast.

"You better wash it really good for Jason," Francine said to me. "Or else he might dump you."

"Whatever. I'll dump him first."

Whenever Francine or anyone else mentioned Jason, I would get this horrible feeling of dread in my stomach, a suspicion that there were still so many things I had to learn and each new thing I encountered reminded me of how far I had to go to catch up to everyone else. I wanted to be *special* but sometimes I couldn't tell if I was *special* or if I was *special,* and even though they were the same word, one singled you out for deep admiration and envy and the other guaranteed you were doomed and worthy only of pity. Was I *soooo special* to be the first girl in fourth grade to have a boyfriend or was I *soooo special* to have a boyfriend so perverted he uncontrollably soiled himself in his sleep? The more I thought about it, the more I wasn't sure. It hadn't even been a month and I already wanted to dump his ass. Who got wet dreams in fourth grade? I stayed up all night playing Bubble Gum Bubble Gum in a Dish just so I wouldn't fall asleep and have regular, *dry* dreams.

I wanted to live a dreamless life in my unconscious and be full of dreams in my conscious life. Also, I hated having nightmares. I hated how, even if you were lucky enough to never have anything terrible happen to you the entire time you were alive, and even if every single thing you wanted was within your grasp, and even if you were the luckiest girl on earth who all the other girls aspired to be and all the boys liked and all the adults found charming and sweet and full of potential, even if everything went right for you and there was no chance of slipping off that path, you still had to contend with your nightmares, how they intruded on you while you were sleeping when the point of sleeping was to skip past the next eight hours so you could get back to living your ridiculously good life that you couldn't wait to wake up to every morning if only you didn't have terrible nightmares that made you feel like your body was detached from itself, like you had floated up into the sky and were now looking down at yourself, at everyone who secretly pitied you, who laughed at you and threaded flowers in your hair not to make you look beautiful but because they knew you were horribly allergic and wanted you to sneeze and suffer all day, and worst of all, you hated how your dreams made you think that the vision of yourself that you saw when you were forced to see yourself the way other people saw you was the real you, which was a confused little girl who wanted someone to pay attention to you, to show you how to be a person because actually, if you really really looked long enough, if you really really didn't look away, you'd see that you weren't just a confused little girl desperate for attention, but a child who was in real danger of becoming someone no one would want to know, and even worse than that, what you feared the most was a day when no one could hear you cry for help, a day you must have been heading for your whole life because there had always been something about you that made it seem like you didn't need any help, which was why your mother reminded you so often of all the other needier, more deserving people in the world, and why your father had to be someone who you only saw a few minutes a day, which, your mother never failed to remind you, was ultimately for you and your brother and you were supposed to be perfectly grateful for it, but all it really felt like was growing up without a father, and it was terrifying—all of it—but especially the moment when everything flashed before you in these dreams where you were crying out and no matter how long or how loudly you cried no one heard, no one came to you. It made you feel helpless because no matter how many times your mother told you dreams were not real life, you could not forget what you saw and what you felt. So there was no rest and there was no escape. There was a version of you that was too selfish and there was one where you weren't selfish enough and you were constantly waking up from one into the other and that was why you weren't sure if you were looking down at yourself or you were looking up at yourself and which one was the real you and which was the dream? There was no telling. I'm sorry, I repeated in my head. I'm sorry, sorry, sorry, sorry, sorry, sorry, sorry, sorry. I stumbled around the house saying "sorry" until I crashed into my brother's door.

Help me, I mouthed and he looked at me like I was a spiderweb he was about to destroy just by waving his hand. "Well? Why're you standing there? Gone retarded again?"

I snapped out of it and went for a classic shadow. "You must be talking to yourself, retard-boy."

"I always knew it was a mistake when Mom and Dad fought for you to be placed out of special ed."

Whenever Eddie was getting the best of me and Francine wasn't there, I had to drag myself to the living room where Frangie sat, drinking soda and watching TV—or sometimes watching nothing at all, because she was weird like that—and I'd ask her to help me come up with a plan to get back at Eddie.

"Frangie, help me beat up Eddie," I said to her after Eddie made up the lie about me getting out of special ed.

"I have an idea," she said. "What if you go buy a wolf and train it to eat Eddie for lunch?"

"Where am I gonna get the money, stupid?" I said to Frangie. "Stupid," I said again. "Just wish you weren't stupid. And anyway, like a wolf would want to eat Eddie. That's like putting throw-up in front of a wolf. A wolf wouldn't eat that."

"I wish I could be a jellyfish," Frangie said to me, fidgeting with the clasp of her corduroy overalls.

"Why?"

"Cause then it would be easy to sting people."

"Wow," I said, shaking my head at Frangie, and then I considered it for a moment. "Actually, yeah. Me too." I patted Frangie on the head the way my father did sometimes when he got home early enough to tuck me into bed. "Let's go get a stick and poke Eddie in the butt with it until he buys us candy. Wanna?"

A few days after everyone found out about Jason's wet dream, I went to school and Francine wasn't there. I missed her and felt dizzy and thought I was going to barf, so I asked Jason to walk me home after school.

"I'll show you my coin collection," I told him when we were in front of my house even though the only coins I collected were the chocolate ones that I had to beg my mom to buy at the supermarket.

When we got inside the house, I yelled out to whoever was home, "Leave me and my boyfriend alone," and then grabbed Jason and pulled him into my room.

"Put it inside me," I said to him, just to test it out.

"What?"

"Never mind," I said. "I'm not really allowed to have anyone over except Frangie. Don't you have to be home?"

"Yeah, but you're the one who asked me to come here."

We looked at everything in my room except each other. "Say the thing you like best about me again."

"Huh?"

"Your favorite thing about me."

"I guess that you're my girlfriend."

"No," I said, "the other thing."

"What other thing?"

"If I say it then it doesn't count."

"Everything has to count?"

"Duh."

We sat in silence again. "It's kind of the same," I said.

"What is?"

"Having a boyfriend and not having a boyfriend. Actually maybe it's more bad now."

"Rude."

"Okay," I said. "Can't you just beat it? Scram? Bust out? Leave me alone? Go away? See you later, alligator? Bye-bye, American pies?"

"You don't make sense and you're bossy," Jason said.

"You act dumb and also, you're dumb."

After he left, I closed the front door behind me and sighed. I suddenly wanted my mom to come home so I could tell her that I had a boy over even though I knew she was already burdened with so much, and the level of care she could devote to something like this was probably so low in the grand scheme of all the things she had to care about that it would annoy her more than anything, which wasn't the same thing as caring. And anyway, even though my mom tried to tell me what to do, the fact was she rarely came home before seven at night, and there wasn't enough time for her to find out what I did while she was away, especially since she often had more work to do once she got home because people sometimes paid her to make their ugly clothes look nicer. She had an old sewing machine that we got from a Salvation Army and it was mostly good except sometimes the needle would break into her finger and then it was days and days of her clutching her swollen, bruised finger, crying that this life was going to kill her, and I would follow her around and blow soft kisses at her finger, which irritated her because my breath was too hot and the hot air, she said, made everything worse. So it was best to leave her alone even though that meant I had to be alone and miss her without letting her know it because it stressed her out to know. Didn't we understand that the only reason me and my brother and all the people we housed in our home weren't already dead was because she, and she alone, carried all our burdens on her shoulders? Um, thanks? I said sometimes to let her know I kinda understood, but that only angered her more, which was how I knew I was useless to her, and that scared me because it meant I really *was* related to Frangie, someone who made everything worse, someone who was so helpless that she sucked the energy and life out of the people who had to look after her, and no way was I going to be a Frangie, no way was I going to be a hangers-on in my own home to my own family, no way was my mom ever going to wish I had never been born the way I wished Frangie had never been born. I vowed never to be my family's charity case.

My parents promised me everything was going to change once my father finished school and got his degree in business, which wouldn't be long now because my father was a superhuman who broke world records in things that no one kept records for, like most accelerated course of study in business while also working forty-plus hours a week delivering Chinese food for this twenty-four-hour place that hired him because my father was a MACHINE who could ride regular bikes like they were motorbikes and he made record-breaking time delivering General Tsao's chicken to people who lived on the Upper East Side and probably didn't know there was never a General Tsao in China. Ha ha ha, I said when my father told me this, even though I hadn't known it either. In the movies I saw on TV, Chinese delivery guys brought cartons and cartons of fried rice and spring rolls and fried wontons to men who lived in their robes and were surrounded by beautiful women who had the kind of tits you wanted to use as shelves. And in these movies, they always had buck teeth and started every sentence with "me likey" or "me no likey" and had high-pitched voices and stomped around with their arms flailing up and down, and even though I could laugh at anything, I never laughed at that.

So things were going to change but I just had to wait . . . with Frangie and my dumb brother. At our house, Frangie would sometimes talk to herself in the living room. Once she put on my mother's push-up bra and clothes and makeup and asked me to stuff socks in her underwear so that she could have a porn star's ass ("What's a porn star?" I asked, and Frangie only smiled knowingly so I slapped her on the mouth and said, "That's not a good look for you") and she walked out of the house like that and strutted around downtown with the face of a ten-year-old girl and the ass and tits of a twenty-year-old. She was like the world's most confusing-looking slut.

My brother was even more of a waste than Frangie was. He had gotten a girlfriend not long after I started dating Jason—this girl who already looked like a woman, like she could be someone's mother—and they hung out in his room most afternoons. He put a flag up on his door whenever she was there.

"That's for you to know that you don't disturb me when this"—he pointed at the flag—"is draped across my door. Got that?"

"Is this house ever going to be just for us?" I moaned.

He ignored me. "What did I just say? You do not ever come in when this is here. Understand?"

I nodded.

"I'm serious, Lucy. Come in and you're fucking dead."

I said, "Come into my room, and I'll freaking kill you too."

"Wouldn't dream of it," he said before shutting the door and staying hours and hours in there with his new girlfriend who had tits the size of Kansas—no the whole Midwest, no the entire continent of North America, no make that the continent of Asia, no Asia plus Antarctica, no actually the whole Milky Way galaxy. Her tits were out of this world. Literally. Everyone I knew was living on a different planet from me and I was the only person left on earth, wandering around dumbly, and it was possible I would have to stay there forever. It wasn't fair I had to be me for as long as I lived while other people got to be other people.

I put my fingers in my vagina, wriggled them all the way in deep until it hurt, and then wiped my fingers on Eddie's door.

"Don't worry, Eddie," I said with my mouth pressed up against his door, "even if you don't come in my room, I'll still freaking kill you." I walked back into my bedroom, locked the door, collapsed onto my carpet, put my fingers back in my vagina, and waited for my mother to get home.

The next day, Francine showed up to school with makeup on and I said, "You look very dumb," before she even sat down in her desk.

During art class, Francine told me that if you have big knockers you can come the second your boyfriend puts it in you.

"I don't care about that," I told her.

"About what?" she asked.

"Coming."

"Ew," she said. We made ourselves sick sometimes just by talking.

"So has he yet?" she whispered into my ear.

"Oh, totally, yeah."

"What?" she screamed.

Our art teacher, Mrs. Feducci, walked up to our table. "Francine, do you want to go to the principal's office for the second time today?"

"No," she said, head bent down.

"Didn't think so," Mrs. Feducci said and then turned back around to help Susanna Lopez with her origami paper crane.

Francine stuck her tongue at Mrs. Feducci, and I giggled into my shirtsleeve. We started to pass notes.

[Francine]	why haven't u done it yet
[Me]	BUSIE n stuff
[Francine]	YEA RIGHT
[Me]	yeah! right! i'm right! you said i'm right!

[Francine]	*I sooooo bet you didn't*
[Me]	no, you said, YEA RIGHT
[Francine]	*um, you didn't do it*
[Me]	fine
[Francine]	*HA! caught you!*
[Me]	but I asked him to
[Francine]	*and?*
[Me]	he doesn't know how
[Francine]	*I'll help you teach him*
[Me]	ok
[Francine]	*ok*
[Me]	but Frangie is gonna be there
[Francine]	*ew*
[Me]	my mom said she has to be there
[Francine]	*she always has to be there?*
[Me]	always and never never has to be there
[Francine]	*not fair*
[Me]	like I don't know

After school, the sky darkened and I didn't know if day had become night or if night had become day, and then I decided that day had become night like in my nightmares that made me believe I was living in a world without day, and under the threat of thunderstorm, Francine, Frangie, and I ran all the way home holding hands, Frangie in the middle like she was our kid. I told Jason that he had to set his stopwatch for ten minutes and only start walking toward my house after it beeped because we had a secret in store for him, and because Frangie was awkward around boys so we had to escort her home first. The only boy I ever really saw her talking to was Eddie.

When the doorbell rang, Eddie opened the door.

"Who the hell are you?" he said, looking down at Jason, who was wearing a big green sweater with a leaf print and dragging his book bag and black down jacket behind him on our steps.

"Get away from there," I said, running down the stairs. "That's my friend from school."

"Um, you mean boyfriend," Francine shouted from a few feet behind me.

My brother looked at me and then looked at Jason and then burst into laughter.

"Is something funny to you?" I asked him and then turned to Jason. "C'mon, Jason, ignore him. He needs mental work."

"You have a boyfriend?" my brother asked me.

"Yeah, so?"

"Do you even know what a boyfriend is? I mean, obviously not," he said, shaking his head. "Look, I have no desire to know anything about you and your weird little friends." He went into the kitchen to heat up some frozen pizzas for him and his girlfriend, and Francine and I led Jason up the stairs into my room where Frangie was waiting.

When we had gotten home ten minutes earlier, we'd ordered Frangie onto my bed and stripped off her clothes. I stashed them in my closet while Francine tied Frangie to my bed with my mother's scarves.

"We're finally going to let you play with us," Francine said. "Aren't you glad? You don't have to wait outside the door anymore." Frangie didn't say anything; she was probably imagining being a jellyfish for all I knew. When I saw how tightly Francine was tying the scarves around Frangie's wrists, I told her to go easy.

"I don't feel anything," Frangie said.

"Really?" I said, inspecting the knots Francine had made and loosening one of them a little bit.

"This is what you play in here?" Frangie asked.

"Yup," Francine said. "Every single day, and now you'll get to."

When we brought Jason into my room, he immediately turned around and reached for the doorknob, but Francine and I were already on it. We blocked the exit with our bodies—me backed up against the door with my hands spread out like they were wings and Francine standing in front of me in the same posture.

"Shrimpson," Francine said, smiling. "You aren't scared, are you?"

"No," Jason said. "Course not."

"Why's your face all red then?" I said.

"Shrimpy, you know you want it. If you didn't, why did you have a wet dream?"

"Yeah," I said. "Why did ya? Huh?"

Jason shrugged. "That's just a rumor."

"Says you," Francine said. "Didn't they tell you in pre–sex ed sex ed that there's nothing to be ashamed of?"

"Yeah," I said, feeling like Francine's echo. "Didn't they tell you?"

"Guess so."

Francine clasped her hands together into a prayer, and I reached around her waist and did the same. "Please, Jason,"

Francine said. "Promise you won't try to leave, or we'll tell everyone you're scared to do it."

"Do what?" he said.

"Just say you promise," Francine said.

"Please, Jason, just promise," I said.

"Fine," he said.

"Say you promise," Francine said.

"Okay," Jason said.

"Say 'I promise,'" Francine insisted.

"He said okay," Frangie said. The sound of her voice startled me.

"This is kind of stupid," I said.

"You say that about everything," Frangie said from the bed. I peeked over Francine's shoulder to look at her. She had wriggled out of the one scarf I'd loosened and had placed that hand across her stomach. I wondered what it would be like if my mother had died like Frangie's, if my father was as unfit as Frangie's father was, and if Eddie moved out to live with his girlfriend. Where would I go after school? Who would take care of me? I felt a deep disappointment in myself that when I looked at Frangie on my bed, I could only picture myself. For a brief moment, I felt like I was going to puke but then Francine was in charge again and things started happening quickly.

"Sit." Francine directed Jason to my chair. "You," she said to me, "kneel down in front of him." I got on my knees and unzipped his pants. "Take it out. He's your boyfriend."

I couldn't find it at first. I wasn't sure what to look for.

"Ugh," Francine said, kneeling down next to me. "Do I have to do everything myself?"

"Hey," Jason said, slapping her hand away and zipping his pants back up. "Who said you could touch it?"

I stood up and realized that everything that was new to me

was yesterday's meatloaf to Francine. The brief glimpse I had of Jason's dick wasn't so much shocking as it was unremarkable. It was this tiny flabby thing and I couldn't imagine it was really capable of all the things we had discussed in pre–sex ed sex ed. "*I'm* his girlfriend, Francine."

"So act like it." She stood head to head with me.

"I'm going home." Jason started to get up from the chair, but Francine held him down without much effort, her arms freakishly muscular from playing softball every weekend. She shook her head with a look in her eyes that had worked on me before too. It was this look that said, Only I know what comes next.

"Not yet," she said and then to me, "We have to make it hard. It's easy. You just put your mouth on it or rub it like this." She knelt back down and ran her finger across the zipper of his pants. Outside, it was almost completely pitch-dark. The lightning was stalled, but I knew it was coming soon.

"I'm not doing that."

"What the hell? First you say you want to, and then you say he wants to, and then he says he doesn't want to, and now you say you don't want to either. What's wrong with you people?" She rolled her eyes and, before any of us could react, she unzipped his pants, grabbed his penis, and put the entire soft, limp little thing into her mouth.

"Mmmn," she said.

"Francine," I said, feeling sick.

"Mmmm mmn mnn."

"Francine," I shouted. "No. Stop it!" I grabbed her by the shoulder and tried to pull her away, but she was so, so strong. She moved her mouth off Jason's penis, which looked smaller than ever, but it was no longer something I could bring myself to laugh at—it was part of my nightmare now. Standing back up, she grabbed ahold of my wrists with one hand, and covered my mouth with the other. The lightning was here now, so was the rain.

"Shhh," she said. "Do you want your brother to hear?"

I heard my brother take a few steps up the stairs, his every footstep sending vibrations through my heart. "Lucy, can you and your friends stop screaming? It annoys the crap out of me and honestly, I just can't be bothered anymore. Do you realize I'm actually trying to study? With my actual girlfriend? Do you realize other people actually have lives? So listen, this is the last time I'll ask you and your friends to shut the hell up. From this point forward, you don't exist. Don't bother me and I won't bother you and everyone's happy."

But I'm here, I said to him in my head. I'm here, Eddie. "What if I needed you to know I'm here?" I said in the smallest voice I had.

"It's time," Francine said. "Jason, get on the bed." She explained to me earlier that we needed to do this, and that there was only one way it could be done, and it had to be done that way because Jason needed to learn how to do it properly so that our first time could be perfect, and what better test case than Frangie? I needed to save myself for when Jason was more experienced so that it would feel good. She told me that I also needed to watch carefully because it wasn't like everyone was born into this world knowing how to be good at sex—she certainly wasn't, and I probably wasn't either—some people had to work constantly at it, like math, like those algebra equations Francine and I got wrong every time, and so that was why everything was the way it was.

Jason climbed onto my bed, one of his legs shaking uncontrollably. Francine tugged his pants down so they were bunched up by his knees. "Why do you wear such tight pants, Shrimpson? You're not some kind of gaylord, are you?" He was trying to straddle Frangie's knees, and Francine was telling him to move up higher, to get closer to her vagina. Frangie's raccoon eyes looked up toward the ceiling. I kept waiting for her to blink, to make a sound, to say she wanted to go home, but she just laid there with one hand tied to my bedpost.

"Frangie," I said. "Frangie, my mom says you should stay for dinner."

"Jason," Francine said. "Move up closer, you retard."

"Frangie," I said. "I still want to be a jellyfish with you."

"Closer. You're still too far."

"Frangie," I said. "I saved an orange soda for you. I'll get Eddie to put your name on it so that I don't forget and drink it by accident."

"That's good." Francine leaned over the side of my bed and grabbed Jason's penis, shiny and gross with her saliva but still tiny and soft. "Now you open her up," Francine said to me. "Do it like we usually do."

"Frangie," I said, putting my fingers on her vagina lips and parting them with my thumb and forefinger. "Frangie, my mom says she'll take us shopping this weekend."

"Fuck, why isn't it working?" Francine said, looking genuinely concerned for the first time all day. She bit down on her knuckles. "Your boyfriend might really be a gaylord."

"Frangie," I said. "You need anything? You want that orange soda? Cheez Doodles?"

"Look at Jason's face. Look at it, Lucy. He looks like he needs to poop."

"Frangie, close your eyes," I said, trying to pull her eyelids down with my fingers, but they were stiffly open, like the lid to a tin of anchovies. "Frangie, please. Please close your eyes." Downstairs, my brother was singing along to the radio, sprinkling little pepper flakes on his finger and licking it clean while his pizzas were spinning in the microwave, out there, my mother was telling someone how she had taken Frangie in as one of her own and no, she didn't treat her any less than her blood children, and even farther somewhere, my father was riding his bike all around Manhattan with a plastic bag tied around his face, speeding past lights like he was light itself, accepting quarters for tips, forcing a smile after each delivery, and as for me, I was waiting for that first clap of thunder, the moment when I could detach from myself again, when I could hover in that space above reality where I sometimes saw myself for who I really was, only this time, I would let it happen, I wouldn't struggle at all, instead, I would allow myself to see what was really there down below me.

Our Mothers Before Them

July 1966

S chools had been indefinitely shut down for a month when the rain started and the children of Shanghai came out in packs to play. The first month of no schools and no responsibilities had spilled feral energy into the streets. Hardly anyone spoke of poetry anymore unless it was coded in another kind of poetry. It was dangerous to be precious about the lakes and the summer willows that had been fetishized by the old masters; now it either served the revolution or it was an act of sabotage. Beauty was a distraction, it was an indulgence, and all the things that carried it, all its vessels, were to be burned. Burn! It! Down! the kids shouted, flicking matches at anything during the hot, dry month of June.

The sudden power reversal—the young and rash were now the enforcers, the ones who dealt punishment—made some kids despotic, some giddy, and some so terrified they went into hiding, though everyone had to come out eventually. The kids who liked breaking shit and the kids who regularly had shit broken across their bodies were the ones who formed packs and marched up and down the streets, carrying glass bottles beneath their arms to throw at any woman who still wore her hair loose and long (that was *piggish bourgeois decadence!*), or anyone who reeked of being an *intellectual,* which could have meant someone with squinty eyes from reading too many books or someone with overly relaxed eyes from a lifetime of being spared hard manual labor.

Anyone could be named a counterrevolutionary, anyone could be made to crawl like a dog through the streets until their knees and palms were rubbed raw to the point of exposing cartilage. Faster, faster, faster, the kids cried. Enough, enough, the adults begged. In another month, some of the children would name their own parents over something as trifling as an expression—maybe someone's mother had *almost* smiled when hearing a story about Mao stumbling on some steps, maybe someone's father had said flippantly one night, *Would be nice to go to bed full for once*—anything was fodder and all gossip could turn into serious allegations that so-and-so wasn't down for the struggle. The kids who were willing to turn in their own parents were rewarded, rose through the ranks fast. Everyone knew the fastest way to the top was to be someone no one wanted to cross. Some of the children started wearing their parents' old green army uniforms, comically big and pocked with moth holes, redolent with black mold. The serious ones memorized every aphorism from Mao's Little Red Book and went around quoting lines like, "A revolution is not a dinner party, or writing an essay, or painting a picture or doing embroidery; it cannot be so refined, so leisurely and gentle, so temperate, kind, courteous, restrained and magnanimous. A revolution is an insurrection, an act of violence by which one class overthrows another," at the slightest offense, like if someone licked their lips when walking past a stall selling hot salted soy out of plastic bags for four cents a bag. The desire to have a midafternoon treat was the desire to feast and the desire to feast was wasteful and self-indulgent, the opposite of resisting bourgeois greed and capitalist filth. The serious kids scrounged up scraps of red silk, inscribed the words 红卫兵 and wore them as armbands. The less serious drew elephantine balls hanging under a tiny penis, or a woman with big juicy tits squirting fat droplets of milk into her own mouth. They grouped themselves according to longtang, and Nanchang longtang had a reputation for being the most ruthless and the most creative. There was no injury too small, no grudge too petty for these children to avenge with the kind of energy that, in another world, at another time, they might have saved for birthday clowns and pony rides.

The day before the rain started, some kids from Nanchang longtang had strung up Teacher Liu to a poplar tree that was still mottled from years back when people had crowded around it to peel off slabs of bark for food. One of the kids Teacher Liu beat the most frequently had a twitchy lip from all the times she'd slapped him across the mouth with a ruler for answering math problems wrong, earning him the nickname "Twitch" (though his closest friends knew that his own father beat him much more savagely than Teacher Liu ever did and it was far more likely that his mouth twitch had come from the time his father tied him to a chair and flicked rocks at his face for hours until finally one of them knocked out his front tooth), and he had come up with the idea of carving $2 + 2 = 5$ down her arm with a shard of glass, knowing there was no greater insult than to brand her with bad arithmetic. She gave the hardest tests of all the middle school teachers, often pre-quizzing her students on units that she only planned on teaching months later. She handed rulers to the good students and made them beat the bad ones. She wouldn't let them stop until all the rulers were streaked with blood or broken in half. Once she had given ten rulers to the most soft-spoken girl in class and instructed her to hit Twitch with them until they were quote unquote "a pile of splinters."

As soon as the announcement was made in early June that all schools were to be closed immediately and students were to devote themselves to the revolution, Twitch began gathering evidence against Teacher Liu. She's a seditious slut, Twitch told his schoolmates. She's been wiping her pussy with images of Chairman Mao ripped out of the newspaper. Her father owned land, did you know that? And refused to give it up too. He had to be purged, that's why she doesn't have any family around because they were all rightists and capitalist sympathizers.

At the break of dawn, Twitch gathered the beefiest and the grodiest of his classmates to break into her home and destroy all her possessions. There's books gilded in gold leaf! Twitch cried upon seeing her library. He flicked his tongue against the filaments of gold, not knowing what else to do and inexplicably drawn to their beauty before snapping back into action and ordering the two biggest boys to drag her out of bed. By the time they had successfully tied Teacher Liu to the poplar tree, a crowd had gathered.

What do you get when you add two plus two? they taunted her, ignoring her pleas to be untied.

Four. It's four.

If you say four again . . . Twitch said, grabbing her pinky finger and motioning to slice it off. Someone who loves the number four so much should only have four fingers. Am I right? The crowd of children had stones in their pockets and full bladders they were planning to relieve on the fresh wounds on Teacher Liu's arm.

Look how fat she is, one kid pointed out. She must have been hoarding eggs and meat while the rest of us were fed shit from our own asses.

Bourgeois scum. Say it! another shouted. Say you are bourgeois scum. Say you've always been a counterrevolutionary revisionist seed of pigshit and you deserve to be beaten blind.

She said it through blubbering sobs, but Twitch was still disgusted by a certain self-satisfied gleam in her eye. He encouraged a couple of kids to force her mouth open while another few took turns aiming piss into it. The especially inventive discussed which branches to climb in order to position their ass cracks at the best possible angle to feed her some of the shit that her bourgeois upbringing had kept her from eating while everyone else lived at the level of dung beetles. Teacher Liu had lived well. It was obvious from her height: only people who came from generations of well-fed families could grow to be as tall as her. Her white skin proved that she descended from pampered thinkers who never had to labor under the sun from sunrise to sundown. Some of the kids talked about making a stew from her bones. We won't even have to season it much! they shouted. Calcium for the people! By late afternoon, the children were bored and starving, having pissed and shat themselves empty. This is just the beginning, Twitch told the others before they all dispersed to go home and eat dinner—flour fried in a bit of old reused oil. The more fortunate kids had a few grains of salt to sprinkle on their fried flour, and the even luckier had a drop or two of soy sauce.

The next morning, it rained and was cool for the first time in weeks, washing away the dust and shards of glass strewn all over the streets. The children were ecstatic. They set their bottles on the ground and stripped naked in the streets. You like what you see, don't you, they said to each other, pointing at the littleness of each other's parts, and flexing the muscles they didn't have.

My uncle wasn't out in the streets; he was indoors. He lived in a modest apartment at the end of Nanchang longtang with my mother and my grandparents. Unlike the kids who ran in packs and stayed outside until they felt like it, my uncle came from a family who could actually afford to eat eggs more than once a year (he and my mother ate them once on New Year's Eve and once on their birthdays, which was unheard of and had to be kept secret). He had only used a match once in his life and it had gone badly, burning the hair on the back of his neck. When he went outside, he went outside alone, keeping few alliances. If he hadn't looked so comically out of proportion—his big watermelon head balanced on a beanpole body—the hooligans of Nanchang longtang would have singled out him and his family for abuse, but instead they were soft on him, treated him like their own personal entertainment. Bighead, Bighead, they shouted at him, have you come to be our umbrella?

Just taking a stroll, he would reply, waving cordially.

When his mother told him he ought to stay indoors more, citing the legend of a village of people who put their children in steel boxes to keep them from growing as an example of what would have befallen him if only she had the means to do it, he was appalled and declared his intention to liberate all the village children from their boxes.

It's just a story, his mother said. It's not real. It's made up. It's for a laugh. You don't have to be the hero for some kids who never existed.

Why would anyone even think of it? my uncle asked. Why did someone have that thought?

Why, why, why? my grandmother said. You waste my time

with these whys. Go do something already so someone can ask you why you did it.

My uncle made a promise to himself that he would never let himself be caged. He would be free, he would always be free, he would stretch his long limbs out with great care and pleasure, he would stand up straight to be that much closer to the sky and feel the infinitesimal growth of his body happening in real time.

The day the rains started, he went outside for his daily stroll around the neighborhood and passed by the poplar tree that Teacher Liu was still tied to, the odor of blood and piss lingering in the air despite the rain. He approached her like she was a display in a museum, taking tiny steps toward her unconscious body.

You shouldn't be here, he whispered. Before he could untie her, a pack of naked boys led by Twitch ran up to my uncle, formed a ring around him and the poplar tree and Teacher Liu, laced their fingers together and sang:

Rain, rain, you make us wish
We had an umbrella
If we had an umbrella
We wouldn't be wet!

Rain, rain, you make us wish
All the good girls
Were wet like you
But look!

There's Chunguang
With his big fatty bighead
Who needs an umbrella
When Bighead can keep us dry!

But your mother's still wet
She's always been wet.
That's how we know
She's a whore!

February–March 1996

"A whore?" I said in Chinese. "What's that?"

"No," my mother said. "You misheard. I said, 'That's how we know all's well.'"

"Oh. Okay."

My mother sang the Bighead song obsessively during the months when we were preparing for my uncle's stay. He was coming to live with us for a few months before starting school in Knoxville at the University of Tennessee.

"What's he going to do in Tennessee?" I asked my mom.

"Make toothpaste taste like Sprite," my brother Sammy interrupted.

"Um, yeah, right."

"Ask him yourself when he gets here."

I was seven and starting to be curious about my uncle again. We were having fish for dinner when my father tipped his chair back and started choking.

"There's Chunguang," my mother sang, her eyes averted to the ceiling.

"Should we help Daddy?" I said, looking at Sammy. I didn't move because often when I knew I wanted to do something I ended up doing the opposite, and my brother, who was good at anything that a person might ever want to be good at and even good at the things that we as a species had not yet conceived of wanting to do, ran up to my father and thumped him on the back.

"With his big fatty bighead."

"Mom, please. Help him!" my brother said.

"Daddy's head is exploding," I said.

Our mom kept singing as if nothing was happening. My brother tried to give our father the Heimlich, which I had also learned in school, but the Heimlich was for bigger things like a hunk of meat, not a slivery fish bone. My father pushed my brother away, pulled some black vinegar from the cabinet, took four huge slugs, wiped his lips, and said, "I'm fine. Vinegar washed it right down. Now, I don't want you kids eating any more fish tonight. We need to save some luck for the next year." He smiled in my direction and I covered my face, pretending to cry because I felt my father deserved better but only pretending because the only person who could make me cry was my mother, who knew it and never missed an opportunity to do so.

Later that night, my brother came into my room and told me, "Mom doesn't like Dad that much and she wants to live with just us. That's why she didn't do anything when he was choking. They're trying not to fight all the time because our uncle's coming so you have to be good and help me take care of Dad."

"How do you know Mommy hates Daddy?" I said.

"Annie. I never said hate."

"So I know she doesn't and who says I have to help you?"

"I'm just trying to talk to you."

I was so sick of him then. I didn't know why my brother had to be so mature at thirteen. Shouldn't he have been surly and rude to me? Embarrassed about the pimples on his face? Hormonally out of control and wanting to nail every girl in sight only to be rejected mercilessly, which would in turn shatter his self-esteem, and as a result of his destroyed sense of self-worth, shouldn't he have turned on me and taken his frustration out on me, instead of being someone who sat me down in my room and refused to speak to me as if I were a baby and instead took me seriously and cared for me and shamed me with his unflinching maturity? What allowed him to be at peace with the world when I was still so behind, waiting for the next several years to hurry up and finish so I could show everyone that I, too, would turn out this way, poised and so incredibly well-adjusted that I was a marvel to be discussed and openly pondered, perhaps even kept in a glass case rimmed with gold in a museum somewhere that charged exorbitantly for admission to see me, the special exhibit people traveled far and wide for.

"I'm not on your side," I said.

"There aren't any sides."

"Everyone's on a side."

My brother came over and sat next to me on the bed. He started to braid my hair.

"Stop it. I don't want you to do that."

But he kept going because he was good at it and he knew I liked having my hair touched, that it made me feel moonstone blue like my favorite crayon color, and feeling that way made me fearless against the nightmares I knew I would have. My mother was the one who taught my brother how to braid hair so that she wouldn't have to do it when she was depressed or stressed out or feeling frantic or in a hurry, or too tired to lift a finger or just wanted to be alone, and we had to understand or else it meant we didn't love her. We had to understand everything, not that we had a choice when she would suddenly stand up and grab her jacket, yelling over her shoulder as she walked out the front door, "Get used to your father's miserable cooking because you won't be seeing me anymore."

Sometimes I covered my eyes before I could see her leave but I could never keep them covered long enough. When I opened my eyes again nothing was ever different—there was my father in his tie, holding a computer programming book he was planning to study on the train to work, and there was my brother, letting his cereal go soggy and lowering his head so no one could see if his eyes were moist or dry, and there was the spot where we first angered our mother, the spot where she pulled at her own hair and threatened to rip it out and throw it down by our feet, a spot we avoided all day, tiptoed around casually, as if it were covered in glass shards, until she came back late in the evening when the darkness that surrounded my house was much different from the darkness that had snuck its way inside.

At school during recess, I tried to sing the song to my friends Sarah and Alexi because I wanted them to know what a dynamic uncle I had and how lucky I was that he was coming to live with us. I stood with them by the hopscotch square and sang in English:

Rain, rain, go away
My uncle's head is big today
My mom is pretty wet today
We're also wet, we're stinkin' wet
We need Bighead to keep us dry today!

"So that's how big my uncle's head is," I told them. "Ha ha, it makes me wanna laugh."

"Then laugh," Sarah said.

"Let's all do it," I suggested.

"Nah," Sarah said.

"Can't," Alexi said.

We stood around shifting dirt underneath our shoes for no reason.

"Why would a head keep a person dry?" Sarah asked.

Alexi didn't get it either. "Yeah, I know, right? I have a head and I still get wet."

"But the mother is wet and the head is big. It's bigger than an umbrella."

"Ew," Alexi said.

"No, thank you," Sarah said.

"Guys, it's so funny. I was laughing so hard before. Tears were coming out of my eyes."

"Not me," Sarah said. "I don't even wanna laugh for one minute."

"Me either. See?" Alexi pulled the corners of her mouth up into a smile and then took her hands away from her mouth and dropped them to her sides. Her smile fell down immediately. "My mouth won't laugh at it."

After that, I tried telling my mother I didn't want to hear that many stories about my uncle, but she claimed deep within my heart I did, and I kept saying, No, I really don't, I'll find out about him when he gets here, and she kept saying, No, but in your heart you want to know everything there is to know about him, and I said, No, really I don't, and she said, But no, really you do, and then I gave in, like I always did. She usually got her way with me, and if she didn't, she cried. No one liked seeing her cry but for me it was unbearable. I tried covering her mouth but that made her cry harder. I covered my eyes but that only made my ears more sensitive.

So I let her go on and on about how I used to love my uncle more than I loved to eat Cup Noodles in the middle of the night, which was my favorite thing to do. It was mostly the three of us who partook but every now and then my brother Sammy would poke his head into the kitchen when he heard our dad pouring water into the kettle and the sounds of us ripping open the plastic wrap. It was one of the rare moments when the shadow that shrouded his face lifted, and he was no longer "let me have my ups and downs" Sammy who made me pay him twenty-five cents just to go into his room to sharpen my pencil on some nights because he needed to be alone for hours, unlike me and my mom who needed to be needed. I respected his wishes because there were other nights when he came into my room and slipped two dollars under my pillow after I lost a tooth because Mom and Dad didn't know about the tooth fairy.

He was confusing that way, my savior one moment, a menace the next. But when we had late-night Cup Noodles he was only ever my savior. He let me slurp from his foam cup, saying he only liked eating the noodles, and he also fished every little dried carrot and pea out of my cup because I hated those things—what person who enjoyed good-tasting things and hated terrible-tasting things didn't? There was a kind of brief paradise in staying up later than was supposedly allowed, in being the kind of family who enjoyed one another's company. I never felt as safe and calm as I did on nights when my family treated ourselves to instant noodles, bloating ourselves with salt before bed.

Apparently the gooey pleasures of eating late-night noodles were nothing compared to the celestial company of my uncle, whose face and personality my mother encouraged me to recall with precision and tenderness even though I was only a baby during the year and a half I spent in China with my uncle and my extended family and I had never heard of anyone remembering what it was like to be a baby, yet my mother demanded it of me as proof that I had a heart, that I remembered the people who loved and cared for me. When I was seven months old, my parents took me to Shanghai and left me there until I was two. Your father was selling umbrellas in the street, my mother told me again and again, the more times she repeated herself, the louder she became. The street! she yelled. The friggin' street! Do you know who else wanders the street looking for money? Homeless drug addicts who give birth to stillborns in toilets!

Is a stillborn baby alive or dead? I asked my mother so many times that I eventually gave up on her hearing me.

Before I was born, my mother and my father and my brother shared a cramped room in Washington Heights with three other families for forty dollars a month. Like my father, the men in the room had come to America to study, they had gotten sponsors in China who believed in them, they had been told they were the chosen ones, the ones who had actually worked their way up to a miracle. They got to America and saved up enough money to bring their wives and children over, too, and one by one, after a year, two years, three years, four years: each and every one of them, just like my father before them, dropped out.

At parties, my father drank until he was red in the face and then talked and talked and talked. "It was rough in those days," he would say. "We thought an education was an education—the finest thing you could get! And an education in America? What could be better? We were clueless. I couldn't get into my own studio once because they didn't believe I was a student. They thought I was there to deliver Chinese food. I walked past gallery openings where every single possession I owned and every cent to my name wouldn't have added up to the value of a single earring hanging from a partygoer's ear. They were interested if you were a dissident who had been beaten and jailed and sentenced to hard labor. But even then, it would have been impossible to make a real living. I had a wife and a kid. And you know how Li Huiling is. She's the work of two wives." Depending on how red my father's face got, the number would change, increasing the redder he was. He'd sigh and say, "It's like dealing with ten completely different people in a manner of hours. Our first year in America, she cried every night, saying things no man should have to hear. Let me die, just let me die, she said to me. Send my ashes back to my mother, she said to me. We were running out of money. Sammy had a high fever when he was eighteen months old and we thought . . . we thought he wasn't going to make it. We had ten dollars to our name. We went to the ER and they asked if we had insurance and we said no. They asked for an address to send the bill, so I gave them my advisor's address. He was a good man. He got the bill and paid for it himself. I never asked him how much it was. Too ashamed. I couldn't afford art supplies. We went through dumpsters in the fancy neighborhoods on trash day, looking for anything edible or wearable." He talked until he was stumbling and then a couple of guys, also red in the face, would hoist his arms around their shoulders and carry him to the bed or the couch and he'd fall asleep immediately, occasionally waking after a violent coughing fit or to puke his guts out. Sammy was usually the one who remembered to set a trash bin next to my father when he got this way. The day after these parties, he would get up before any of us to make breakfast, betraying no trace of pain.

My mother didn't need to drink to talk about the old days. She didn't need to slur and lean against partygoers. She had me. I was her receptacle and I permitted her to speak endlessly. "Can you imagine? We were with the brightest and the best. These were people who placed number one and two *nationwide* in their subjects of study. And *every single one of them dropped out.*" Whenever she talked this way, she paused frequently to check my face for a response. If I didn't express enough concern, compassion, pity, or horror, she would start her story over again. If I failed to show the right response three times in a row, she would become frustrated and threaten never to speak to me again. If I somehow miraculously showed the right face, she would go on. "Then again, none of them had the potential your father and I had. Your father was a painter, you know. He made sculptures too. Long ago, back in China. I watched him destroy all of them one night in a panic with a hammer. I had a brick saved from when I was planning on smashing my own head—don't worry, that thought never lasted more than an hour. Anyway, I used that very brick to smash his sculptures into bits. We tossed the broken shards into the Huangpu River. Did any of those men who came to America to study ever make anything so incredible that it had to be destroyed? No, they were philistines. They were mercenaries. You wouldn't believe what your mother was capable of. Your mother met a German tourist outside of the Summer Palace in Beijing and he told me that I had 'vision,' that I spoke English like a character from a Jane Austen novel. He gifted me his camera so I could capture the world through my eyes. He was probably in love with me. His wife wasn't too happy he gave away their camera. Well, I took it. I was only twenty-two! I had never seen one before but I was like one of those savants. You know the ones who sit in front of a piano for the first time and start playing Beethoven? That was me exactly. I made a short film and had to go underground. There were plans made for me to seek asylum at one point. Do you know how good you have to be to get to that point? You basically have to be a genius! So your mother was a genius. So what? For what? So your daddy and I could go to America because *he* was offered a scholarship? So we could find out a scholarship was nothing? *Nothing*. There are no Chinese artists in America, did you know that, Annie? It's like a human saying they want to fly with hawks. You can't! You're the wrong species. So your father failed. So he had no chance and he failed. So we had to live like animals, squeezed up in one room with five mattresses on the floor. We were woken up in the middle of the night by some little girl moaning about her itchy legs and how she wanted to burn them off. I was *eight months pregnant* and this girl just cried and cried and cried. Do you know what I said one time when I couldn't take it anymore? I said, 'Take her to get them amputated!' No one else was offering any solutions! So I offered one. She was the one who named you. Did you know that, Annie? Can you imagine your poor mother coming back from the hospital with you and having to go right back to that room with all those people? All those failures. Can you?"

I nodded. I had heard this story so many times before.

"That little girl was called Christina. She said I should name you Annie. Her legs were covered in scabs. Her parents did nothing to control her. She told me the little orphan Annie was a great American hero and that I had to name you after the greatest female character in American film history."

"I thought you said you wanted to hack off her legs?"

"You're not listening," my mother said. "I was supposed to keep making films but I was born in the wrong era. Do you know what happened to all the great people I grew up with? They went to jail. They were tortured. They were sentenced to hard labor and worked to death. To literal death. Have you ever seen someone *literally* drop *dead* with *exhaustion?* Have you ever seen someone *cry to death?* Literally . . . *cry* . . . *to* . . . *death!* These people took their own lives to cut the misery short. These people were disappeared. Do you know what it means when someone is disappeared?"

"It means they're dead."

She shook her head in that way where I couldn't tell if she was disapproving of my answer or disapproving of what had happened back in China. "All for what? To move here in search of the good life? How is living in squalor with three other families in an airless room the good life? I was constipated," my mother continued, "the whole time you were in my belly because all we could afford to eat was white rice, without any flavor, without any meat or vegetables, just plain white rice. We became petty thieves. We'd go into a supermarket and rip open a Cup Noodles and pocket the flavor packets. We would stretch them out over the course of a whole week, sprinkling little bits of it over our rice, and that was it. Can you even imagine? Can you?"

I could not. I wasn't there for it and the parts I was there for, I couldn't remember.

"We had to spend all our money on you. We had to eat less frequently because of you. You needed so much from us."

"I'm sorry," I said. Three months after I was born, they saved enough to leave that "dungeon of suspended farts," as my mother so delicately put it to me one time when she felt like I wasn't giving her enough acknowledgment of how much she had endured to bring me into the world and keep me alive. In the new place my parents frequently ate raw eggs because the stove was broken and their landlord was an out-and-out crook. My mother said my father was too complacent, too willing to suffer, he didn't complain enough. "That's the American way! Complaining! Did you see in the paper yesterday? Someone scalded their tongue drinking piping hot coffee from McDonald's and they had the gall—the *gall*—to sue McDonald's. On what basis? On the basis that the McDonald's employee failed to warn them that the coffee was hot. Coffee *is* hot. It's *always* hot. And this shyster got a million dollars. Do you know what your father would have gotten? Nothing. He would've gotten nothing." It was true that my father rarely complained except when he got drunk at parties, and even then, it wasn't for a purpose, it wasn't to get ahead or to earn money, it was just overflow. That was why he failed to make a big stink about how the landlord never made good on his promise to fix the stove, and why he didn't fight back when the landlord started turning off the heat from eight A.M. to six P.M. on the weekdays because he believed honest, hardworking Americans were supposed to be at their jobs during those hours and no, he didn't expect less from a building occupied by Asians and black families, and no, he would not make exceptions for the hooligans who wore their pants well below their crotches so that their penises looked like guns peeking out above their belt loops, and yes, it just so happened that the kids who let their penises poke out like guns above their pants were all black, but no, that did not mean he was racist in any way against black people, he just didn't need to see so many penises pointed at him when he stopped by his own building and that was all. According to my mother, the black kids dealt drugs and bought space heaters with their profits, among other things, so they were fine with the heat being off all day, but my father sold umbrellas, so what was he going to buy? More umbrellas, my mother said bitterly before I could answer.

She told me I was lucky to have been in China for that year and a half, the hard years when she didn't know if she wanted to live or die, and I thought maybe if I were really lucky I'd have a mother who didn't feel like dying, and even if she did, maybe she could keep that to herself, because maybe, just maybe, if she kept her sadness to herself, it would go away on its own, or at least soften, like all the times I kept my anger to myself while waiting for her to notice that something was wrong and I needed to be held, to be told I was her beloved and it broke her heart to know she had hurt me. But what usually happened was my mother wouldn't notice, and after a few hours I would forget my anger and be happy to put her clip-on earrings in my hair and show her the dance I made up with Sarah and Alexi, a dance so wild that it shook all the earrings to the ground, and then my mom and I would swoop down and compete against each other for who could collect the most. Sometimes she let me win and sometimes she was vicious, clawing the earrings away from my fingers, but the point was that if I could forget my anger then she could forget her sadness.

The memories I had of China—of my uncle and my grandparents whom I lived with—were all given to me by my mother. She told me everything whether I wanted to hear it or not. "Everyone loved you the most and said you had inherited my exact personality. Don't forget you were competing with boys over there! You know how Chinese people are—boys this, boys that. But our family's different. My parents raised us differently. They never made me feel like I was any less than your uncle, and I always felt that my mom and dad gave me the same amount of love as they gave your uncle, and that's why I made sure you were loved even though you came second, and even though you aren't a boy. That's what makes our family special from other Chinese families, and that's why Mommy is different with you and Sammy compared to other Chinese mommies. Did you notice how all the other moms make their kids go to Chinese school on Sundays? Did Mommy make you go to Chinese school this year? Did I? Mommy *suggested* that you go to Chinese school because why would a Chinese person not want to learn Chinese? It's like a snail wanting to learn how to fly instead of snailing around like a snail is supposed to do. It's not natural and Mommy wants her children to do what is natural for them, which is why Mommy doesn't push you and Sammy like Peng a-yi. Did you know she makes her kids take violin lessons in the morning, then Chinese school, then math tutoring, then English tutoring, then pre-PSAT-SAT tutoring, then ninth-grade biology tutoring for sixth graders, then badminton, and then piano! That's how these women are, and you know what? I'm not going to subject you to that. Even if these women look at me like I want you to never go to college and never find a great job that earns enough money to take care of Mommy when Mommy goes blind and accidentally soils herself five times a day, because you know what? Those women couldn't be more wrong. Mommy actually wants all of those things for you, but I'm not going to be one of those women who has to control everything. I won't! That's why Mommy let Daddy go to America by himself and live two years in dangerous neighborhoods where Daddy had a really good chance of dying before having a chance to give Mommy all the things that a daddy should give a mommy, and all the things your daddy should give to your mommy's favorite two people—you and Sammy. Except you weren't born yet, but Mommy had a feeling that the two people she was meant to love forever and ever in life couldn't possibly just be Sammy and your father. Oh, certainly not. Can you believe your daddy wanted your mommy to have you when he couldn't even afford to take your mommy out for dinner? Not one measly dinner! Did you know Mommy only agreed to go to America and bring Sammy with her because Daddy was such an extravagant liar? Lie number one: he said he had a lovely place for us. Lie number two: he said he was making so much money he would soon be able to buy Mommy a *diamond* ring. Lie number three: he said people here are free to pursue what they want. Unlike China, in America you can make a living doing anything. Lie number four: he said we would love it in America. I could keep going but our lives would come to an end before I get through all the lies your daddy fed your mommy. Daddy is delusional. Daddy is a person Mommy tolerates but you and

Sammy are my loves. I was wondering . . . who do you love more? Mommy or Daddy? You don't have to answer right now, but you should know that when Chen shu shu asks you at a party in front of everyone and everyone is waiting for you to say the answer and you don't say anything, it embarrasses Mommy, and it makes Mommy cry, and that's why Mommy didn't pour you a soda with ice at the last party. I promise I didn't forget. I was in the bathroom sobbing my eyes out because you hurt me so much when you wouldn't answer Chen shu shu, which is why Mommy hopes you can think about this question right now and come up with an answer before next Friday since Chen shu shu is coming over for dinner and he's going to ask you again and if you don't answer, you'll make Mommy so sad that I won't be able to eat anything and then Mommy will get so weak that eventually Mommy will have to die and then you'll be all alone, except for Daddy and Sammy, but Daddy will probably be so devastated I've passed on that he won't even remember to make dinner for you and Sammy and then you know what? I'll tell you. You'll regret taking so long to figure out the answer to the question of who do you love more: Mommy or Daddy?"

She talked me into falling asleep when I was perfectly well rested, she talked me into tears when I didn't want to hear any more stories about her youth, the way she had suffered, how she married a man who would only continue to make her suffer, how my brother's main accomplishment in life so far was making her suffer, how she suffered when my father convinced her to take me back to China to live with my grandparents and uncle for a while until my parents were more financially secure, how she suffered while I was away in China, how she suffered the day she drove alone to the Charleston airport in South Carolina to meet my distant aunt Cheng Fang who agreed to bring me back to the United States from her trip to Shanghai, and how in the airport arrivals lounge the first thing I did was kick my mother in the shin repeatedly and head-butt her when she tried to pick me up. I honestly didn't recall doing this, but my mother insisted that I had behaved monstrously and would never let me forget how I hurt her that day, the day she waited a year and a half for, and how one day, I would turn on her again. Her predictions bewildered me. How could I, who clung to her in the mornings right when I woke up, who crawled into bed with her at night even though I was supposed to be sleeping on my own, who only made things for her in art class and never my father, never Sammy, never any of my friends, who set up a lemonade stand with Sarah and Alexi and spent my share of the profits on a glass vial that contained a grain of rice with my mother's name on it—how could a person so pathetically lovestruck for my mother as I was become someone who would one day callously abandon her?

For my mother, the good life had long expired, there was only struggle and pain left to endure, so when her mood lifted so tremendously at the news of my uncle having finally secured a visa, I was taken aback.

"Our life is finally just beginning," my mother told me after reading a letter from my uncle. He was coming in a month.

"Mommy," I said, pulling her hand. "Mommy, tickle me already."

She ignored my request. "You'll see your mommy like you've never seen her before." That night, I saw her arranging old photos of her and my uncle on our living room carpet with such intention and focus, I imagined she was an intrepid adventurer laying down a path. One of the reasons I studied her so closely was because I wanted to track how she ended up in these secret places I couldn't enter. How did she get there and why couldn't I follow her? But it was no use. She frequently disappeared without warning and I had to tell myself that if I wasn't a part of it, then I wasn't a part of it, and I would learn to savor that too.

August 1966

Twitch had a first cousin everyone called Goober, who had been so severely malnourished as a baby that he walked with a permanent limp and had a tendency to repeat the same phrase for a week at a time. He was rumored by the other kids to be so stupid that he once stood up before he was done shitting and walked around the rest of the day with a broken turd sticking out of his ass. The day after all the papers reprinted Mao's speech at Tiananmen in front of a million pulsing Red Guards, Goober made the mistake of going around Nanchang longtang and telling all the kids hanging around outside that he saw his father wiping his ass with the front page of the *Jiefang Ribao*. The next day his father was rounded up by a mob of kids and flogged publicly for hours. The kids, not satisfied with the beating, decided to shove a bundle of sticks up his ass so he would never shit on Chairman Mao again. Twitch had been one of the kids who kept gathering sticks even when the enthusiasm from the crowd had died down, and for several days afterward, the children of Nanchang longtang heard Goober's mom wailing deep into the night until one day she was gone too.

You you you you you you you you you turned turned turned turned turned turned her her her her her her in in in and and and and and and and and and him him him him him too too too too too too, Goober stuttered at Twitch, following him for blocks and blocks until he collapsed in front of the entrance to my grandparents' apartment.

Don't, my grandmother said to my uncle and my mother, even think about going out there. It was mostly directed at my uncle, who had been watching from the window and saw Goober twist his stumpier leg and land hard on his good one. If you have a death wish, fine, but I won't let you bring it on the rest of this family.

For the rest of August, my uncle Chunguang was nowhere to be found and neither was my mother, who had very recently become beautiful and spent her first year of high school walking around town surrounded by a procession of girls far less attractive than her, and trailed by several love-sick boys who swore monuments looked more statuesque when she passed them, trees renewed their verdant leaves when she leaned against them, snow melted into gold when she stepped in it, and birds flew drunk into lampposts and dropped dead in the street after passing over her (it was the idea that my mother could be responsible for the decline of a species that pleased her the most).

Don't think they won't come after you just because you have a decent face, my grandmother said to my mother after finding out what the Red Guards had done to Teacher Liu. Don't think these delinquents are above slashing that precious face of yours. You'll be a carcass before you're a beauty queen.

No one has said a word, my mother replied, preemptively defending her long hair, something that not a single other girl in their longtang still dared to have. That night, my grandmother hacked my mother's hair off with a kitchen knife while she was asleep. "I knew she was going to do it," my mother told me when I was older and more eager for these stories. "I was surprisingly calm in the morning when I woke up and saw that she had chopped it all off. I tried in vain to tie a chunk back onto the hair I had left. It was for my own good. She was right. Pretty didn't spare you."

My uncle was less convinced of the dangers my grandmother spoke of. Why can't I just go around the corner and back?

Why why why, my grandmother said. You waste my time with these whys. I'm going gray from trying to figure out how to burn the last of your father's books without anyone noticing and you're sitting here asking me why?

Twitch and the other kids with armbands came knocking on my grandparents' door a few days after Goober's mother disappeared.

We're looking for our umbrella. Where did he go? they asked my grandmother. We want to thank him for keeping us dry all those days it rained like hell.

He's with his father in Baoshan, my grandmother told the children. They're laboring to bring a plentiful crop for the fall.

Twitch had lost interest the minute he peered inside my grandparents' apartment and saw that it was completely bare of books and artwork. Just two beds and a bamboo slat on the floor with the sheets neatly made up, a cracked kitchen table and a chair with a broken leg. C'mon, let's go, he said to the other kids. We'll find some other freak to be our shade.

Far above the children loose in the streets, my uncle was seated on a chair that he had found in the hallway of his apartment building and had dragged up four flights of stairs to the roof. He was naked from head to toe, muttering, You can't tell me what to do, you can't tell me what to do, you can't tell me what to do, you can't tell me, you can't, all the while clutching his exposed penis, which he feared would turn red from the sun that beat down on him without mercy, without knowing.

The day my uncle was to arrive in New York, my family piled in my father's 1988 silver Nissan Sentra, and in the car I grabbed for Sammy's hand every time I thought I heard a strange sound coming from the engine or whenever I thought I saw a little stream of smoke rising from the hood. I imagined our car bursting into flames and exploding like in the action flicks I watched with my father on the weekends. "Could we survive that?" I asked my father after seeing Jean-Claude Van Damme emerge from a totaled car that had flipped over three trucks, crashed into a library, and exploded into flames after skidding across an oil slick.

"No," he said. "We'd be long dead."

As my father was getting a parking ticket from the machine, my mother lowered her face into her hands.

"You're already crying?" my brother asked her.

"If you hadn't seen your sister for seven years, you'd be crying too," my mother said in between loud gulps of air.

"Doubtful." He snatched his hand away from mine. "Do you really need to be doing that right now?"

"Sorry," I said.

"Just keep your hands to yourself."

After we parked, my brother was contrite and went off to buy me and our mother a Sprite and a Sunkist to make up for his moodiness.

"You don't have to pay me back." He had our mother's can of Sunkist between his legs because she couldn't drink anything too cold. It makes my throat feel like a lion trapped in an iceberg, she said once.

"It's still too cold," my mother said when Sammy offered her the soda.

"I'll fix it." I took the can from Sammy and slipped it down my pants. "It's always warm in there." I gave him my classic both-eyes-closed wink that Sammy pointed out was really just a drawn-out blink.

"That's disgusting," my mother said. "Who would want to drink that?"

I ended up drinking both and asking Sammy to take me to the bathroom three separate times. As we returned from the third bathroom trip, people on the flight from Shanghai began streaming out of the arrivals gate. I recognized my uncle immediately, though it wasn't exactly a great feat of psychic prowess since my mother showed me pictures of him every day for hours until I felt like attacking someone more helpless than I was. He had big, frizzy hair that I learned later was permed, and was several heads taller than most of the other Chinese people in the terminal. I could not stop staring at his mouth, unsure if I really saw what I thought I saw—that every single one of his teeth was crooked and black at the roots. Later in our lives, when everyone who took care of me when I was a child started to raise the question of who would take care of them, my mother would call me in the middle of the night to tell me that Uncle Chunguang had lost his last tooth on his fiftieth birthday, and I would grieve for him as if he had lost his arms and his legs, too, wailing alone in my dorm room, pounding my fists against my chest until I knocked the wind out of myself, falling onto my bed and lying there on my back, breathing shallowly, realizing that my mother had gotten to me after all. Her hysteria would not end with her passing because it had already been passed on to me.

He came for me first, picked me up and raised me as high as his arms extended. It was my first memory of looking down on so many people at once—I felt like we were all strangers meeting in the same giant living room. He set me down and crouched to my height. "Do you remember me?"

I nodded shyly to please him, permitting a tiny lie, something I had only done previously for my mother.

"You should," he said. "You peed all over me before boarding your flight back to America with Auntie Cheng Fang." Everyone laughed except me. My uncle patted my brother on the back and then decided to pull him in for a full embrace. "You know the drinking age in China is unofficially whenever the hell you want, right?" My brother smiled and I glanced at my father, trying to imagine Sammy's face turning as red as his had been at all the parties this year. My uncle motioned for me to get on his shoulders. "May I?"

I nodded.

"Guoqiang, nihaonihaonihaonihaonihaonihaonihao," my uncle said, cradling my father's hands in his and shaking them vigorously. "Happy belated eighteenth birthday, brother!"

"Spoken like a man with the energy of a boy," my father said. We had celebrated his forty-fifth birthday the week before with Chen shu shu and the usual suspects. My gift to him was hiding in the bathroom for the last hour of the party to avoid the question of how I ranked my love.

My uncle hugged my mother while I was still perched on his shoulders. I felt my sneakers graze my mother's shoulder blades. She was crying silently for once, not making a show of herself, not proclaiming that she had been cleaved apart, leaving us responsible for holding her up, for mending her.

"You won't believe what Ma made me bring in my suitcase."

My mother held on to Sammy's shoulders for support, still unable to speak.

"Sugarcane."

A new stream of tears ran down her face.

"Have you ever," my uncle asked Sammy, "seen anyone so emotional over sugarcane?"

Sammy shook his head. "Get ready."

"Oh, I've been preparing."

It was lovely to be above it all and when my father motioned to leave, I felt the pleasure and panic of doorways that had once seemed impossible to reach looming ahead of me. I felt sure I was on the verge of something wonderful. I wanted to come right up to it, and shake its hand and say, I'm ready I'm ready I'm ready I'm ready.

At first, it seemed like nothing was changing. I was shy around my uncle and Sammy was helpful. Sammy showed him the public bus system, how to use tokens instead of exact change, the way to the nearest McDonald's and the trick of asking for the secret two cheeseburgers deal, which was only forty-nine cents more than the regular meal. He took my uncle to the library and showed him the selection of Chinese books, cassettes, and videos. He explained that at self-serving soda stations like 7-Eleven, the way to go was to fill your cup with only soda, no ice, that way you get twice as much drink.

My father got my uncle a job delivering Chinese food through an old friend he knew back in the days when they sold umbrellas in the street. Now his friend was the owner of a Cantonese restaurant on Bayard Street even though he was from Jinan.

"They don't know the difference here?" my uncle asked.

My father snorted. "These people don't know the difference between Japan and China. You'll see soon. Everything here is Hunan Garden or Great Wall restaurant and nothing to do with either. Lao wai only know how to order three things: sweet-and-sour chicken, beef with broccoli, and lao mian, but they pronounce it low mee-en."

My uncle was amused. "Sweet-and-sour? So the lao wai here have a taste for Shanghai style."

"If you can even call it that."

"Do you remember," my mom interjected, "when Ma traded a stalk of sugarcane she had smuggled back from that farm for extra flour-ration tickets?"

"Oh yeah, to the really weird dude who consorted with the long-haired Canadian who came and taught English at our middle school for a month before he disappeared. Didn't he hide the sugarcane in some hollowed-out tree one time?"

"I think that turned out to be a made-up story."

"Well, anyway, remember how excited we got when we came home to those lumps of fried flour and we'd dip it in expired soy sauce that was all gooey? It looks like that crap."

"Oh, c'mon. You're exaggerating."

"It's not exactly like that stuff," my father said, "but it might as well be. You'd be lucky to find a speck of meat inside all that fried dough."

When we took my uncle to the supermarket for the first time, he started laughing at the concept of a supermarket that didn't sell food.

"Where's the food?" he kept asking. "Where do they keep the food in this food market?"

"Right here," I said, gesturing toward shelves of cereal.

"And here," Sammy said, pointing at another aisle for chips.

"Those are boxes," my uncle said, "and those are just bags."

"We're taking you to the food," my father said. We brought him to the produce and fruit section, which did seem really sad—wilty greens and all manner of lettuce sprayed by jets of ice-cold water.

Normally, we never went to American grocery stores; we shopped at Chinese supermarkets in Flushing or Elmhurst, but every once in a while on his way back from work, my dad would stop by the Key Food on College Point Boulevard and check to see if the three-for-one-dollar cilantro deal was on. As soon as I remembered that, I told my uncle that he didn't need to worry, we only shopped where Chinese people shopped. He would see soon—there were other supermarkets that had long aisles of greens with names that had not yet been given English counterparts, where you could buy fish heads for a buck and a three-pound bag of pork bones for two.

"So Americans don't eat food," he said, still unable to recover from the lack of food we found on our grocery trip.

My father nodded. "They just eat boxes, brother."

My mother wanted to have a welcome party right away for my uncle but there was no time. It took him a few weeks to acclimate to his new job—he frequently mixed up chow mein and lo mein and had to work extra hours to make up for his errors. "Will someone set these lao wai straight?" my uncle complained after his first week.

"Chicken lo mein is Sarah's favorite food and egg rolls are Alexi's," I said.

"You see?" Sammy said. "You gotta get into the American mindset."

"They aren't egg rolls," my uncle said. "They're tough rolls of fried flour with cornstarch and MSG."

Then once my uncle got used to the job, some issue came up with his student visa and he had to take the bus to D.C. to sort it out and returned with a mysterious illness that lasted ten days. "I've figured it out," he said. "It's too sanitary here. There aren't any germs! If I ever go back to Shanghai, I'm a dead man."

"I don't get it," I said.

"China's filthy," Sammy translated. "Though you're probably inoculated because you were there when you were a baby."

"I don't get it."

"No one does. Just accept that and move on."

"Your qin jiu jiu will explain everything to you, Annie," my uncle promised, using a word I didn't understand, and when I didn't understand a word I imagined a hole where the word was supposed to land. Sammy was the most attentive to my bouts of blankness but he wasn't always in the mood to do something about it. My uncle, on the other hand, was like my mother in that he could talk for hours and never needed space like Sammy did, but, unlike my mother, when my uncle spoke at length, it didn't leave me smothered. "You know, in Shanghai, you had way too many uncles."

"I don't remember any of them."

"Neither does your daddy," my father joked. "And they're my brothers!"

"Well, I couldn't stand to be just another uncle. I wanted to be your best uncle, the one you love more than anyone. So I asked you, Am I just another jiu jiu or am I your *qin* jiu jiu? And you said qin jiu jiu. So that's what you called me from then on. Qin means something really dear to your heart. You agreed I was the most cherished uncle of all your uncles and so I became your qin jiu jiu."

Without precedent, my mother was elated to hear this story about my time in Shanghai even though it didn't involve her.

"This is why we have to have a party. For your qin jiu jiu," she said.

"Isn't my favorite niece's birthday coming up?"

"May tenth," my brother confirmed.

"Well, then, the party should be for Annie," my uncle said.

My mother was uncharacteristically excited to celebrate me and didn't even try to make it about her. "Eight birthday cakes! Eight presents! Eight different birthday outfits!"

"Eight days of Annie," my uncle said.

"Can I have eight days to myself? That'll be my present to you," Sammy said, already weary of us. "Or at least eight hours."

"Eight days before my baby is no longer a baby," my father said. "It's happening too soon."

"With her, you might have to wait longer," Sammy said.

"There's nothing wrong with staying small," my uncle said. "As long as it's what Annie wants."

"I get to choose?" I asked. I had never been given the choice before.

"It's your life, little lady," my uncle said.

"Look at what being big gets you," my mother said, pointing to my uncle's head.

"Huh?" Sammy said.

"It's true," my uncle explained. "I had this big head when I was in the womb."

"You know this story," my mother said to me even though I didn't. "Your grandmother couldn't push him out in the final moments of giving birth. It was no joke."

"Your mother had to go and get the guy who was mopping blood off the floor of this rural hospital. She brought him to your grandmother thinking he could help."

"Ma was screaming. I mean actually screaming. Pleading with God to let her get through this."

"And cursing our father," my uncle added. "She really gave it to him."

"Ma was like, If you ever try to come near me again to make another of these, I'll slice it off."

"So your mother goes and she gets this guy who is basically the janitor, and she's like, Attention! I've brought help. You have to remember this was back then. There were no specially trained doctors in the country. They got some teenager with a month of training to deliver all the babies. It was normal for the child—"

"—and the mother—"

"—to not survive childbirth."

"So at this point your uncle is half out but it's the wrong way. His head was still stuck inside your grandmother's belly. There was something like half a minute left before he would have suffocated and come out a stillborn."

Dead, I realized, a stillborn is dead.

"The dude was unfazed. He instructed your grandfather to grab your grandmother by her shoulders. He was like, You got a grip on her?"

"And then he grabs your uncle's tiny legs and yanks him right out. Your uncle was delivered by a country janitor," my mother said, laughing.

"There'd be no me without your mother," my uncle said. "I owe her my life."

My mother cleared her throat. "Childbirth," she started to say, and then trailed off. We waited for her to continue, but she had nothing left to say.

The morning of the party, everyone had tasks except me, because I was too small to be useful and I was the guest of honor, so my job was to sit around and be cherished, except everyone was too busy to pay me much attention. My father was marinating the meat and combining packages of Cup Noodles to make a monster pot of ramen.

My mother was mending my party dress, which I had

snagged in our doorway the weekend before, ripping a hole through both the bodice and the skirt. When I showed my mom, she was furious for days, threatening to make me go naked to my own party.

Sammy was busy baking cupcakes and mixing up eight kinds of frosting and showing my uncle how our oven worked. "Do they not have these in China?"

"Nope," my uncle said. "Well, unless you count those useless makeshift furnaces that were supposed to produce steel."

My father grunted. I had heard him ranting about those backyard furnaces at a party earlier this year. "Remember when we were told to throw all our kitchen implements in? That was supposed to get us on par with England. Whose ass were we supposed to be eating? Our own, apparently."

I got bored waiting around for the party to start. It was hours before anyone would pay attention to me. I fingered my presents and played with the bows until one of them fell off. I brought that one into the kitchen and asked my parents if I could open it before the guests came, but my mother said that would mark me as ungrateful. The plan was for the presents to be unwrapped one by one in front of all the guests.

"Is today for you or is it for Annie?" my father asked, opening a beer.

"What kind of question is that, even?" She slammed my party dress down on our dining table, which doubled as our living room coffee table since our dining room was also our living room and also temporarily my uncle's room. "Of course it's for our daughter. It's her frigging birthday, why wouldn't we want it to be the most memorable, lavish birthday to remember? Why else would I be mending this dress and jabbing my own finger with a needle? Look at this!" She held up her hand. "Do you see how many times the skin's been pierced? I need reading glasses. Why? Because I've been squinting my whole damn life since meeting you. Squinting at every seam. Reading books by candlelight like a goddamn bum and now my eyes are ruined and we can't afford to get a proper prescription."

"Calm down," Sammy mumbled. "No one even likes the unwrapping presents part."

"No one likes it?" My mother was enraged now. "Everyone loves it! I leave parties early when they skip that part. It's a birthday party. We specifically instructed everyone to bring presents. More than one if they can swing it. And on short notice too. This is what we told our guests and now, an hour before they're supposed to show up, suddenly everyone wants to scrap it? Where was this last week when we agreed to have the party? Where were you all when I was out buying presents for Annie and hiding them under the bed and waking up before all of you to carefully wrap each and every one so it would be a surprise? No. No! I won't let you look at me like I'm the one who's being unreasonable. Don't look at me like you're afraid of what *I'm* going to do. I'm the one who's afraid of what you people are capable of." My mother was holding my dress like she was going to rip it down the middle.

"Hold on a second," my uncle said, approaching my mother the way cops on television approached a highly dangerous criminal who was holding a gun to an innocent bystander's head, though in this case, we were all the bystanders; all of us were hostage to my mother's outbursts. "All this talk about gifts reminds me that I still haven't given you the gift Ma got for you."

They went into his room, a little curtained-off area that was really still the living room. Originally, my father had bought all these materials and tools to build a temporary wall, but my mother kept accusing him of scaring her, accusing him of wanting to bury my uncle alive like in that one story about the wine cellar, and my father wearily replied that she was the one who was concerned about her brother's privacy and anyway, it was bricks in the story and it was meant to be taken as an allegory. My mother accused my father of condescending to her so he relented and worked on putting up a curtain instead, which angered my mother because she said a curtain provided no privacy at all! So it was back to the wall, which not only still scared her but she also claimed that she had bumped into it in the middle of the night and nearly broke her nose, so it was back to the curtain, but my mother hated the color of the curtain my father brought home from the store, she said it reminded her of puking when she was pregnant with me, so it was back to the wall, then the curtain, then the wall, then the curtain again, until finally my father blew up at her and told her that if she didn't stop it, he would harden his heart and leave her. My mother was never one to be fazed, least of all by my father, so she ran to her bedroom to collect her things, shouting the whole time he wouldn't dare leave because he was a coward and who was it that kept him fed and clothed the time he was nearly kicked out of school? Who was it that supported him when he could barely keep himself upright? Who was it that stuck by him when he couldn't get a second-year scholarship, and while taking care of their infant son no less! Who? she screamed. Say who or never see me again.

Who, my father said finally after polishing off half a bottle of Johnnie Walker Red.

That time she was gone for three days. In her absence we did not eat Cup Noodles. Sammy suggested it to wound my mother from afar, as a kind of revenge, but I told him we had to wait. We had to honor her even if she wouldn't have done the same for us. When she finally came back, I waited for my father and Sammy to toast to me, to say, You did it, Annie, you brought her back. She would have been lost to us without you. But they never did. They forgot how serious I had been about the noodles when my mother returned with a curtain she liked—eggshell white, she said, the only acceptable curtain. They forgot that my mother cared about the little things and so did I. In a few days, we all forgot, because these were just little episodes, one after the other, all of them the same, another scar that faded enough to be just another mark we carried.

My uncle took my mother behind the dividing eggshell-white curtain and they were in there for a while. When they came out, she was holding a microphone.

"Your mom is going to sing for you, Annie. She's a gifted singer, did you know that?"

"Don't tell me—" my father started to say.

"He got me a karaoke machine!" My mother unraveled the cord and then bent down to hold the microphone up to me like it was my turn to say something.

"Thank you, jiu jiu."

"Qin jiu jiu," he corrected me.

"Thank you, qin jiu jiu, for getting Mommy that microphone."

"Two microphones!" He pulled another one out from behind his back. "For duets. Did you know your mother and your father sang the most beautiful duet on their wedding night? Your mother—she's not just some run-of-the-mill talented singer. She was the most talented singer in Shanghai. Producers literally pounded on our door to try and sign her. They wanted to make her the Chinese Shirley Temple. They said A-Ling had it all, beauty and talent."

"Your grandmother wouldn't let me. She said it was a dirty business. They were liars and crooks, she said to me, and I'm not feeding you to those sharks. She told me my entire life I was hideous. Disgusting to look at, and it would destroy me if I went with those producers. They were setting me up for public humiliation. Well, I was only ten! I didn't want to be publicly humiliated, and how was I supposed to know I was pretty? The person I trusted the most told me every day I should cover my face so as not to scare people in the streets."

"Your mother was stunning. I mean, she's still got it, but she was a head turner as a young girl. She had a voice like a nightingale too. But it's good Ma kept you away from those producers. You would have never met Guoqiang and never had Sammy and Annie, my two favorite people in the world."

My mother got up and drew the microphone to her lips and spoke into it, breathy and slow. "Yes. It. Was. A. Good. Thing. In. The. End."

August 1966

The dispute started when my grandmother announced that they were going to have a guest stay with them for a few days. There was an air of secrecy to the whole thing. My grandfather even came back from Baoshan for a day and was extremely occupied drafting papers and meeting with several people my mother and my uncle had never seen before. He and my grandmother spoke in hushed tones about making arrangements to "send her up north," and then by nightfall, he was gone again. My grandmother decided the guest would sleep in my uncle's bed, since it was the most firm, and my uncle would sleep on the floor. She scrubbed the sheets and aired them out in the sun and laid a wrapped-up dried plum on the pillow as a special treat for their guest.

Why don't we get special treats? my uncle asked.

You're alive, aren't you? You want a better treat than that?

Everyone I know is alive, my uncle protested.

And still, my grandmother said, you want more treats.

Finally, in the middle of the night, without even hearing an audible knock, my grandmother got out of bed, opened the door, and quickly pulled in the woman standing in the doorway. Her head was totally shaved and she wore a ratty long-sleeved cardigan over another sweater riddled with holes and tears even though it had been over a hundred degrees that day and not much cooler at night. She immediately started to weep, bracing herself in my grandmother's arms.

There's no need for this, my grandmother said. Everything has been taken care of. Save your tears for something worse.

It's Teacher Liu, my uncle whispered to my mother. It's definitely her.

No, it can't be. I thought she committed suicide.

Well, it's either her or her twin or her ghost.

Deep into the night, when everyone was asleep, my grandmother heard a scream and leaped out of bed to rush to Teacher Liu's side.

It's okay, it's okay, she said. No one is coming for you. You're safe. But it turned out to be something else altogether: my uncle had spent the past six months erecting a house made of boogers on the wall he faced at night, and what Teacher Liu saw when she woke up from uneasy dreams was my uncle's dried snot meticulously arranged into a two-story Spanish-style villa, glistening from the glow of the street-lamps outside.

The next morning, my grandmother stood over him and instructed him to destroy his creation, booger by booger, until there was nothing left.

She didn't have to make such a big deal about it, my uncle said, shooting dirty looks at his teacher, who was wrapped up in blankets and eating porridge. And anyway, he continued, I saved her and she never even thanked me.

No, my grandmother said.

Yes, I did—I untied her.

No, my grandmother repeated, and slapped him clear across his cheek. You don't know her.

She's in our house. I'm looking right at her. How are you going to say I don't know who that is?

We don't know her. She'll be gone tonight. Do you understand me? You don't know her. She was never here and I don't want to hear another word about it.

My uncle put his hands over the side of his cheek that she had slapped. I hate you so much, he told my grandmother.

And I don't care, she replied, stepping into the kitchen to prepare a wet cloth to run over the faint, oily marks that still remained on the wall, the only evidence that once, a house made of snot had resided there and its creator could not have been more proud.

May 1996

For the first two hours of my birthday party, I stayed by my uncle's side. As soon as my mother pulled him away to introduce him to a guest who had recently come back from Tennessee on business, Chen shu shu made a beeline for me. I had refused to answer his question all night but he wasn't giving up. "Can you at least say if you love *me*?"

I didn't answer.

"Surely you *like* me? C'mon, Annie, we're old friends! Who do you like more—me or your uncle?"

"Qin jiu jiu," I said.

"Okay, now we're getting somewhere. What about your mother or your father? Who do you love more?"

"I love them both equally."

"You have to choose."

"I love my mommy and my daddy the same," I said, careful

to say my mother first and then my father. My mother had a way of knowing who was talking about her even if she was on the other side of the room. She probably heard every instance her name was invoked when I was in Shanghai and she was in New York. She probably sensed from across the world that after a month, I stopped calling out for her, and she would probably never forgive me for it.

"Did you forget about your mother?" she would ask me. "Did you remember my face? Did you ever hear my voice in your head? Did they even tell you you had a mother back in New York or did everyone cut me out of the picture?"

"I . . . I . . . I . . ." I could never get past those I's, which was disastrous because my mother was looking to be disproved, she was looking for me to deliver a speech that directly counteracted the one she had concocted in her brain, so it wasn't enough to say, "No, I didn't forget you, Mommy," whenever she brought up that year and a half. What she wanted me to say was: "I can't even begin to imagine the pain you must have felt being ripped away from me when we had such a close bond and when you already had to go through the trauma of being separated from your family to come to America to be with Daddy who failed to deliver on every single promise he ever explicitly *and* implicitly made. And then to think that your one and only daughter was in Shanghai, reunited with the family you missed so much that it made you go crazy with grief, and on top of that, I wasn't even aware of all the sacrifices you had to make to keep me safe and loved, and then to think every day that passed, I was less and less aware of you as my mother and as the most important person in my life so by the time I came back to you in America all I wanted to do was head-butt you in the face, which left lasting psychic scars as well as physical ones. It really is true that you have had one of the most unfair, terrible lives any person on earth could have and I'm so sorry that you've had to go through that."

My mother kept tabs on every single thing that could hurt her so I had to say her name first to Chen shu shu, who was still grilling me, unsatisfied with my answer.

My uncle broke away from his conversation to intervene. "She loves everyone! There's no one sweeter than little Annie."

Xiao Ming a-yi came over and took Chen shu shu's cup away from him. "One an hour," she reminded him with a look in her eye that said, Better if it's zero.

"That's a really nice dress." Chen shu shu fingered the raised mesh polka dots on the top layer of my skirt. "Show Chen shu shu how you twirl like a princess."

"You know," my uncle said, coming to my rescue again. "I've worn a dress before. In public."

"You?" Chen shu shu slapped his knees with laughter. "I didn't know you swing that way."

"Oh, I swing every which way," my uncle said, winking at me, which either meant he really did or he really didn't, but either way I had no idea why it was so funny.

"Hey, Li Huiling," Chen shu shu shouted. "Did you know your brother's a cross-dresser?"

"He was," she said, smiling. "For a day. Are we telling that story now?"

"Story time," Chen shu shu said, shushing the party chatter and indicating that people should gather around to listen.

"I used to be jealous of A-Ling when I was a kid. I thought it was really unfair my sister was allowed to wear dresses *and* skirts *and* pants, but I was only allowed to wear pants."

"Chunguang was always concerned with what he wasn't allowed to do. He used to get into massive fights with our mother over how he wanted to wear dresses too."

"Wow," Sammy said. "You guys really are related." My father raised his glass of Johnnie Walker and clinked it against Sammy's can of Coke.

"Naturally our mother thought I was being ridiculous. She ignored me and let me fume for days. I was a crier back then. One time she finished knitting an entire sweater while I stood there crying in front of her. She tuned me out like I was street noise." My mother nodded enthusiastically. "Anyway, so I run out of school early one afternoon and I go through my sister's clothes, pulling out all her best dresses, and I change into one of them. The nicest one, of course. Well, not as nice as Annie's dress, but it was really something. Our mother pulled out all the stops on that one—it had silk sleeves and those nice twirly clasps around the neck." The women at the party all looked at each other knowingly, nodding their heads like yes, yes, yes, it must have been a fine dress for a girl back then.

"Go on, Chunguang," Chen shu shu said, putting his arm around my uncle. "Tell us about all the men you picked up in that tasty little number."

"Well, I'm pretty proud of myself, right? So I go outside where everyone's hanging out and I go, Look at me! Look at me! Who says only girls can wear dresses?"

My mother was already laughing at an ending that she knew but the rest of us were still waiting to hear.

"A crowd starts forming around me. Everyone's coming out of their houses to look at me prancing around in a dress. I hear this one kid saying, Bighead Chunguang is a girl! and I get this sinking feeling in my gut that I've made a huge mistake. The crowd is growing around me and the kids are yelling, He's a girl! Bighead wants to be a girl! and the one who started the whole thing—you guys remember Twitch? Some of you must have known him."

"His dad used to beat the lights out of him," my father said.

"The teachers too," Ling shu shu said with his mouth full of cake.

"Didn't people say he got into a bare-knuckle fight with a PLA soldier when he was still in middle school?" Peng a-yi asked from the kitchen where she was washing out the container she had used to bring her delicious cold noodles with scallion and so much raw garlic and chili seeds that for an hour after eating them, I felt like the clouds in my head had parted and everything was crystal clear.

"Oh, there were some stories," my uncle said and then turned his focus to me as if we were having a private conversation and everyone else was eavesdropping. "Annie, you had to see this guy to believe it. He really knew how to get into trouble. Even as a kid he knew how to make people afraid of him. So he walks through the crowd and looks me in the eye with the most evil, twisted smile on his face and he goes, Let's see if he's a boy or a girl. There's only one way to find out.

"I'm all of six years old at this point. I have no idea what he meant by 'there's only one way to find out' but my gut told me I did not want to know. I'm thinking I'm done for and in my head I keep hearing your grandmother's voice: Do you have to be interested in everything? Can't anything be off-limits to you? Suddenly, your mother appears—out of nowhere! Annie, I'm not exaggerating—you have to listen to your qin jiu jiu— your mom here had a smile that could melt the coldest of hearts. So she gets in front of me and flashes a smile at the crowd and says, Does no one have a sense of humor anymore? And then the weirdest thing happens. The crowd just sort of melts away. People stop shouting and the kids holding up rocks put them down by their feet and shuffle away. Even Twitch, he starts scratching his head and mumbling about how he has to get up early the next morning because there was talk of a fresh restock of eggs at the distribution center and his mother wanted him to be in line by four A.M."

"That really happened?" I asked, glancing in my mother's direction. "Mommy? Did you really save qin jiu jiu?"

"What can I say? He's my baby brother."

The partygoers raised their cups and cheered. "To boys who wanna be girls!" Chen shu shu shouted.

"To beautiful girls who save the day and become beautiful women!" said Wang shu shu, who always found a way to sit next to my mother at parties when the night really got going and he had switched from Heineken to Johnnie Walker. Sometimes he'd announce to the whole party that my father had it *made*. This guy, Wang shu shu would slur, must be doing something the rest of you fools haven't figured out yet.

I knew my mother was hoping to be the last toast of the night but Wang shu shu's toast was too long and convoluted and no one was able to repeat it word for word. "To beautiful girls . . ." people said and then trailed off.

"And to Annie!" my uncle added, raising his glass higher than anyone. "Happy birthday to our princess!" It was the first time anyone had ever toasted me and I noticed everyone raised their glass except my mother. There would surely be hell to pay. It would come back later during some argument that had nothing to do with this, but the memory of how she was robbed of an important moment because of me would most certainly be the thing that would push her over the edge.

"All right," my mother said, putting a stop to the clapping and the birthday wishes. "Let's test out this karaoke machine."

My brother went to help my uncle set up the machine,

pulling out several shiny round laser discs. "Who wants to go first?"

"Let's hear a duet from husband and wife," Peng a-yi suggested.

"Fine idea," Chen shu shu agreed. "Annie, now pay close attention. I'm going to quiz you on who was the better singer afterward." The guy wouldn't let it go. He wanted to send me to my deathbed.

My parents huddled over the song list for a while. "A love song," my father said, "for lovers!"

"Never say that again," my mother said, but she was pleased. She had often accused my father of being developmentally challenged when it came to romance. "You can't get your wife of sixteen years some flowers? You don't know how to put music on before dinner? You've never heard of candlelight? When we go into a store and I say, Oh, I love this dress so much, it's my dream dress, you don't think to take a mental note to come back the next weekend to buy it and surprise me with it? I know, I know, I know," she'd say before my father had a chance to say anything. "You work, you study nights and weekends to get more work, you do everything to put food on the table. Well, that's the bare minimum a man is supposed to do, so don't give me that crap. You think you're entitled to this life, but you have to *earn* it."

My father was useless at charming my mother except when he struck gold and found that sweet spot between his fourth and fifth drink at parties and was suddenly in possession of the kind of confidence that made my mother respect him but not so much that she felt threatened by him; it was then and only then that he remembered to pull out her chair before she sat down and was coordinated enough to twirl her like they were ballroom dancers. He pretended one time to be Gene Kelly at the end of a long party full of lingering guests who didn't want to go home. He followed the last few out into the street and waved at them under his umbrella as they drove off into the night. He folded his umbrella and twirled it in a half circle. "I'm singing in the rain," he belted, tapping his feet, showing us moves we had never seen his body make until that moment. "You're my Debbie Reynolds but even more stunning," he serenaded my mother, refusing to come inside. "I'm bringing Hollywood home, honey."

Sammy had to drag my father back inside and peel his wet clothes off him. "Go get a towel," he told me, "and a hair dryer unless you want Dad to die of pneumonia."

I always suspected it was that very possibility—that my father could die making a fool of himself—that had pleased my mother the most that night.

Now my father was considerably less cute to my mother but that was why the drinking was so crucial—so he could obliterate the growing record of debts that had piled up between them and be free to enjoy himself for once. "This is dedicated to Annie," my father said into the microphone as the music began. "Happy birthday, my dear daughter. May you one day give your father and mother the pleasure of singing this song at your wedding."

"Up in the trees the birds have become pairs," my mother sang, delicately pressing her forefinger and thumb together like a Beijing opera star.

"Green waters," my father sang, stepping up to my mother and cupping her cheek, then gesturing at some far-off place, *"clear mountains carry little [____]"*

They took turns singing to each other and turning to us at the end of each line. It was a Chinese that was somewhere between the Chinese I understood and used with my parents and a Chinese that I only heard during the big CCTV Chinese New Year's all-day gala when all the big pop stars and movie

stars and famous singers from the past got together to entertain the country. "It's our Oscars," my mother explained.
"Except it's bigger than the Oscars and more interesting in
every way." This year, she took a day off work to watch the
show morning till night, pointing out her favorites. "That's
my favorite singer, and her, too, and also him. He's the most
talented movie star of the last twenty years. No one's funnier
than her. He's an incredible game-show host. There's another great singing pair. The person on the left, yes, she's my
favorite entertainer."

"How many favorites do you have?" Sammy asked.

"All of them. I love all the great entertainers our country
has produced."

"Damn," Sammy said. "Proud much?"

"Very," my mother answered.

"From this day on, we won't accept [_____ _____] suffering." My
mother's eyes were closed as she sang—she didn't need to
look at the lyrics on the screen.

My father, on the other hand, staggered closer and closer
to the TV. *"Husband and wife are going home together."*

"You work the fields and I'll weave the cloth."

"I'll bring back the water and you'll flower the soil."

"[_____ _____] may be broken, can [___] wind [___] rain."

*"As long as a husband and wife love each other, even suffering
is sweet."*

"You and I are like [_____ ___] birds."

My mother started singing the last line, *"[_____ _____ _____
_____ _____ _____]!"* and my father joined in halfway through. I
wasn't sure if it was because I was so entranced by their voices
mingling together, without strife, or because the words were
new to me, but I didn't understand the ending.

"Hao ting!" the guests cheered. "Zai lai yi ge," they begged.
"Chang de xiang ge xing!"

"Who sang it better?" Chen shu shu asked me. "Annie, isn't your mother a natural? A great talent?"

Wang shu shu agreed vigorously, taking the opportunity to congratulate my mother, touching her with too much obvious pleasure on his face. "We have a real-life star among us!"

"Hardly," my mother said, her face plump and shiny with joy. "My notes were way off. I'm rusty, and don't get me started on Guoqiang's timing."

"I'm telling you, Annie," my uncle said. "Producers were trying to break our door down. But your grandmother said no."

"She practically locked me in the house like I was a prisoner," my mother added.

"A shame," Chen shu shu said. "They should've have cast you in the movie."

"Well," my uncle said. "A-Ling would have been a year old, but yeah."

"Sammy," I whispered into his ear. "Did you understand it?"

"Barely. I just know it's some old song about a goddess who falls in love with a mortal."

My father overheard Sammy. "No mere mortal! The most honest, hardworking man for miles around. He sold himself into indentured servitude to pay off his family's debt. He meets a woman one day not knowing she's the youngest daughter of a great and mighty god. And you know what, son? She doesn't want to go back up there. To heaven. No, she wants to come down to ren jian. The human world. Where we're all condemned to. But she doesn't see it that way. To her, our world is a kind of paradise. That's where her man is! And she wants to be with her man." He started singing the woman's part, *"Ni wo hao bi yuan yang niao."*

"What's what?" I asked.

"She says, You and I are like the mandarin ducks."

"Huh?" Sammy said. "Chinese ducks?"

"Mandarin ducks, son! They are *always* together. Where there's one there's another next to it. I challenge you to find me a solitary mandarin duck hanging out."

"That's okay, I'm good," Sammy said, though my father was no longer listening.

"Can't do it! Not possible! You can *only* find mandarin ducks in pairs. That's how they are! When one duck dies, the other drops dead right away!"

"It's quite disturbing," my mother said.

My father was smashing his words together. All the adults were. "So this goddess decides she wants to be with her man. That's right. Her man is so important to her that she'd give up her immortality—her life in the realm of the gods—to be part of this world right here with all its misery and indignity. To be one of us."

My mother looked like she was far away. "These old folk songs romanticize love too much."

"How the hell else would love be portrayed if not roman-tic?" Chen shu shu objected. Xiao Ming a-yi took the drink out of his hand and said, "No more." Chen shu shu barely registered her presence.

My mother continued as if she hadn't heard Chen shu shu. "She gave up paradise—her birthright to paradise—for a man."

"And for the human world," my uncle added, sensing my mother was about to cry. "There's no better world than the human world—isn't that right, everyone?" He raised his glass and cried, "To the human world!" and we all cried after him, "The human world! The human world! The human world!"

My uncle was furious my grandmother had made him destroy his booger house. He asked my grandmother if she would like it if he ordered her to break all of her bowls and rip her best shirt to shreds.

No, I would not, she said. But that's because it's not your place to tell your mother such things.

So I can't say anything? But you get to say whatever you want to me?

If I tell you to bend your head down to my feet and lick the dirt from my shoes, then you must do it. If I tell you to go out into the jungle and catch with your bare hands a serpent that is capable of laying golden eggs, then I better not see you again until you've brought back those eggs. If I tell you to cut off strips of your skin to make a pair of leather gloves to keep me warm, you should already be sharpening your knife and searching for the warmest part of your body to hack off. But as my son, you cannot so much as tell me what I should make for dinner on any given night. Do you understand me?

My uncle felt sick to think he was condemned to such a servile position simply because he was born a son to my grandmother and he would remain her son for the rest of his life. It infuriated him how my grandmother was so cavalier and unapologetic in the way she ordered him around, how she assumed that his only task was to obey her, how she so readily refused him his own personhood and volition.

I'll put it right back up, he said, after Teacher Liu left. Tonight, I'll pick my nose dry and put them all right back up. And if you stop me, I'll tell everyone she was here. Let's see how you like it when they destroy your things.

I'll pick every last booger off the wall and stuff them right back into your nose. And if you tell a soul she was here, I'll strangle you myself and leave your lifeless body out in the street with my handprints on your neck so no one will dare come near this family.

You don't scare me, my uncle said. And you don't own me. I'll run away. You'll wake up one morning and I'll be gone and you won't know how to find me.

Is that right? Do you mean it, Chunguang? Do you stand by what you say? That I don't own you?

Yes, I do, he said in between loud sniffling. You don't own me and I hate you and won't do anything you tell me to do. You think you can bully me. You can't. I'm free. I'm my own person.

I ask you again. Do you stand by what you say? That you want to be free from me? That you won't be bound to me?

Yes, my uncle said. I already said yes, didn't I?

Then give me those socks, my grandmother said, pointing at his feet. You won't be needing those since I knitted them for you.

Fine, my uncle said.

And your shirt, and your pants, and come to think of it, all of your clothes.

So my uncle took off his shirt and his pants and his undershirt and stood there in his underwear.

Don't be shy around your mother. If you are going to be free, don't half-ass it. Give back everything I ever gave you and you're free. Just like that. You're no longer my son. I'm no longer your mother. I don't owe you anything. You don't owe me anything. Come on. Take those off as well.

Fine, my uncle said. Take it. All of these clothes are garbage anyway.

Don't you dare stand there as if this is still your home. Since you are no longer my child and I am no longer your mother, you won't be living here anymore either. Is that clear? You can't very well say you won't listen to your mother and still allow yourself to eat food I bought and prepared, and sleep in the bed I paid for with money I earned, and tuck yourself in blankets I sewed for you. Now, if you want to be truly free, then be truly free. Live outside where the pigeons can peck you to death while you sleep, and if not to death, at least they will take your penis and your ass and your mouth and your fingers and your toes, and when that happens, you won't be coming back here. You go and find the other kids who don't need their mothers. You go and do what they do and see how many years you have left. I can tell you now you won't need all your fingers to count them. But go see for yourself. You are free now just as I am now free from you. I'm no longer responsible for you and you no longer have to listen to me. This is the agreement you insisted on. I won't be opening this door to you anymore. So scram. Get the hell out of here. Consider yourself unwelcome. You have nothing to do with me and I have nothing to do with you. This house is no longer your home. Get your ass out of here. Goodbye.

June 1996

After my birthday karaoke reignited my mother's starlet ambitions, her bid for attention moved its target from just me to the whole world.

"Why do you think I made that film?" my mother said one night around the dinner table. "It wasn't just so I could talk about it. I wanted people to see it. It was an incendiary object. I wanted it to break glass, to shatter old ideologies and open up new [_____]." More and more she used words I didn't understand. "The irony, right? You have to have bourgeois upbringing and education to know what a cancer it is on the people."

"Well, where is it?" my brother asked.

"The film?" my mother said.

"Yeah, can we watch it or what?"

"We don't know where the copies are," my father said. "Or if there are even any left. We had to destroy the tape. We gave a copy to Ling and he's in Kuala Lumpur, the last I heard. And then some went to these Norwegian student filmmakers who we haven't heard from since Tiananmen."

"It's all going down the drain. Things are [_____ _____ _____ _____ _____ _____ _____ _____ _____ _____ _____ _____ _____ _____ _____ _____] over there," my uncle said. "You guys have mostly been here this whole time so you don't know but . . ." He trailed off and stood up. "All right. Off to work." He was still working the night shift at the restaurant my dad's friend owned, so we had gotten into the habit of eating dinner on the weekends extra early.

"Already?" my mom asked. "Stay for a song. Just one?" My mother now started and ended every day with song, cradling a microphone whether it was plugged in or not, serenading us with love songs from her favorite singer, Teresa Teng, the angelic Taiwanese pop star who had been Jackie Chan's lover for a minute in the late seventies. "We used to bootleg her tapes," my mother said. "Everyone said I looked like I could be her sister."

Sammy rolled his eyes. "Her prettier sister, right?"

"No," my mother said, surprising us. "No one was more beautiful than Deng Lijun." When news of her death came over the evening CCTV broadcast the year before, my mother shrieked and dropped her Cup Noodles to the floor. I had been standing next to her and some of the broth splashed onto my feet, scalding me.

"Ow, ow, ow, ow, ow, ow, ow. Mommy, that was really hot."

"No, no, no. This can't be, this can't be, this can't be, this can't be," my mother had cried. She beat her fist into her chest and smashed the cup and the noodles and the still partly dehydrated peas and carrots and scallions and corn with her slippered feet. "They killed her. They killed her with their bare hands. I can see the marks on her neck."

"It was an asthma attack, honey," my father had said. "She had been in bad health for a while."

"Lies," my mother had cried. "She was murdered." For weeks after, our house filled with her songs.

"Look at the moon," my mother told me the night Teresa died. "No one sang more gracefully or more lovingly of the moon than little Deng. Her English name was Teresa and I wanted to name you Teresa, but your father said we ought to embrace American idols. What crap. I should have gone with my initial impulses. From now on, you're Teresa. Teresa, my heart, should we get McDonald's for breakfast tomorrow?"

I didn't answer because I wasn't sure if she was calling out for me or her favorite singer.

"Hello? Are you asleep? Where'd you go, Teresa?"

"Are you talking to me?" I asked.

"I'm talking to Teresa," she snapped, tears dripping down her cheeks.

Now, a year later, she was singing more and crying less. And by the time school let out for the summer my qin jiu jiu really was qin. He was precious to me, as miraculous as my mother had prepped me to believe. When we didn't clap loudly enough to satisfy my mother after another rendition of "Yue Liang Dai Biao Wo De Xin," she threw the microphone across the room. "You'll give your father a standing ovation for the 'Macarena' but you can't throw your own mother a few measly claps? How about 'Good job'? How about 'That was great, Mom'? Nothing?"

My uncle picked up the microphone, neatly wrapped the

cord around it, and put it back into the sliding glass case in our entertainment center. "They did clap," he said. "Your kids love your singing. We all do. You can't get upset if things don't go exactly as you envisioned them. Your emotions take a toll on them." He meant me and Sammy. We were talked about in those days. We were considered. It made me feel like royalty. Now when my mother was on a roll, one of her soliloquies about how life had mistreated her and saved an especially cruel fate for her and her alone, as long as my uncle was home and not out delivering food or attending English language meet-ups at the public library, he would stop her mid-sentence and remind her that their mother wouldn't have stood for this kind of self-pity. "If Ma could hear you," he'd say, "she'd come to New York and slap those complaining lips right off of you."

"Well, she's not here, is she?"

"She's not here because she's at home taking care of our father—her husband. She's looking out for him. Don't you want to be able to say the same?"

My mother let him say these things to her. Since my uncle moved in with us in April, she hadn't threatened to leave or tear out her hair or rip off her fingernails one by one and flick them against our faces so we could feel a fraction of the pain she felt. Instead she'd sniffle and straighten up like she was getting ready for battle and then go into the bathroom for a few minutes and come out with water drying on her face. She didn't apologize but she didn't go on and on either. It was during those periods of uneasy calm, when Sammy and I wondered how long her restraint could possibly last, that we were finally as doting and caring and considerate toward our mother as she had been berating and unreasonable and furious with us. We'd make sure to apologize anytime we walked past her too quickly and we'd remember to leave a bottle of

Sunkist out on the counter so she could enjoy her warm soda with the rest of us, who always had plenty of chilled sodas since we were in the majority with our preference, and though she clearly enjoyed our penance and attention, it was nothing compared to the rapturous delight she expressed whenever we outdid her by blaming our father for anything and everything that could possibly bother her before she had a chance to.

"Don't worry, Mom," Sammy said in the aftermath of one of these de-escalations, "I'll never attempt art when I get older. Only a sadist—a self-centered sadist—would put his family through that."

"Yeah," I chimed in. "It's really unfair for the person who has to marry him."

"No, I would never attempt art. That's a death sentence right there," Sammy continued.

"Two death sentences!" I said.

"Well"—Sammy hesitated—"unless it was someone who was *actually* talented."

"A star!" I cried. "Like Mommy!"

"It's true, Mom. You've got a voice like the queen of the mermaids. I can only imagine what kind of vision you had behind the camera."

"That's old stuff," my mother said. "Kids, I want you to be the first to hear this . . . your mother has decided to become a novelist. It's a much worthier endeavor. Not nearly as frivolous as singing or as decadent as directing."

My uncle cocked an eyebrow. "What do you plan on writing?"

"The untold story of my life," my mother said. "And your life and our mother's life and all the family stories no one has the guts to tell."

"Well, I hope you won't savage your poor little brother in it," my uncle said, winking at me.

"Or me," I said, winking my exactly-like-a-blink wink, the precise mechanics of which I was refining in secret because my uncle said it was charming and part of my personality and thus something I should cherish and cultivate.

My mother, however, was uncharmed and refused to make any promises. "Art does not pledge loyalty to the petty feelings of its subjects! There cannot be any restriction on the truth!"

My father looked up from his *Programming in C++* book. "I don't recall you saying that when I was in grad school."

"And I don't recall you making anything anyone wanted in their home or gallery," my mother retorted.

"And this book you're writing . . ."

"Will be on every bookshelf in every library and every bookstore!"

I backed her up. "It'll be taught in every school. Right, Mommy?"

"That's right, my baby."

"Are you writing it in Chinese or English?" my brother asked.

"What do you think?"

"I don't know." I could tell he wanted to say, "Chinese because your English is broken," but he knew that would upset her. No broken person in the history of the world had ever wanted to be described that way. He was sparing her because she demanded to be spared.

"If only," my mother started to say, "one of my kids could read and write in Chinese."

"Now, that's a big endeavor," my uncle said. "I'm only semiliterate myself. It takes a special kind of nerd to slog through all that memorization."

"Your uncle is being humble," my mother said. "Don't listen to him. In a few years, we'll all be calling him Dr. Li."

"All right, sis, it's just a master's degree."

"So now you think grad school is a good thing again?" My father tried to enter our conversation but no one was listening to him.

Sammy offered to be my mother's research assistant, her own personal historian and archivist, since he had a gift for keeping track of details and was a natural interviewer. "I'll go through the family documents. I'll record the oral histories of all the people who are still alive."

"What documents? What people?" my father asked.

"I wanna start Chinese school this summer," I said. "So I can translate all your books, Mommy."

"My sweet angel girl," my mother said, her eyes brimming with tears. "I thought you'd never ask."

"You pitched a fit last year when your mother suggested you start attending on Sundays," my father reminded me.

"Will you look at your kids," my uncle said to my father, always the person who attended to anyone who needed attending and tried his best to not adhere to the hierarchy that my mother wanted us to adhere to. "What would A-Ling do without them? What would you?"

My father looked at us like we were potatoes trying to be oranges. The way my mother egged us on, the promises she begged us, explicitly and implicitly, to make if we wanted to avoid imminent and future breakdowns, must have riled him.

"My book will open with the story of Bighead!" my mother said.

"Now, what did I say about painting me in a good light?"

"It'll be better than good! It's art." My mother was gleeful and seeing her this way, I felt infected.

"Mommy will tell the story of qin jiu jiu!"

My mother grabbed my hand and we started to sing the Bighead song.

"Now, stop that," my uncle said, feigning like it didn't bring him any pleasure. Even Sammy was humming along. My mother and I danced around my uncle in a circle, like the kids had done in the summers when there was nothing to do. I locked eyes with my father as I passed him and then broke the gaze. He must have been wondering how and why he had helped to create me—what part of him did he pass on to me, and would I nurture it with the same patience and care I was nurturing the part of me that was my mother, who never, ever, ever gave anything a rest?

August 1966

My mother was the one who went up to the roof after a few hours had passed, when the children of Nanchang longtang, tired and hungry and uncomfortable with being anointed the stewards of anarchy, haunted by the rumors of where they were going in the fall and how long they would be going there for, began to make the trek home, hoping this was the night when there might be a little bit of pork fat to eat for dinner. It was my mother who found my uncle, his little naked boy body shivering under the dimming light, his face swollen and long strands of mucus falling from his nostrils to his lap. She was the one who brought him a sheet to wrap around himself and the one who wiped his nose with a handkerchief and coaxed him into coming back downstairs. She was the one who took him down to my grandmother and said, Forgive him. He's sorry. She brought him a bowl of rice seasoned with a few drops of soy sauce, and when he was still hungry afterward, she went into the kitchen and asked my grandmother in the softest voice she could muster, Can you slip some pickled radishes into my bowl? I'll tell him I stole it. We both know he won't eat it if he thinks I asked you for it. It's okay, Ma, he learned his lesson and he's hungry. Remember what we said? We don't let anyone in this house go hungry.

It was my mother who tucked him in and told him that there exists a sort of love in the world that only survives as long as no one speaks of it, and that was the reason why he would never have to worry because my grandmother was never going to be the kind of mother who held her children in her arms and told them how smart and beautiful and talented they were. She was only ever going to scold them, make them feel diminutive, make them feel like they were never good enough, make them know this world wouldn't be kind to them. She wasn't going to let someone else be better than her at making her children feel pain or scare them more than she could, and to her, that was a form of protection.

That's how we will be with our own children, my mother told my uncle, proud that she had realized this. Because we'll learn from our mother who learned from her mother who learned from her mother who learned from her mother before her and all the mothers before them. That's how I imagine we'll be, my mother said, watching my uncle's mouth open slightly, allowing a trickle of drool to escape—his nightly ritual before falling asleep.

August 1996

My mother insisted on a going-away party for my uncle before he left for Tennessee to start his master's program in chemical engineering. My uncle was reluctant but we all agreed there had to be a proper send-off.

In the weeks leading up to his departure, my mother had reverted back to her twice-daily breakdowns. "You can miss the first month, can't you?"

But my uncle wasn't having it and shut down all her attempts to bargain with him. "And what? Keep delivering food? You don't actually want me to mess this up, do you? You gotta move past the first layer of sentiment—that's just reaction, an attempt to circumvent any kind of pain. Deep down, you want me to go. I know you do."

I had trouble accepting it too. "Will you come back right away?"

"He'll come back for Christmas," my father said. "We already got his ticket home."

"Why why why why why why?" I moaned, climbing all over my father and smacking the bony parts of his body.

"That's what he came here to do. That was his plan, my little ape." I was eight now, but still had the tiny lanky body of a monkey, helpless and prone to being swung like an object.

"It's true," my uncle said. "You better stay small and adorable for your qin jiu jiu. I'm kidding—I want you to grow if those bones of yours want to stretch. Remember: you can be who you want to be, okay? And you," he said, speaking to Sammy, "you're gonna have to be the man of the house because this one"—he pointed to my dad—"needs to retire soon. And Sammy? Make no mistake about it. You've already grown into a fine young man. You're five times the man I was at your age."

Chen shu shu and Xiao Ming a-yi were the first to arrive, and right away he and my father egged each other on to take three shots for my uncle. Then Chen shu shu ordered me to sit on his knee and drunkenly proclaimed to everyone that if Xiao Ming a-yi finally came to her senses and left him and he was still single when I turned eighteen, he would marry me. My parents laughed and clutched at their bellies, and I thought, Great, I'm getting married to a pervert in ten years. People were drinking fast, just as Sammy warned me earlier when he came into my room and told me to brace myself. "When adults are sad, they bury their feelings in drink."

"I just don't get what's so good about alcohol," I said.

"Let's hope neither of us ever do."

A few of the guests drank too much and started talking about the old days, who turned in whom and who got beaten and who lost their minds.

"This is a celebration," my father said, climbing onto the couch and interrupting the somber talk. "We're all of sound minds, aren't we?"

Some of the guests nodded and the drunk ones ribbed each other and jokingly accused the other of lunacy.

"We're all still here, aren't we?" my father said. "We all came to this country with not a dime in our pockets, did we not?"

"Dad, can you help me with the helium? It's not pumping properly," Sammy asked, offering my father a dignified exit off the couch.

"Some of us are broken down. But not my brother-in-law. He's . . . he's . . . he's . . ."

"Okay, okay," my mother intervened. "That's enough."

"Annie," my father said after slumping back down onto the couch and tapping the seat cushion next to him. "Come sit with Daddy."

"Okay."

"Daddy's drunk."

"I know. Do you want some coffee?"

"You know how to make coffee?"

"Qin jiu jiu showed me."

"You're a miracle daughter. You really are. I lucked out with you and Sammy. I will do everything in my power to give you the life I lost out on. Daddy's old, you see. But Annie, you're still young."

"If I'm so young," I said, "then you can't be that old yet. As long as I'm still little, you can't say you're old." My father pulled me in so close to him that I couldn't breathe. I struggled to escape but he wouldn't let me go.

"One second longer. Let Daddy hold you."

A tear rolled down my face, the first of who knew how many for him and him alone.

Chen shu shu came over and broke our embrace to ask me the dreaded question, "Do you remember what I asked you at your birthday party? You said you needed to think it over and I said, Okay, but I'm gonna need an answer before your uncle leaves."

I looked at him with pure hate. "No."

"C'mon, now," he said. "You've deflected long enough. Everyone wants to know the answer. We've all been waiting and now you've had enough time to think this through. Who do you love more? Your mother or your father?"

I shook my head.

"C'mon, little Annie, it's easy. Just say 'my mom' or 'my father.' Here." He put his fists out in front of me. "Just pick one of these and I'll tell you if it's your mom or dad."

I shook my head again.

"All right, all right," my uncle said. "Let that one go. She doesn't want to answer right now."

"Pick one! I can tell you already know your answer. Share with Chen shu shu. Just whisper it into my ear."

There was some amused laughter followed by silence as my mother made her way to the door. At this point in my life, the sound of my mother slamming the front door should have been only as shocking as the sound of a car key turning on the engine, or the sound of the blinds squeaking when my father pulled them up in the mornings, or the sound of my brother pushing his glass of orange juice back and forth on the kitchen table whenever he was anxious about a test, but there must have been some shred of hope I couldn't bear to give up that prevented the sound of the door slamming from becoming familiar to me, and so it chilled me as it always did and always would. No matter how long the intervals between each outburst lasted, it was still a shock when the period of respite ended.

This time I ran out after her. She was standing against our Nissan Sentra, hiding her face in her hands.

"Are you okay, Mommy?" I asked.

She shook her head and then picked me up and sat me on the hood of the car. "He's a horrible man," she said.

"Daddy?"

"No. Chen shu shu. I hate that he asks you that stupid question at every party in front of everyone. You shouldn't have to answer that. No child should. He's a horrible, awful man. He's a drunk, Annie. I won't stand for him bullying my daughter."

My uncle emerged to join us under the stars. "Everything okay here?"

My mother nodded. "I can't stand that guy."

"Should I go in there and kick his ass back to Hunan?"

My mother laughed and then broke down in tears. "It's a cruel thing to ask a child."

"He's an idiot," my uncle said. "He forgets his own name after a few drinks."

"Please don't cry anymore," I said. "It makes me cry when you cry."

"Really?" she said, separating my hair into three sections and loosely braiding it the way she taught Sammy to when I couldn't sleep at night and she wasn't available to soothe me.

I didn't have to answer—I was already crying.

The front door opened again and this time it was Sammy.

"Okay, seriously, guys? Dad is starting to talk about Leonardo da Vinci. It's getting to the point where people are gonna start throwing tomatoes."

"Sammy!" my mother said, exuberance creeping back into her voice. "My eldest boy! My brilliant son! Should we go back in and save the guests from your father?"

"Uh, yes," he said. "I'd say the situation is dire."

My mother lifted me off the hood of the car.

"Am I too heavy?" I asked her.

"A little," she said but didn't put me down until we got to the front door.

"I don't like making an entrance," Sammy said.

"Then you and I can go in through the back," my uncle said.

"Annie and I have no problem going through the front. Right, Annie?"

"Right!"

The four of us went our two ways and ended up in the same place. "The party's not over!" my mother announced as we reentered the crowd. "Is the microphone plugged in, Sammy?"

He went over to check and gave my mother the thumbs-up.

"Can you play 'He Ri Jun Zai Lai'?"

"Lai lai lai," Chen shu shu cheered, oblivious of all that he had set in motion.

My mother began to sing, *"Beautiful flowers don't live long."*

My father was shouting about da Vinci's notebooks to Xiao Ming a-yi, who was nodding politely.

My uncle saw I was trying to follow along with my mother's voice and losing the thread. "After you leave tonight," he said in English, "when will you come back?"

"Sing it with me," my mother said. "For my brother!"

"Ren sheng nande ji hui zui,

"bu huan geng he dai."

I noticed my brother was singing the chorus—he had been listening all along, he had been learning the words I skipped.

My uncle was still translating for me. "She's saying there are so few opportunities to be happy in this world, Annie. So you have to take them all. When they present themselves, you take them."

"And drink up!" Chen shu shu cut in. "No need to censor yourself for the little one. That's what your mother's singing: Don't wait until you're unhappy to drink! He wanle zhe bei zai shuo ba!"

"Lai lai lai," my mother spoke into the microphone, beckoning me and my uncle. Her voice was girlish and soft. She departed from the script even as the music continued. "Come everyone, come gather around. Have a glass on me and my genius son Sammy and my brilliant little brother and my sweet, beautiful daughter. They live up in the skies and the rest of us are condemned to solid ground. We must toast to them! To those who choose to stay in heaven." She was a poet sometimes, my mother.

"A toast!" everyone agreed, raising their beers and whiskey glasses.

"What about me?" my father asked right as the music stopped. Everyone laughed.

My uncle said, "And to Guoqiang!"

"To Guoqiang!" the people said.

This time my mother raised her glass of orange soda higher than anyone and when the toast was over, she put down her glass, took the pins out of her hair, and let it all drop down. For a brief second, I could not see her—her face obscured by her long mane of hair—but I was certain it would not be long before she revealed herself again.

"And to my qin jiu jiu!" I cried out.

"To qin jiu jiu!" everyone repeated after me, raising their glasses for the third time.

My uncle picked me up as Sammy released the balloons he had pumped full of helium on his own, without anyone's help. He raised me to the ceiling and I locked my legs together and held my arms out as if I were a plane and the red and blue and purple and green and silver balloons I pushed out of my way were the clouds parting for me as I made my ascent into the unknown territory of the skies.

The Evolution of My Brother

I.

We were alone most afternoons. On one of them, we searched my room for candles. We found one that I liked: white with Colombian coffee beans clustered around the bottom.

"Eat it," I said.

"No," my brother said, furrowing his eyebrows, turning away.

"Eat it, eat it, eat it, eat it, eat it." I backed him into a corner with the coffee end of the candle pointed at his mouth.

"Stop it, Jen-naay," he said, stepping back, "or I'll enable my force shield to turn your bones into dirt."

"Okay, fine. Let's light this and then blow it out. Let's do it like twenty times in a row. It'll be just like our birthday."

"Why twenty? That's too many."

"Fine, twenty-eight it is."

"No. That's more than twenty."

"Okay, okay, fine. Fifty-five, if you insist."

We set the candle on our living room coffee table. I told him to stand back while I lit up the match and touched it to the wick. "You first."

He crouched down on the ground, closed his eyes, and leaned in close. Neither of us expected the front of his over-grown bowl cut to touch the flame, to curl up immediately, to change color as if he had gotten a badly bleached body wave. If he were old enough, I would have laughed and said, "Cute pubes." But instead, I covered his face with my hands and pulled out the burnt ends. The little crisps disappeared between my fingers when I rubbed them together. It smelled just like popcorn.

"Let's not tell Mom."

"Okay, Jenny."

I picked out the rest of the burnt strands, and the two of us ate them from my cupped hand while we sat on the couch, my arm around him and his feet wiggling like noodles in boiling water, our eyes staring straight ahead, as if the opening credits were coming on.

The next summer, I pulled him inside my room and locked the door. I was supposed to be teaching him addition, but I tossed the workbook on the floor and stuck a pair of head-phones on his head.

"Good thing your head's so big."

I turned the volume up. He was five and starting kinder-garten in three weeks. I was going to be a high schooler.

"So the casbah is like a huge palace," I said. When he started to get that distracted look on his face, I turned up the volume another few dials and told him to pay attention. "This is important," I said. "When kids on the bus ask what you're listening to, you just say: PUNK ROCK MOTHERFUCKER!" I folded all his fingers down into his palm except for his forefinger and pinky.

"What?" he shouted. I pushed one of the headphones away from his ear and held him by the shoulders.

"Look at me." We stared at each other. "You're listening to punk rock music, the most rockin' music ever made in this extremely unrocked-out world. So you just listen to this on the bus and school the shit out of the other kids about rocking out."

"Why?"

"You're a punk rocker now."

"Can you make me cereal with milk?" he asked, handing me the headphones.

He came in holding two pieces of ham stuck together and wearing a Mickey Mouse sweatshirt over a hand-me-down turtleneck that was so old and stretched out on him it reminded me of our neighbor's Dalmatian after he was neutered and had to wear a big plastic cone around his neck. I had said so the last time my brother wore it. (We were outside throwing sticks for our neighbor's Dalmatian to catch and my brother asked me what neutering was and I said, "Hold on, I'll get some scissors and show you," which earned me an appalled look from our neighbor, and I was immediately embarrassed because I knew he found me odious and cruel.)

I felt bad whenever I saw my brother wearing my old turtlenecks and when I saw him eating food supplied by our mother. Our mother had a habit of shaping food into hard tangerines. She'd cram his mouth so full of food that I'd find him sitting on a couch, dazed and unable to close his mouth or swallow. I'd pick him up and carry him to the bathroom so he could spit everything out into the toilet. I pitied him because I knew he would never have an easy relationship with food, not now and not when he was older either.

"Please stop feeding him," I said to my mother once.

"You must be kidding," she said. "You were the one who begged me for an extra five dollars a month to feed African babies."

I was reading a magazine when my brother walked in, his mouth overflowing with half-chewed ham, and instead of taking the two slices of ham away and showing him the proper way to eat and instead of re-cuffing his drooping turtleneck so it didn't look quite so pathetic, I ignored him and pretended I only cared about the new sweater-skirt combos for autumn. When he wouldn't leave, I told him, "You have to."

"No." He folded a slice of ham into his mouth. "No, I don't."

I nudged his shoulder. "Yes, you do," I said, bumping the other slice of ham out of his hands.

"Hey," he said, butting his head against my stomach. We started using knuckles, fingernails, pillows, magazines. He kicked my leg, and I struck his cheek, the ham side. His mouth opened, and big fat tears slid down his cheeks and into his open ham mouth.

Seeing him like that made me feel like a monster. "Spit it out," I begged.

It would be my fault later in his life when he wouldn't take packed ham and cheese sandwiches to school, and even later, when his teacher made a phone call to our mother, concerned that he had refused to eat the ham sandwiches the cafeteria had prepared for the annual seventh-grade overnight trip to Boston. It was my fault. It had always been my fault. It would be my fault again in the future; it was endless. "Please," I whispered. More pieces of chewed-up ham slid out of his mouth. He tried sucking some of them back up in between gaspy breaths. I cupped my hands together and offered them to him. "Just spit it out in here." The ball of ham in his mouth seemed to be expanding from the addition of all his tears. "I can't see you like this."

Later that day, when we were getting ready for bed, I showed my brother how to pull back his lips to look at his gums, and when he did, I found a little piece of uneaten ham stuck between his incisors.

"Can I have it?" I asked.

"Why?" He smiled wide, baring his teeth so I could pick the piece of ham out. I popped it into my mouth. It tasted so, so salty.

He had a temporary stutter where he would add the sound "ma" to the beginning of certain words. Sometimes, when he called out for me, he would say, "ma-ma-ma-ma Jenny." It sounded like he was saying, "my-my-my-myyy Jen-neeeeeeee." I liked being his property.

"It's very common," the speech pathologist told us. "It's a tic, almost like clearing your throat compulsively before speaking."

"Is it significant that he often does it before saying my name?" I asked, hopeful.

"Not particularly," the speech pathologist answered.

"She's a quack," I said to my parents when we got home. "I don't believe a word she says." I went and found my brother pacing around in circles in the TV room, taking great care to keep the speed at which he paced perfectly steady. "Say it again."

"What?" my brother asked, continuing to circle until I stood in front of him, blocking his path.

"Say, 'my Jenneeeeeeeee.' "

"My Jenneeeeee," he said, pushing me away and continuing to circle.

"No. Say it like you did the other day. Ma-ma-ma-myy Jenneeee."

"Ma-ma-ma-myy Jenneeee," he repeated after me, completing another perfect circle.

It wasn't the same. He was growing up. He was growing out of his speech disorder. From that point on, in order to be his, I had to request it.

When I was fifteen, I spent three weeks in California studying philosophy at Stanford University with people who made me feel like I was part of a tribe—their tribe, not mine, but a tribe nonetheless. All I had wanted for so long was to be part of a family that wasn't mine. To have an excuse to love mine less, an excuse to run away instead of staying so close all the time. "Why," I wailed to our parents the week I got back, "do we have to do everything together? Why can't you ever go someplace without us?" My brother was standing as close to me as he could without touching me. I had warned him that if I felt any part of his body touch mine I would saw it off. "Why does it always have to be the four of us? Do you really think I'm going to live here forever? Maybe *he* will," I said, pointing at my brother, "but not me."

"You should have stayed in California, then," my mother said.

"If you want to stay home while we go to Home Depot, that's no problem," my father said. "It's fine. We'll take your brother with us."

"Jenny's not coming?" my brother asked.

"If you come one inch closer to me, I swear to God," I said.

In the weeks leading up to my Stanford trip, everyone had

been extremely tense. I was about to experience my first taste of independence and I wanted to celebrate, but my excitement had been deflated by my mother's moping, my brother's tears, and my father's absence—he seemed to be staying late at work even more than usual. Everything became an argument—whether I was going to check one bag or two, whether I should buy a phone card now or wait until I got to California, whether I should try to find used copies of the assigned books or buy them new at the Stanford bookstore. The one thing we didn't ever bring up was money, how I had convinced my parents to spend nearly six months' salary to get me to California and cover tuition and room and board, how I had sold them on the necessity of all of this. I wasn't thinking about how the first time either of them had ever traveled anywhere significant was to America from Shanghai, with nothing more than eight boiled eggs in their pockets, fifty dollars that were confiscated at customs upon arrival, and a suitcase full of pots and pans and one broken broomstick for fear that they would not be able to find or afford these things in America. And anyway, that trip didn't make them *travelers*, at least not the way the people I met at Stanford would speak of travel; that trip just made them immigrants, it made them charity. They became people to be saved, to be helped by institutions and individuals. I didn't want to be saved, I wanted to be a member of the institution organizing the charity, the philanthropist dripping with generosity.

At one point, in the early years of living in New York, they became friends with another Chinese couple who showed them how to scavenge for edible food in dumpsters. This other couple was saving money to bring their little girl back from Shanghai, where they had sent her to live with her grandparents after a long struggle with their finances.

"Essentially, they were broke," my mother told me. "They

were irresponsible. They talked constantly about their little girl. I think her name was Christina. Every time we came across a carton of tangerines or something, the mother would say, 'Our Christina only eats sour fruit.' They were odd. They were the kind of people we didn't know to stay away from back in the day. Just compare them to us. Your father was not only able to save up enough money on a student scholarship—a student scholarship!—to buy you a one-way ticket to America so we could be together, but he was also able to save so well that he could afford to gift me a real gold pendant necklace and you a keyboard because remember how in Shanghai when you were small, you said you wanted to play the piano?"

My mother made it all sound like a fairy tale and I didn't want to point out that we were also separated for more than a year, when I was in Shanghai and my parents were in New York saving up enough money to reunite us.

"But," my mother continued as if reading my mind, "it's not the same as that family, you know. They were wild. They had so many problems. What kind of person can't afford their own apartment after six years in America? What kind of person brings their child to America only to send her right back for a full year? And what were they doing to change their situation? Eating out of dumpsters? Selling chips from Atlantic City at an inflated rate to the elderly who didn't know any better?"

"How long were you friends with them?" I asked my mother.

"Oh, you know how these things go. We would see them here and there and then they disappeared and we found out that they had gone to North Carolina to live with the woman's brother. They came back with some unlikely plan to make money and then disappeared again for a few weeks and turned up with no mention of what happened to all that talk about starting up a tutoring business or whatever their idea was. That's the kind of people they were. Show up out of nowhere and then disappear for weeks and then reappear. We fell out of touch. It wasn't accidental. Eventually I think the man got a job in an office and it turned out that his wife was pregnant with their second child. We ran into a mutual friend a few years ago and they said that they live on Long Island now. New Hyde Park, which means they must have gotten it together. Anyway, it's not important. All that's important is what happens to our family. Our family is just too lucky. I've got you and your brother and your father and we live in this gorgeous house, and every day I wake up and feel so lucky."

"Reel it in a little, Mom," I said, rolling my eyes. I knew in the very fuzzy part of what I paid attention to that my parents had suffered, too, they had struggled, too, and whatever happened to them in the year before I was brought to America was somehow related to their refusal to ever order beverages at restaurants because paying an extra dollar or two for something they could get in bulk for cheaper activated some kind of trauma inside them. It really did. But even more astounding was how they never stopped me or my brother from ordering those drinks, though I rarely did anyway, because . . . because of what? Because I was closer to that time of their lives when they had suffered and lived without much energy to dream? Or was it because I didn't like the sickly sweetness of regular sodas and preferred rarer drinks, like a tart, fresh-squeezed lemonade or a non-carbonated fruit punch with a bubble-gum aftertaste? I used to order those at Sizzler without even thinking in the days before my brother was born.

"You guys get one too," I would implore them. "Let's all get fruit punch." But they insisted on the old tried and true formula: my father would order the steak dinner, which we would split three ways, and then my mother would get the salad bar buffet and I would get my fruit punch and all three of us would eat off the endless plates my mother brought back—mac and cheese and buffalo wings and fried chicken and spaghetti with meatballs and boiled string beans and broccoli and fried rice and rotisserie chicken breast and sometimes king crab legs if we were fast enough or lurked long enough and shrimp scampi and fillets of rubbery fish coiled inside of themselves on a mound of congealed buttery sauce. We would go through seven or eight plates of food and then rest for a bit or jump up and down to make room for round two, which was just as long but slightly less vigorous as we tackled another five or six plates of food. By the third round, we were slumped and sluggish with our belts undone, and then it was on to dessert. I would get vanilla soft serve with rainbow sprinkles then the swirl with no sprinkles and then chocolate with M&M's and then a dozen chocolate chip cookies and one of each kind of cake—chocolate, butter-cream, carrot, red velvet, cookies and cream, pound, me-ringue, whatever. It all went inside and we burped the memories of the night for hours afterward. Sometimes we would wake up still full, our bellies round and the skin over them stretched tight like a drum. After my brother was born, we stopped going to Sizzler—he was too small and we were too greedy and too broke to tempt ourselves with any more nights out. The three of us had to look out for him first and each other second. At least, that was how we would have liked someone else to describe us—a pack, a unit.

But now I wanted to be free. I wanted to be free to be self-ish and self-destructive and indulgent like the white girls at the high school my parents worked so hard to get me into, and once they did, once we moved into a neighborhood where no one hung out on the streets, where everyone was the same pasty shade of consumptive blotchy paleness, all it did was make me want to get away from my family. I envied white girls whose relationships with their parents were so abysmal that they could never disappoint them. I wanted white parents who didn't care where I went or what I did, parents who encouraged me to leave home instead of guilting me into staying their kid forever.

The morning of my California trip, my mother kept bringing up how she didn't leave home until she was thirty and even then it was only because my father was immigrating to the United States. "For a long time, I considered just not going."

"Well, I'm not waiting until I'm thirty to leave home. You need to realize I don't have the same life as you."

At the airport, I avoided looking in her direction. It was bullshit that she made her sadness so known, and took up all the space my excitement should have filled. My family waited with me at the gate until the very last minute and then, as they walked me to the boarding line, my mother staggered and stopped in her tracks as if she had been stabbed and leaned against my father with the weakness of the dying. "Are you sure you want to go? It's not too late to stay."

"No," my father said. "That's not an option. Everything is going to happen exactly as we agreed. We want you to do well. We're proud of you, okay? We'll see you in three weeks." My mother's tears triggered a crying jag from my brother as well, and my father had to hold him back from running after me. It was strange to walk past them and wait in the back of the line to board the plane, knowing they were watching me go. I resisted looking back until there was only one person ahead of me in line. When I turned my head I saw the three of them huddled together—only my father was waving at me as my brother and my mother clung to him. It was a family formation that finally did not include me. *I'm freeeeeeeeeeee,* I thought as the agent scanned my ticket and then immediately began to panic when I realized I had missed my opportunity to say goodbye. I heard my brother shout out, "When're you coming back, Jenny?" and then the door closed behind me and I hardly thought about them again for the next three weeks. It was only later, much, much, much later, that I understood and accepted that my parents paid for me to be free. All of it, I realized, had to be paid for by someone.

"You'll drive a Mercedes, and I'll drive a Porsche when we grow up," he said to me while we sat on the curb waiting for the ice-cream truck.

"I can't even freaking ride a bike," I said, staring down the street, waiting to see if anything was coming.

On my ninth birthday, my mother was rushed to the hospital. Ten hours later, she gave birth to my brother. When we were both old enough to care, our mother told us that he was born at 10:22 in the morning.

"When was Jenny born?" my brother asked.

"Nine twenty-eight at night. But that was in China," she reminded us. "It's a twelve-hour time difference, plus you count an extra hour for daylight savings."

"So?" we said.

"No," our mother insisted. "You two were meant to be twins, but somehow you"—she pointed to my brother—"were stuck in my belly for an extra nine years. So lucky, you two."

We rolled our eyes. "Whatever."

* * *

When I got back from California, I was so tired from not sleeping for three weeks straight that two different flight attendants had to wake me up after the plane had landed and taxied. I slept straight through the car ride home and when we pulled up to our driveway, my brother tugged at my arm and asked if I would play with him.

"Now? I was going to go to sleep."

"But it's not even nighttime," he said, his bottom lip quivering.

"He's been waiting three weeks to play with you," our mother said.

"Fine. Let's play Monopoly. I'll let you be the car."

The next thing I knew it was four P.M. the following day and I was in my bed.

I cried out for my family and immediately the door swung open to reveal my brother had been waiting on the other side.

"What happened?" I asked him.

"We were playing Monopoly and you said you had to lie down for a minute and then you were asleep."

"Why didn't you wake me up?"

"I tried. I put water on you. And I set the timer to one minute and put it on your pillow next to your ear. I was blowing my breath into your nose and I tried to pull your eyes open but they kept closing."

"And?"

"You kept sleeping," he said, his voice breaking. "We only played for five minutes."

"Oh," I said, rubbing my eyes. "I'm sorry. I promise we can play tonight after I write an email to my friend, okay?"

"What about now?"

"I just said I have to do something first."

"Okay, Jenny."

The email took me hours and by the time I was done, it was

too late to play Monopoly. I called my brother into my room so we could hang out before bed.

"Did you really miss me all that bad?"

"I cried every day. One time for three hours and twenty-two minutes," he said, precise as usual. "I didn't even have time to play."

"Because you were crying so much? No way."

"Yeah way."

"What about the time you called me and all your friends were over playing baseball? You didn't cry that time, did you?"

"Yes."

"Yes, you cried?"

"Yeah."

I wanted to write another email to the boy with the pink button-down shirt who pulled me into his room one night when his roommate was out getting ice cream and took pictures of me. I missed California, missed the sweetness and newness of a boy, any boy, telling me cheeks were meant to be pink, and so I was meant to be in this world. But I was back in my old life now. I couldn't even properly daydream without thinking about my brother crying alone while his friends were running around in our backyard. How did he do it? How did he find his way into everything? Even in my most private memories, the ones I told no one, sooner or later, he showed up, the perpetual invader, his small face asking me if maybe I'd watch him play a scary videogame and stand in front of the TV to block out the ghosts when they suddenly appeared.

My brother wanted to hook up his PlayStation to my TV on the one afternoon I actually had a friend from school coming over to watch three movies in six hours, so I picked up one of the videocassettes I had planned on watching and flung it across the room.

"You always do this. I have to spend every single day with you. Every freaking day and every freaking hour. I'm so sick of it."

"So?" he said. "So what? I still get to play in here cause Mom said."

"Mom said crap. Get out before I push you out." He was sitting on the ground and I grabbed him by the ankles. He pulled little white curlies out of my carpet as I dragged him into the hallway.

"Never coming in," I yelled after slamming the door against his outstretched palms. A second later, he was pushing his tiny hands through the wedge of space underneath my locked door. I took my slipper and whacked the tips of his fingers like he was a bug. I heard him crying on the other side. His fingers were touching my rug again. I took a glass of ice water from my desk and poured it all over his fingers. I heard the sound of my mother's footsteps, thumping up the stairs from the basement den.

I threatened him, "I won't stop until you stop."

"I won't stop first, I won't stop first," he repeated. I slumped down against the door and reached out a hand to stroke his little wet fingers, but they were gone. The footsteps stopped. I heard my mother scoop up my brother and knock on my door.

"Say sorry."

I took my slipper and started hitting my own fingers as hard as I could.

"Say sorry," my mother said, louder. "You can kill yourself if you want, but first you have to say sorry to your brother."

I took my dictionary off the shelf and dropped it on the floor.

"Don't you dare," my mother said, hitting her elbow against my door.

"Ye-yeah, ma-mom's ga-going to punish y-you ma-ma-ma-ma-my Jenny."

"One day"—I sighed—"you are going to have to stop missing me." I pressed my chin against the spot on his head from where his hair swirled out. "Okay?"

"Why?" he asked me.

"You just have to get used to it." A week ago, our father had gone to Cleveland for some work business. "How come you don't miss Dad?"

"He's coming back Friday."

"So what? When I go away, I also come back. Why do you miss me and not Dad?" I wanted to shake the answer out of him. "Why do you miss me more? I want you to give me a really good answer or else I won't ever stop asking you."

"I don't know. I just do."

"Then I'm going to keep asking you. Why do you miss me but not Dad? Why do you miss me but not Mom? Why do you miss me but not anyone else?"

"I don't know, Jenny." He was crying now, and I shook my head.

"I'm not a nice person, am I? You ought to make me pay one day."

"Okay," he said, tears rolling down his face. "Then give me all your monies."

"Okay."

"I'll buy you a Mercedes with some of it."

* * *

Before dinner, I dabbed some of my mother's lipstick on my lips. Tangleberry.

"Lemme kiss you on the cheek," I said. I puckered my lips and moved in close.

"Are you wearing lipstick?" he asked me, arching his neck away from me. I had already pulled that joke on him three times that week.

"No," I said, lightly pressing my lips to the back of my hand. "See? No lipstick." I knelt down next to my brother and kissed his cheek hard enough to dimple it.

When we went to wash our hands in the bathroom, I remembered the mirrors and shielded his eyes with my hands as we were going in. "You're my robot and I control everything you do!"

"Okay, Jenny," he shouted back.

The summer after he finished second grade, there was a Saturday when we were inseparable for an afternoon, going around every room in the house arm in arm, which was hard to do because he was so little and only came up to my waist. I had to bend down really low, so low that it made my back ache but I didn't care. We walked in circles, chanting, "We! Are! Best! Friends! We! Are! Best! Friends!" until our dad emerged from hanging up laundry in the basement and watched us with an empty laundry basket balanced against his hip. He shook his head and laughed.

"You're both ridiculous. Come up here, I want to show you two jokers something."

We walked up the stairs arm in arm, following our father down the hallway to my room.

"You see that hole?" he asked, pointing to my bedroom door.

"Yeah," we said.

He took the laundry basket and hurled it through the hole in my door. There was room to spare.

"You"—he pointed at my brother—"kicked that in because you"—he pointed at me—"wouldn't let him in." He looked at us, arms crossed. "Two minutes later, you're running around in circles saying you're best friends? You should be jesters of the royal court."

We were silent for a bit. And then we said, "So what's your point?" For the rest of the afternoon, we went around arm in arm, still chanting, "We! Are! Best! Friends! And Dad! Is Such! An I-di-ot!"

Our mother came into my room when we were having a sleepover—my brother on the floor and me in front of the computer—and yelled very fiercely, "Go to sleep or never sleep in your sister's room again." I felt partially responsible because if it hadn't been for me farting the entire chorus of "Row Row Row Your Boat" for my brother and making him laugh so hard that our mother heard it through the walls that separated my bedroom from hers, he would have never gotten yelled at. I knelt down on the floor and asked him if he was okay.

"Are you thirsty? Hungry?" He nodded his head. "Be right back," I said. "Don't fall asleep." I came back up with a turkey sandwich and a cup filled to the brim with water. While he ate I was reminded of the time when I had come back from a bad day at school and shut myself up in my room and watched taped reruns of *Late Night with Conan O'Brien* for three hours. When I realized I hadn't heard any sounds from my brother in several hours, I went downstairs and found him sitting less than a foot from the television, watching *Fresh Prince of*

Bel-Air and eating peanut butter with a plastic ice-cream scooper. Oh, I murmured when I looked inside the peanut butter jar: a hole right down the middle.

Even now, I wondered if I had done right by him as I held out my hands below his chin to catch stray crumbs.

Whenever my brother and I start listing our grievances against each other—who wounded who more—my brother inevitably brings up the time I tried to kill him.

"You tried to kill me. Remember?"

"What? I never tried to kill you. That's crazy." But he swears that I did, that once, I asked him to take his plate of pizza downstairs and he wouldn't, so I pinned him to the floor of his bedroom and held a knife up to his throat.

"It was probably a butter knife. You can't even cut paper with those things."

"No," my brother insists. "It had sharp edges. You were going to kill me with a knife." And it was true, he was right. I had been so angry that day because I made him a lunch of microwaved pizza, which I had cut into twelve neat little squares since he was so picky and only ate food that had already been pre-arranged into bite-sized pieces he could chew once and swallow immediately, and despite my having gone through the trouble of making a perfect meal for him, he didn't show any gratitude at all. He refused to eat. I told him if he wasn't going to eat it then he needed to put the plate of untouched food back in the refrigerator, but he refused to do that as well, so I took the knife I used to cut the pizza and held it up to his face. "You deserve to die. You make me want to kill you sometimes. Maybe this time I will."

It was an act of desperation. I should have told him, I would never hurt you. I would set fire to any tree harboring branches that might one day fall on your head, cut the arms off the first kid who tries to punch you in the face, pave down and smooth over the bumps on our street where you always trip, go into your nightmares and vanquish the beasts who chase you so you never ever have to be afraid. But what right did I have? When would I finally get it? That *I* was the one he needed to be protected from?

Once when we were napping side by side on our parents' bed on one of the many afternoons we were left alone, I dreamt we were fighting on opposing sides of a civil war. When the war was over, I knelt down by my brother's injured body and hacked him into four pieces. It was up to me to give him a proper funeral, but I had only two hands and couldn't figure out which parts of him to carry back and bury and which parts to leave behind.

One winter, when I was home from college, I went outside in the dark, crossed the playground behind my house, and followed a narrow road up a hill. I forgot my glasses and for a while, I sat on a patch of grass, looking down at the town where I spent my adolescence, the town my family had moved to not long after my brother was born. The streetlights appeared as big as tangerines, blurry and orange. What I wanted was for someone to come looking for me, for someone to worry about me, for two adults to argue about me. I wanted everyone I knew and everyone I could know one day to wonder about me, to think of me as if I were the last Popsicle on earth, and oh no, before anyone got to eat me, I had already gone ahead and melted entirely! What I wanted was for someone to kneel down on the ground and lick the red sugary water of mememememememe curving and rolling down streets half-paved in asphalt. I worried about a world where my existence barely mattered. A world where I did not exist at all. Maybe that was the world I was headed to. Maybe that was the world I deserved.

After a month of kindergarten, my brother still couldn't write his name on a sheet of paper, and the teacher, Ms. Notice, was concerned and sent him home with a note.

"A notice from Ms. Notice," I said, skipping around our living room, the happiest I'd been all day. He smiled when I ripped it up into four pieces, but pulled at my sleeve when I put one of them in my mouth. "You'll die."

"I won't." We worked on spelling his name for a good hour.

"The letters go next to each other, retard," I said.

"Ass."

"What?" I looked at him in shock. "What did you say?"

"Penis."

I was tired. I felt on the brink of a deep, stirring sleep. "Let's go outside and throw the ball around." I took the pen from him and flung it across the room.

We went out in the lingering September heat. I threw the ball up and neither of us caught it. Then my brother picked up the ball and threw it into the tree. It was stuck up there. "You're good at throwing. I've never seen a ball go so high."

"I know," he said.

I wanted to hug him, to kiss his cheek until it was sore, but I knew he was getting older. He would protest, he would one day no longer hug his arms around my legs because he was short, or make a fist around my pinky when I picked him up from school, or crawl into my bed with his wet hair and face, no longer say *it hurts me to leave you* before going to his friend's house, or *I missed you all day* after coming back, because he would get old, and I would get even older. Maybe we would grow apart, he would develop a personality that I would know nothing about, we would start our families, have children of our own, and there would come a point when in thinking about "family" we would think of the ones we made, not the ones we were from. From that point on, I would refer to him as "your uncle" and he would mostly refer to me as "your aunt" and it would take a long time for our children to even understand that we were siblings first, but more than that, our children, just as we hadn't, would likely not think much about a time before they were born, a time when he was my brother and I was his sister, and together, we were our parents' children.

II.

The year I moved out to California for college, we talked on the phone every week. It was hard to hear him through all the tears in the beginning. Then it was every other week, and by the time I was a senior, our mother had to order him to stay on the phone for at least five minutes a month.

"Do you miss me?" I asked him during one of our recent five minutes.

"Yeah, kinda, but sometimes I forget about you."

"I would never forget about you."

"Do you want to talk to Mom?"

Now I had to learn about him from my mother. Last week, she reported over the phone, he ate a penny. "Total freak thing," she said.

"Let me talk to him," I said.

"Hold on, I just have to check if I have any money in my wallet."

"Why?"

"Your dad and I have started giving him a few bucks to talk to you."

"Fucking fantastic."

When he was five, he told me he had put his finger down his throat and accidentally threw up a bit. "But, I swallowed most of it back down," he had said at the time.

"You only did it the one time, right?"

"I did it other times too."

"How many other times? Two? Three?"

"Fifty to sixty."

"Holy shit. I don't get it. Do you not like the way your body looks or something?"

"I just wanted to see what would happen if I put my finger down there."

"You know what happens—you throw up, develop an eating disorder, and then you die."

"You can die from that?"

"From making yourself vomit every day? Oh, for sure."

"No, from putting your finger down your throat? What if you die right after doing it?"

"What is with you? Stop putting your finger down your throat, dude."

"Get this," I told my friends at school the next day. "My five-year-old brother has an eating disorder. How is that even possible?"

When my brother was starting third grade and I was starting senior year of high school, our grandparents came and lived with us in New York for six months and brought an electric bug racket from China with a tag attached that had a skull and crossbones above big bold letters: WATCH OUT! ELECTRO-CUTES PROBABLE.

"What the heck are electrocutes?" my brother asked me.

"Oh, it's a typo. It means you could get electrocuted if you touch the racket when it's on. So, don't touch it, okay?"

"Never," our mother said, popping her head into my brother's room. "Never never never never never never never ever touch."

"Okay, okay," my brother and I said. "We get it. Can you please get out?"

But my brother was haunted by the racket. He rolled up pieces of paper and pressed the tips against the racket.

"I saw sparks," he told me later.

"Seriously, stop obsessing. Leave it alone, okay?"

But he couldn't. He wanted to put his finger on the racket. He said his friend Harrison touched his lips to the racket and had to wear a bandage over his mouth for a month. All the parents we knew were calling up their parents in China to tell them to stop bringing over the electric rackets. "Do you want your grandchildren to have lips or not?" I heard my mother asking my grandmother in the kitchen one evening.

"I touched it," my brother told me the same week his friend Harrison burned off his lips.

"Oh my God. Why?"

"I just did it for a second, to see what would happen. For some reason my brain is telling me to touch it again. What happens if I put my mouth on it?"

I took the batteries out of the racket and tossed them into a pile of logs in our backyard. The year after that, I went away to college, and in my extended absence, my brother found the electric racket hidden behind a suitcase in the basement. He told our parents to get rid of it permanently, and they laughed and called me on the phone and said, "Your brother is still our little sweet baby. He's just trying to get attention, you know?" To that I said, "Please. Please pay attention to him, then," and to that my mother said, "Of course I'm paying attention. You think I just ignore him?" and to that I said, "Why do you always call me when I'm trying to study? Every minute I talk to you is one point less on my midterm next week."

Several years after my brother tried to burn his lips on an electric bug racket, and many years after I accidentally burned my brother's hair with a candle, I found out he would sometimes light a candle and wave his index finger back and forth through the flame. Sometimes, he would hold a knife up to his own throat and inch it along the growing hairs on his neck, daring himself to get close enough to draw blood. He would swing his keychain near his mouth, letting the key graze his lips. He would dip the key into the back of his throat until he gagged before yanking it back up. "I just wanted to see what would happen," he said to me on the phone, again and again and again. "I kept thinking, What if I swallowed the key? What if the knife pierced my skin?"

"What if," I said. "What if you start wondering what would happen if you jumped off a bridge? What if you start wondering what would happen if you held a loaded gun to your head? What if you die trying to figure out what if? Then what? Then you're dead."

After my brother ate the penny, he called our mother at work and told her that he had eaten something he wasn't supposed to and that his stomach felt weird and he wanted to go to the hospital. She rushed home, weaved through traffic on the LIE, and drove my brother to the emergency room, where, behind partially closed curtains, a doctor with a glass eye put his finger up my brother's butt and said, "You have some hard stools lodged up there. Other than that, everything's fine. But tell me something. You're thirteen years old. Most of the kids who do this kind of thing, eating pennies and quarters and tree bark and tacks and Happy Meal toys—you name it and

I've seen it—most of the kids doing things like this are four and five years old. You're thirteen. Don't you know better?"

"Did it make you feel bad?" I asked my brother on the phone after our mother bribed him with a twenty to talk to me.

"No," he said. "I didn't care that the doctor put his finger up my butt."

"No, not that. I mean when the doctor said the thing about you being too old to eat pennies."

"I wasn't eating pennies."

"Swallowing, whatever. Did it make you feel weird when the doctor said the thing about you being too old to do this kind of thing?"

"I guess. Dunno."

"Why did you eat the penny in the first place?"

"Not eat, swallow."

"Whatever. Stop being so specific about everything. Stop correcting. Why did you try to *swallow* the penny in the first place?"

"Uh-un-uh," he responded, his shortcut for *I dunno*. "The thought just came into my mind. I kept thinking, What if I swallowed a penny? What if it got stuck in my throat? Would I die from a stuck penny? I was thinking it so much I couldn't sleep. I figured, instead of wondering what if, I should just do it. I'm not stupid. I just wanted to know."

"But you can't know. And if you die from these experiments, you still won't know. You'll be dead. Dead people don't know because they're dead. Are you depressed or something? You can tell me. It's okay to be depressed. I can help you."

"No," he said. "It's not that. I just can't stop wondering, What if?"

"It's perfectly normal to be depressed at your age. I mean, look at how I was. A complete fucking nightmare of a human being. Do you remember how I would just shut myself up in my room and sob over nothing?"

"True. You were an extremely difficult teenager," my mother said. "So listen, your brother went to play videogames. He said his five minutes were up."

"Can't you give him more money?"

"No. Not right now. He has too much to do."

"You just said he went up to play videogames."

"What are you having for dinner tonight? Anything yummy?"

"I don't know," I said, petulant. "Pennies stir-fried with garlic."

He was three and I was twelve when our parents bought our house in Glen Cove. We had successfully done something people studied in academic textbooks—we became upwardly mobile. We moved from our mostly working-class Puerto Rican and Korean neighborhood in Queens to a named community (its namesake was J. P. Morgan, the very tycoon my father worked twelve hours a day for, the reason why we never ever saw him) in a mostly upper-middle-class white neighborhood on Long Island. Everywhere we went and looked there was unused space, there was room for two people to never have to touch each other or breathe in the same approximate air. There was silence to fill, grass that had never been trampled on, trees with undisturbed spiderwebs. Between the ages of twelve and seventeen, I was the first person to come back to the house on weekday afternoons. I had about forty-five minutes to myself before my brother came home, five hours until I had to cover up everything that went on in our house before our mother returned from work, and eight or nine or ten hours before our father came home and checked in on us. We would wait up for him in our pajamas, having done everything we needed to do that day besides see him. Sometimes if I was in a selfish mood, I'd pretend to be asleep in my bed to avoid the five or so minutes I had with my father at the end of the day—it wasn't like I was ever going to know him this way. But still, adding another day to the stack of days I missed out on knowing my father was immense and weighed on me like a millstone in a fairy tale. In a way, we *were* in a fairy tale—all those hours my brother and I spent alone in an empty house together, and all the times I tried to get my brother to believe that our parents had died, that I had just gotten off the phone with a police officer who found them mangled and lifeless, covered in the bloody shrapnel of a massive car wreck.

"It's just you and me now," I would say to him. "Who do you think is going to take care of us?"

"Our aunt and uncle will," my brother would sob. "We'll go to China and live with Grandma and Grandpa."

"No can do. They already said they won't take us. It's in the will. If Mom and Dad die, we're on our own."

We were already on our own. We lived in a split-level house with windows on every level, sliding French doors in the kitchen that led out to a small deck, two skylights and floor-to-ceiling windows in the living room, four sets of windows in the family room, two windows in each bedroom. We were told to keep all the blinds tightly shut and all the curtains closed. "So that no one knows you're home alone," our mother explained. Sometimes though, I would pull up the blinds anyway. I would draw the curtains and let in the light from outside. So what if we were seen? So what if our secret was revealed? What did I care if someone saw me at home, eating cake and drinking coffee, heating up frozen pizza in the microwave and cutting it into bite-sized pieces for my brother? Why *shouldn't* someone have seen me holding up a fireplace poker high in the air, aimed at my brother's forehead for no other reason except that he annoyed me, when all he had to defend himself against me was a useless plastic bat—why shouldn't someone have seen and intervened? I had never been a worse adult than when I was still a kid.

"Will they take us away," my brother asked our parents, "if they see us?"

"Yes, they will," our mother said.

"Jenny," my brother said, pleading with me one of the afternoons when I told him that our parents had died in a car accident. He was pulling on my arm to stop me from drawing up the blinds. "We can't let anyone see us."

"You stupid idiot," I said. "Everyone already knows."

I am home this week, visiting my family before I go back to my life in California. As soon as I enter the front door, I remember my old self—restless, moody, lonely, rageful. When I go through my closet, I find my old laptop from high school that my brother would use from time to time, afternoons when he wanted to be near me but I didn't feel like interacting with him so I would give him my laptop. There weren't any computer games installed. He mostly drew pictures on Microsoft Paint that he tried to show me but I always said, "Later, when I have time." After I went away to college, he used my laptop a few more times to write poems for school. One of them was about me and he read it out loud over the phone:

> "*I have a sister*
> *Once she chased me with a big metal thing.*
> *I found a yellow plastic bat*
> *And I fought back with courage!*"

The Evolution of My Brother

"So did you win the poetry contest?"

"No, the kid who wrote about his grandmother who survived the Holocaust did."

"Seems rigged," I said.

"It's not."

I look at the poem again and then go through some other files, including one called "Fight on Dirt," a painting of magenta, lime-green, and teal-blue stick figures on brown mud. I see another file named "Power Rain," which I remember seeing a long time ago but never opened. I wondered briefly back then what "power rain" was—massive droplets of rain, each one fat enough to contain an armed soldier ready for combat, hitting the ground, causing tremors in the earth?

I open up the file and realize the full name is actually "Power Rain Jurs." Sour tears well up in my eyes and fall into my mouth. I feel self-conscious and stupid crying for myself—for my shame, for my regrets, for how quickly a childhood happens. I wish I had acted better. I wish I had been the kind of sister who was patient enough to show my brother the proper spelling for "Power Rangers."

Whenever I'm home for a few days, I start to feel this despair at being back in the place where I had spent so many afternoons dreaming of getting away, so many late nights fantasizing about who I would be once I was allowed to be someone apart from my family, once I was free to commit mistakes on my own. How strange it is to return to a place where my childish notions of freedom are everywhere to be found—in my journals and my doodles and the corners of the room where I sat fuming for hours, counting down the days until I could leave this place and start my real life. But now that trying to become someone on my own is no longer something to dream about but just my ever-present reality, now that my former conviction that I had been burdened with the

174

responsibility of taking care of this household has been re-vealed to be untrue, that all along, my responsibilities had been negligible, illusory even, that all along, our parents had been the ones watching over us—me and my brother—and now that I am on my own, the days of resenting my parents for loving me too much and my brother for needing me too intensely have been replaced with the days of feeling bewil-dered by the prospect of finding some other identity besides "daughter" or "sister." It turns out that this, too, is terrifying, all of it is terrifying. Being someone is terrifying. I long to come home, but now, I will always come home to my family as a visitor, and that weighs on me, reverts me back into the teenager I was, but instead of insisting that I want everyone to leave me alone, what I want now is for someone to beg me to stay. Me again. Mememememememe.

I burst into my brother's room without knocking and he's playing a game on the computer with such concentration that I can't get him to look at me even as I'm pulling the swivel chair he's sitting on away from his desk.

"Stop," he says. "What are you, an animal?"

"Remember the time I burned your hair and it smelled like popcorn?"

"Yeah, so? Why do you always talk about that?"

"It's funny to me."

"It's stuff that happened when I was little."

"You look so old now," I say. "You're going to be taller than Dad."

"Knock next time," he says. "You always just barge in."

"Well, that's what you always did when you were little and I let you do it so many times. Don't you owe it to me to let me barge in a few times?"

"That was then."

"Well, this will be then one day too."

"That makes no sense."

"That's because sense isn't made, it's learned."

"Yo, you really need to get out of my room."

At night, when everyone is sleeping, I sneak into his room like I used to when he was little. There were nights when I missed him, when I stayed up too late on my own after insisting that he couldn't sleep in my bed with me, after insisting that he had to learn to sleep multiple consecutive nights in his own bed, nights when I stayed up trying to be my most romantic self, when I stared at myself in my bedroom mirror, flirting with myself, seducing myself, laughing at my own jokes, playacting the kinds of friendships I fantasized about having once I was no longer in this house. On those nights, there would often come a moment when I suddenly missed my brother so much that it was physically unbearable and I would creep into his room and watch him sleep, his little chest and his little face and his little knees smashed up against the mesh barrier that my parents installed so he wouldn't roll off his bed. My brother never slept in the center of anything—he was always against some barrier.

I'd kneel down next to him and kiss his pillowy cheeks or run my finger across his long, curled eyelashes that looked so angelic and heavy when wet. I'd stroke his hair from the little swirl in the center of the top of his head where it all seemed to originate. I'd take his fingers and wrap them around my pinky. I wanted him to wake up and hang out with me and when he wouldn't, I'd pull his eyelids back and reveal the whites of his sleeping eyeballs. "Can you see me?" I'd clap my hands loudly next to his ear. Sometimes I'd pull him up like he was a marionette and I was his puppeteer. Through all of it, he would just sleep and sleep and sleep, even the few times when I dragged him fully out of bed and made him stand up-right on his tippy toes, and when that wasn't enough to wake him up, I grabbed his shoulders and made him do jumping jacks by pulling his arms up over his head and then letting them slap down hard against his legs. One time, he opened his eyes, though even then, he didn't remember seeing me the next morning. There was no way to stir him.

For years after I went away to college, he was afraid to sleep on his own. The first few months, he slept in my bed, but once our mother insisted on washing the sheets and pillows, he was no longer comforted by it. He slept in our parents' bed after that for a little while, and then when he was too old to sleep with them but still too scared to sleep alone, they hid a twin-sized mattress on the floor next to their bed. It was positioned in such a way that anyone who peeked into our parents' bedroom would not see it.

"It's on the floor," my mother said, "so he can't fall on the floor! It's been working out great."

"You always want a baby in the house," I accused my mother the year he started middle school. "You don't even know who you are without a baby, do you?"

"And you," she said, "don't know anything."

Last year, I helped my dad take the mattress into the garage and cover it with plastic.

"Are you crying?" I looked at my mother and then looked away.

"You could have just left it there," she said to my father. "It's his choice if he wants to sleep there or not. And now he doesn't even have the choice."

Even though I tried to distance myself, I felt complicit in her tears. I didn't want my brother to grow up either, just like my mother hadn't wanted me to grow up nine years ago. I was the same as her—someone who nurtured my pain as if it could stop things from changing. No matter how many times I saw my mother's watery eyes in my doorframe the summer before I left for college, it wasn't enough to stop what had been put in motion: that I was leaving home and I wasn't going to wait until thirty to do it.

Next year my brother will be in high school and when I was in high school, I had a kid brother who grabbed my leg and walked with it in his arms through our house when it was cold, sat on my shoulders when it was hot to get closer to the ceiling fan, and slept in my bed when he missed me, which was all the time. I kneel down by his bed and kiss him on the cheek, no longer the pillow cheeks I remember from years ago, but now bonier and dotted here and there with pimples. I hold his hand up like he is my king and I am his loyal servant, and I kiss it, bring it up to my heart, hold it there for a moment, and say, "With all my regard." I don't let go of his hand right away. "Don't forget me." He stirs, and I wonder, for the first time, why it should be so important that he remembers me, that he remembers all of it? "Or forget me," I add, placing his hand back underneath the blanket. "Or forget some of it. Or remember me. Whatever. It's your life."

I leave twenty dollars on his desk to secure time for our next phone call. I want it to be possible for us to share a home again but I'll be gone from this house in a week, and he will maybe tell our mom about a dream he had where he was swatting this giant bee away from his cheek, and finally, it came right for him, and no matter how much he ducked or swung his head, the bee remained close, and when it finally stung him, it was a soft puff, not bad at all, and then, it was on to the next dream.

My Days and Nights of Terror

I say everyone, at least everyone who was ever me in elementary school, has known a clinger, a pest, a gnat who won't go away, a stalker who would go so far as to ask God himself to insert her right into your bloodstream if He could . . . if He would. Someone who would stop at nothing to infect you, crushing every single one of your body's defenses until you were resigned to slow, excruciating disease, until you were as poisonously entwined as two separate people can be—one a host (you), one a parasite (her)—so that with every passing day, you (the host) are dragged closer and closer to death as she (the parasite) inflates herself with your blood and your flesh, bringing her closer and closer to glory!!!

If you don't know what I'm talking about, consider yourself lucky that no one would go to such lengths to parasite onto you. Me, on the other hand? Too helpless, too tasty and succulent to blend in, to not be noticed, to not be someone's prey. And that someone? That someone who ruined my health, whose very existence diminished me, the girl who literally chased after me like a poacher desperate for ivory tusks or a ravenous wolf about to pounce on a poor little rabbit, for me, that person, that fatal cancer, that bloodthirsty wolf, that greedy cutthroat poacher was Fanpin Hsieh.

In the mornings, I watched her out of the corner of my eye during the Pledge of Allegiance. I did what I was told and pressed my right hand halfheartedly against my heart as we recited the Oath-to-Lick-America's-Balls-Even-Though-They're-Dirty-in-Order-to-Certify-That-America's-Wonderful-and-Tolerant-Even-Though-It's-Not, but not Fanpin. She always seemed to be lightly cupping the bottom of her breast, the left one, the one that had already grown into something substantial enough to touch by the time we were nine.

She looked like an alien. (But then again, I was an alien, too; that was the box I had to check on every form. Did aliens have unalienable rights? Were we entitled to liberty and justice?) Alien or not, Fanpin moved her body like she had been in it far longer than the rest of us. Not only did she know all the curse words, but she also knew how to use them correctly. She was the kind of person who didn't know how to take no for an answer. She thought "no" still had the potential to mean "yes," which, to be fair, so did I, but for her it didn't stop there, she also thought there was a "yes" hidden in "no way" and "get out of my face" and "can you not talk" and also "no way José" and "you stink like liquid dumps, get away" and also "noooooo" and also "shut the hell up" and also "guess what? I hate you." Nothing stopped her, especially me. She considered me her best friend and I considered her my worst nightmare come to life. At recess, she seemingly never ran out of ideas for us to do together:

—Mande, let's take off our pants and go bare-assed
    down the slide!
—Um, no thanks.
—Let's see who can poke the other person's eye out
    first with these pens my mom got me from
    Taiwan.
—Poke your own eyes out and leave me alone.
—Can you hold still so I can practice my
    roundhouse kick on your head?
—Uhh, let me try to get as far away from you as I
    can.

I prayed for someone to intervene, to take Fanpin's attention off of me. At the start of fourth grade, I thought my
prayers had been answered when some of the more outgoing
kids tried to make fun of her, but she was peerless in her ability to deflect insult.

Natalia Diaz, who had the nicest, most luscious curls of
anyone in our grade, said, "Fanpin loves fans and pins!" (Too
simplistic and dim-witted to affect her.) The class clown
Min-ho So said, "Fanpin, spell I CUP. Bet you can't." (She
pointed at his crotch and said, "Pass, even though I've seen
you piss yourself.") Jason Lam, the shrimpy kid who was always the first to step so that no one attacked him for being
small said, "Look, Fanpin! Boyz II Men just crossed the
street." (She punched him in the arm and said, "Do I look like
a gaylord to you?")

Yasmine Williams got a bunch of her friends to sing, "Fanpin is a ma-aa-aaa-nnn. Fanpin is a ma-aa-aaa-nnn." (She
went up to the offending singers and knocked them all out
with a quick swipe of her arm.)

Another time some Vietnamese kids went up to Fanpin

and said, "Ewwwww, we heard you like touching girls." (She raised her fists and said, "Nah, but I am going to enjoy touching you, and by touching I mean punching.")

It went on and on like that until everyone gave up and moved on to easier targets. As for me, I didn't even bother trying because for one, unlike the other kids in my class, I had to deal with Fanpin outside of school, too, and for another, I tended to avoid anything that involved speaking in front of others. I had only begun to learn English two years ago and even though I pretty much mastered it within a year, I still had trouble pronouncing certain words. Sometimes I inflected my sentences in a manner that gave me away, and revealed my alien soul, my true FOB origins: a lowly immigrant with a shit-stained anus for an anus who added the word "riiieeeght?" to the end of every sentence. *Minhee is so cute, riiieeeeght? The kimbap at Kay's is so much better than the one Jun's mom made, riiieeeeght?*

I worried about how I was seen, who I was seen with, and what kind of abysmal creature other people thought I was—these fears disfigured me though the damage was invisible to my parents, whom I could never compete with as they were always a hundred times more worried, more fearful, more occupied than I could ever be. They worried about me growing up in this neighborhood and attending an elementary school that had been mandated by the school board to offer pre–sex education sex education in fourth grade because we had been identified as a high-risk population. They heard all the rumors and and repeated them back to me. They especially latched onto the ones that involved some poor girl who went from bringing home straight A's to taking a nosedive into junkiedom—everything from stealing money from her parents to selling her body for more quick fixes to stints in and out of jail to winding up pregnant by some other junkie who also tested positive for HIV, and finally OD-ing in a sad gargle of bubbling blood and vomit and shit smears in a gutter somewhere, leaving the fate of her innocent unborn baby totally uncertain. All these stories involved great leaps of disaster, buckets of drained blood, older-men-predator types who could somehow convince even the most clear-eyed girl to do anything, and frequent references to the "problem with America," which, as far as I could tell from what my parents discussed, had everything to do with the extremely disturbing phenomenon of American parents not loving their children at all, and knowing this about themselves, and in spite of this, still insisting on raising children and having more children, creating generation after generation of children who were never loved, are never loved, and will never be loved.

"Why do they do this?" my mother asked one evening when I brought her and my father our class field-trip slip to sign so I could spend the day at the American Museum of Natural History. "Why do they want to sign away their children's right to learn *in school*?" At home, we spoke in Chinese. None of us knew how often and how badly the other made mistakes in English. None of us knew the other's humiliations.

"My teacher said it's another," I started to say and then hesitated and used an English phrase, "component to learning."

"Co-what-what to what?" my mother said.

"They think it's just as vital as studying math and science in school," my father explained. "Regardless, it looks like they want us to sign off on you spending a day *not* at school."

Still, my mother wasn't satisfied. "Why do these people have kids if they aren't going to ever love them?"

Sometimes, I took my parents' rhetorical questioning as a challenge and tried to answer. "Maybe it's because so many parents are junkies," I started to say but as soon as I said the word "junkie" in Chinese, they flipped, asking me how I knew about drug abuse, was it because some nefarious drug kingpin had lured me into his lair, was it because I had been convinced by a stupid girl to try drugs, was that why I no longer flinched when the doctor told me I needed a few more booster shots? Because I had been sticking heroin-filled needles in my veins? Was that why I had slumped over one time while watching Looney Tunes in the morning, because the crack had worn off and my body was in the process of organ failure and total shutdown? Was that why I wanted to buy new clothes, because some gangbanger had told me I was a tasty little morsel and I should come by his van sometime? Did I know there had been 344 murders committed in our borough last year? Did I know that there was still time left in the month to make it 345? Did I want to be the 345th murdered person in Queens? Did I? Did I?

No, I said and then no again and then no again and then no to all the other questions. Still no, I said, and still no. By the end of their questioning, I was too battered to respond and so they took it as a sign that I was actually hiding something. That I didn't realize how dire the situation was. The more my parents fretted about my survival, the more it seemed like it was a miracle I was alive at all. If I somehow escaped drugs, pregnancy, pimps, and gangbangers, then I would still have to deal with my parents, and the constant unloading of their fears made it impossible for me to fear the feared things themselves as all my time was taken up fearing my parents would never stop fearing.

I moved from Shanghai, China, to Flushing, Queens, in the middle of second grade to reunite with my parents who had immigrated to America a few years before me. On the flight, I was put under the custody of a "family friend" whom

I had never met before though he swore he was there at my birth, which I couldn't argue with because no one can remember their own birth and so it was the perfect lie that could never be disproven. The trip left me rattled and terrified. Several times during the flight I woke up lying on the floor of the aisle with everyone looking at me, having not a clue how I got there. It was abject and then suddenly I was in America.

Almost right away, my dad began to regret all those months he spent waiting in the American consulate, filling out paperwork for my sponsorship to come to America. He checked my arms for track marks and had a home kit to measure my blood pressure for signs of hypertension, sign number one for drug addiction, according to the latest literature. My mother checked my vagina every few weeks, making sure there weren't any signs of having been tricked into participating in gangbangs with older men. America was crawling with rapists and addicts, fucked-up nurses at free clinics who gave you a live dose of HIV instead of the measles vaccine because they didn't like the shape of your eyes or because they didn't like the way your glasses slipped down the low bridge of your nose or how your head sloped in the back while the front of your face was as flat as an ice hockey rink.

"Don't be an idiot," my dad used to say to me in Chinese.

"How?" I asked.

"By getting yourself killed."

"Oh, right."

"These kids here have death wishes. It's always the ones born with the right to live who want to die. These people have never been forced to suffer and that's why they seek it voluntarily. Do you know how easy it is to get mixed up in the wrong crowd? Do you know how easy it is to throw your life away? Do you realize how *fun* self-destruction looks at first?"

I nodded furiously. I knew, I knew it all, he and my mother told me a thousand times.

"Are you trying to teach our daughter how to become a sex-crazed drug addict?" my mother asked him in Shanghaihua. "Are you instructing her on how to do it? Step by step?"

"Far from it."

My mom and my dad spoke to each other in Shanghai dialect in front of me when they were discussing things that I wasn't supposed to be privy to. They thought for the longest time I couldn't understand because back when we all lived in Shanghai, none of us ever spoke Shanghaihua to each other; my father's family came from Shandong and my mother's family came from Wenzhou. I remember hearing the strange cadences of the Wenzhou dialect whenever I went to visit my mother's mother's house, how it sounded like an argument between people who really loved each other. My other grandparents spoke in heavily Shandong-accented Mandarin, saying za men instead of wo men and loo instead of lü. I started speaking that way, too, until everyone laughed at me and said I was talking like a little farmer girl, and I said, Then we're all farmers! Shandonghua was everywhere in my grandmother's house in Shanghai where the three of us used to live in a tiny sunlit room that overlooked the garden. We slept in a bed so tiny and narrow that my mother and my father had to sleep on their sides. Usually they faced me so they could talk to each other in the mornings while I pretended to sleep between them, but sometimes we faced in the same direction, like taco shells stacked up against each other—those were the days that they thought I forgot, or never knew about in the first place.

That was the secret to being me back then: if you never say a word, people will think you don't know anything, and when people think you don't know anything, they say everything in front of you and you end up containing everything. On the inside, I was vast. But on the outside, I was a known idiot. Nothing that came out of me had any resemblance to what I thought I had inside of me. My parents talked to me like I was the kind of person who would enter an unmarked van full of leering, strange men just because they said there was candy. My teachers talked to me like I still colored outside the lines and couldn't do two plus two without those red and yellow plastic counters to aid me.

"My wife," my father would often say in Shanghaihua, "you know that if I had my way, I'd send these kids *and* their parents to ten years of hard labor in Manchuria. See how much they like running around with their pants half-down and their shirts half-open then."

"Oh, yes," my mom would say. "Yes, yes."

At least my parents always agreed in the end and I took that to be a small, throwaway sign of their love. I hoped and hoped it would remain that way forever but it never lasted long. They couldn't seem to go more than a few weeks without blowing up over the same things—she irritated him and he disappointed her and because of innumerable miscalculations they accused each other of making, and thanks to the other, my future was a foregone conclusion: ruined. The question of whose fault it was had no resolution. Why didn't he get a proper education back in Shanghai? Why did it take him so long to finish his university studies? Why did he choose to get a PhD in English literature of all things when he knew he was at a disadvantage with his thick accent? Why didn't he just stick it out a few more years? At least then he would have the degree he came over here for and people back home wouldn't think of him as such a colossal failure. She asked him these questions over and again until things were slammed and broken and in return, he asked her what the hell did she think he was doing now and furthermore where the hell did she think they came from? Did she somehow grow up in an alternate universe where schools *weren't* closed for years? Did she somehow live in a country where they *weren't* subjected to the fucked-up genocidal whims of a demagogue? Did she know *anyone—anyone!*—who had a *choice?* Didn't she herself throw several tantrums when he said he was considering just staying in China and taking the government position he had been offered after graduating from school? Wasn't she the one who insisted only someone who had surgically replaced their brain with their rectum was incapable of seeing that *obviously* going to America to pursue a PhD at NYU was the far better opportunity? Wasn't she the one who complained without end about how he wasn't dreaming big enough for her? How *everyone* was going to America and making it so why couldn't we? Not everyone had lived in a cocoon of protection as she did back in Shanghai, he spat at her; not everyone felt as entitled to their dreams as she did.

They'd argue until it was the next day and I would wake up thinking it had all been a dream—my mother crying that she could have been an interpreter at the UN and my father laughing and mocking her, saying, They wouldn't have hired you as a janitor. The insults they traded back and forth until finally my father ended it by striking her in the face or grabbing her arm so hard that it made her laugh like a crazy person. Go ahead, she would say, I dare you to break it. I dare you to achieve something. Be the man you think you are.

It was nightly and it was ugly and they sure as hell didn't try to protect me from hearing it, so every night there was one more scream I couldn't unhear, one more crazy peal of laughter that ended in things shattering, one more argument I could not unknow. I had my own shit, my own fears. The only thing that helped was when I could share some of them with my parents, and they listened and held me and petted me without leaving their nervous shaking imprinted on me. I needed reassurance and I wanted calm, but there was little occasion for that so I went to God instead. Every night before falling asleep, I got into my bed, stared up at the ceiling, and prayed:

Dear God, never ever let me become like those Korean girls in my class who have really ugly cheekbones and smell so bad and can't pronounce words right. Yesterday when Minhee read aloud from Bridge to Terabithia *she was trying so hard to get each word right and you could tell because there was this little spit bubble on the side of her lip and it was disgusting and later she pretended like she wasn't almost crying when the substitute teacher said, "Jesus, have we gone back in time to first grade? Can any of you read a sentence? I don't see how the school board thinks it's a good idea to assign this book when it has clearly gone completely over your heads. My God, how were you allowed to graduate from third grade? Did you kids really pass the statewide English test with this level of reading and writing? Unbelievable. This is a new low, folks. I'm talking rock bottom," and kept looking over at us and sighing and closing her book and standing up from her chair like she was about to leave, which was probably why Minhee went around the playground at recess asking everyone if they wanted a "Korean massage," and if you shrugged or asked, "Um, what's a Korean massage?" she'd thump your back really hard and was getting so crazy about it that she actually made Eric Cho choke. Everyone laughed and was like, "Eric Cho-oked! Eric Cho-oked!"*

So please, God, show me some mercy and don't let people think I'm like Minhee Kim because she's a degenerate and I bet she's going to join a Korean gang when she gets to middle school, something I won't ever do, which already makes me so much better than her, and please also, if you remember, give me boobs before sixth grade and my period before seventh even though I heard most girls get boobs in fifth now and little nubbies in fourth and their period in sixth, but then again, most of those girls are really fat and they all say that I'm anorexic, which I'm not. By the way, God, can you also make those girls stop calling me anorexic? I can't help being the way I am, and it's not like I flaunt it or anything like that Lucy girl who is always saying stuff like, "Oh no! I'm so tiny the wind is gonna blow me away!" when it's really windy outside. I just happen to have to poop a lot and my mom says my grandfather was the same way. He was on the toilet all the time. Apparently just like me, he needed to poop immediately after every meal and that was why my grandmother said he was just skin wrapped around bones because he weighed so little. So yeah, it would be great if you could help me out. Thank you, God. Good night.

Wait, also protect my mom and my dad and my grandparents in China and also my cousins and my aunts and my uncles and their families of cousins and uncles and aunts and things like that and also my mom's friends and also my dad's friends and also my friends' families and also their friends and anyone else I forgot, but . . . you're God, remember? Since you are God (and why would I be praying to someone who wasn't God, and how would I even know to pray to someone who was only pretending to be God, that makes no sense), you probably know everyone I am thinking of right now, even though I can't exactly go through every single person I want you to protect for me because I don't want anyone to be sad and it would even be okay if you didn't protect me as much as everyone else because it's not a big deal if I'm sad sometimes. I just wish people didn't have to die in real life and in movies and in books and in dreams and in my imagination. Sometimes I imagine myself dead and then I can't sleep, but don't worry about me. I'll be okay. Good night.

* * *

The year I immigrated to New York, my mom was working as a bookkeeper for a shipping company in Jamaica, Queens, and Fanpin's mom was working part-time for a Taiwanese newspaper and had walked into my mom's office to try and sell her boss on the idea of buying ad space in the paper, but my mom's boss was a patriotic mainlander who had issues with the *Shijie Ribao* for being an apologist for Taiwan. It escalated quickly and Fanpin's mother was asked to leave and never return. My mom ran out after her to apologize on behalf of her boss, who was an asshole and a half, and the two of them bonded over all the assholes and a half in their lives. After chatting a bit, they realized they lived just blocks from each other and that their kids went to the same school but different classrooms. I'd see Fanpin now and then, weekends when my mom's face was more or less unbruised, she'd bring me over and I mostly sat around, shy and unwilling to leave my mother's side. My mother had to speak for me, chalking it up to the fact that I was still learning English and wasn't comfortable playing with other kids in English yet.

"Oh, but Fanpin speaks some Chinese," her mother said encouragingly, tricking me into feeling okay about going with Fanpin to her room but as soon as she shut the door, she spoke to me in a rush of English, and I didn't know what to say back, so I just stood there, looking at her collection of tiny knives and G.I. Joe figurines that she had neatly spread out on her dresser.

"She's not very bright," Fanpin said to her mother as I was leaving with mine. Fanpin's mother admonished her but the damage had been done. I had to continue going over to her house to please my mother. In fourth grade, I had the misfortune of being placed in the same class as her, which meant more Fanpin but also meant that I had moved up from the remedial classes I had been in for second and third—I was with

the *okay* kids, not the *bright* kids, but the *okay* ones. I thought
my father would be pleased but he was disappointed.

"You should be in the gifted class," he said. "You should be
with the top kids. Not failing is no accomplishment."

"I'm sorry."

"Don't be sorry, just be better."

"Okay."

Once Fanpin and I were placed in the same class, she insisted on walking me home every day after school. "I'm your
knight in shining armor." She grinned.

"You're my blight in shining armor," I said, trying out a
new word on her.

"You really don't know how to speak right." Her voice was
slightly softer than how she usually spoke to me so I knew she
was impressed. I lived on Ash Avenue and she lived on Dela-
ware; since the streets went in alphabetical order it made
sense for Fanpin to walk me home though it had a gleam of
inequality because I didn't want to be escorted.

She insisted and had a million and one reasons for why it
wasn't just her right to escort me, but her duty. "You know we
live in a kind of crap neighborhood, right?"

"Yeah," I said. I knew. I knew too much and never enough.
"But you live in a house and you have your own bedroom."

"So? A house in a crap neighborhood is still a house in a
crap neighborhood."

When we got to Ash Avenue, we kept walking because Fanpin insisted she had something really special to show me—
her mother had bought her a VHS tape of *Lady Chatterley's
Lover* and there was one scene in particular she thought I
would really like.

"Fine," I said, "but I have a lot of homework."

"We have the same homework, dumbo. We're in the same
class, remember?"

"It takes me too long to alphabetize the vocab words. I wish we could just alphabetize our streets. Ash, Beech, Cherry. It would be sooo easy."

"Well, I don't," Fanpin said.

"You always go against me."

"It's not that. It's just if everything is easy we'll never learn. It's supposed to be hard. That's how we know we're learning."

She had a point and I found myself nodding like the Korean kids in my class did during church service. I knew how vigorously they nodded because one afternoon Fanpin and I snuck into the back pew of Flushing Memorial Presbyterian on our way home from school to spy on Minhee and her crew, but what we stumbled upon was so new to me, so unknown, I forgot to think of ways to make fun of them and instead just stared, wondering if this was something I would do one day.

"What are they doing?" I murmured to Fanpin.

"Praying," she said.

"That's praying?"

"Yeah. Don't your parents take you to church? Don't you speak to God?"

"No," I lied. I spoke to God every night, but I had never known how to pray because my parents didn't believe in God.

"God is money," my father told me after slamming the door on some Jehovah's Witnesses one evening. "God is having medication when you're sick, babies that have a chance to live out their adult lives." He was sputtering the way he did when he'd had it with my mom. "Your mother's grandfather was tortured. Where was God then? Where was God when they were torturing that poor old man?" The word for "torture" in Chinese sounded like the word for "bean." Like a cute, round, soft bean. It stretched for miles—it was appropriate to use when describing one kid making a mean face to another kid just to be annoying, and it was appropriate to use when describing a group of Red Guards accusing their history teacher of being a bourgeois landlord and dragging her out of the classroom and forcing her to crawl on her hands and feet across a path paved with coal cinders until they bled, then stringing her to a lamppost while students pushed thumb-tacks into her forehead for being a "bourgeois pig who valued intellect over class struggle" and so deserved to have her brain permanently injured, and deserved to be beaten with sticks and belts and clubs spiked with nails and deserved to stand under the sun while boiling water was dumped over her head until she lost consciousness and was placed into a gar-bage cart to die. When my father brought up torture again in the context of my mother's grandfather, I was ready to bite my lip so hard that it bled, I was ready to grind my teeth against each other until I had a headache for the next three days, I was ready to pull my sleeves over my hands so I could secretly dig my fingers into my palms until skin broke.

"They tortured my great-grandfather?" I asked my father while holding up the pamphlet that read in big block letters: WILL THIS WORLD SURVIVE? My father had thrown it onto the ground in disgust and I picked it up after him.

"They tortured him to death. To *death*. They took all his paintings and dumped them in the river. They burned his books and ripped up his scrolls. They emptied his booze down the toilet. They literally torched his family history that had been scrupulously recorded and passed down for gener-ations. In a matter of minutes, it was all lost. Forever. They demanded he give up his own home so they could turn it into a shoe factory. He began coughing up blood. He was so mad. He forsook God. He had no paper to write on. He was a poet without paper! His home was emptied of beauty. He was a lover with nothing to love. Your great-grandfather owned the most beautiful estate in Wenzhou. It was a dream home he built with his own hands. He hadn't harmed anyone. He was known as the most generous man in the village. He *volunteered* himself in the early days of the party. He joined the army because he *believed* in the Communist utopia. He *convinced* other people in the village to collectivize when no one else was willing, and this was how they repaid him. They dragged him out and forced him to kneel in front of his own children! Do you understand, Mande? Can you explain what kind of God oversees this? Can you imagine continuing to pray to this God? Your great-grandfather died standing up, writing his last poem in the air, scribbling with his fingers. He was engaging with ghosts, he handled ghost objects for a brief time in the real world. His children thought he was going mad. He took ten shots of baijiu, one after another, like a general about to take his men into a losing battle, and after gulping down the tenth shot, he died."

"Where did he get the alcohol from? I thought they drained it all."

"There was no booze. There weren't even glasses. He was holding air, he was already a ghost and his body took another few days to catch up. He took empty shots of nothing and dropped dead."

"Dropped dead?"

"Dead. Died. Diiiiiiiieed. He was in perfect health and then he was dead. People died of anger back then. They died of humiliation, they died of sadness, they died of longing. They died of shame. Families were separated. Husbands and wives assigned to provinces thousands of miles away from each other. My mother and father saw each other five times in ten years. I saw my father a total of three times after my ninth birthday. People my age walk with canes because they were sent to the countryside and worked to exhaustion. Tell me what prayer will do for them. Go on."

"Religion was banned in China," my mother added, saying nothing more of her grandfather. "It was illegal to pray. You could be jailed or beaten if someone snitched."

"And that's why . . ." I started, then hesitated, "God is money?"

"Listen to your dad. He's right. It was illegal to have money. Or it was impossible to have it. It's hard to explain because it was a different world."

My head was spinning. I prayed for a God who would show me there was a God. I prayed for the past, which had already happened and was too late to change, but still, I thought, what if God could? What if the past could be healed? What if my parents could unlive what they lived through and still be my parents, then what? I began to kneel because Minhee knelt. I clasped my hands because the Korean kids clasped theirs. I learned in school that everywhere in the world except Europe, people didn't know how to pray and God had to be brought to them, and everywhere God had to be brought to, it seemed people disappeared, died, lost all dignity, and/or were forced into lifelong servitude. I didn't want anyone to bring God to me. I didn't want to die standing up. I didn't want to live in servitude to the people who claimed they found God first. I would learn in secret, I would become fluent with God. I had to.

Fanpin was already fluent. "I speak to God every night. My mom and I do it together. We go to church and do it with everyone else." Her mom was from Taiwan and my mom was from mainland. According to my mom, that made all the difference.

"It means they fled after the civil war. They were on the losing side, of course. It means they went to school. They live now the way people in China did sixty years ago. The women don't work. They have multiple children if they can. It's the old country, they live like it's still 1920. It's not normal. The men are vicious. They have free rein to beat their wives. It's not looked down upon over there." She had a strange look in her eyes, one that told me she wouldn't elaborate further on the hypocrisy—I would have to get older and find out on my own.

"Can you show me how?" I asked Fanpin after we spied on Minhee and her friends.

"Sure," she said. "It's easy."

Fanpin wasn't all bad. Just in front of the other kids, she was. At school, I pretended I barely knew Fanpin, even though I went over to her house all the time. I pretended like I didn't know what Fanpin's room looked like, like I had never laughed along with her at the part in *Tiny Toons* when Babs floods the entire town to get back at Buster, like I had never helped her bury her pet cat Lucifer, who died when she was in third grade and smelled so horrible that I had thought for sure someone in her family had soiled their pants during the goodbye ceremony. I pretended I had never got down on my knees with her and repeated after her: *Dear Heavenly Father, thank you for blessing us with another day. We bow our heads in supplication to you, to show the immensity of our thanks, insufficient as they are to Your glory and Your blessings. O Father, grant us Your benediction. Watch over us through our hours of darkness. Protect us in spirit as well as in body when we sleep. Help us to confront tomorrow with unwavering faith and without fear. We are forever Yours. We place all our trust in You. We open our hearts to You and we implore You to guide our minds, fill our imaginations and control our wills so that we may be wholly Yours, dedicated to You and only You. In Your Holy name, we thank You for drawing us into Your heart. May You use us as You will, always to Your glory and Your honor and to the splendor of heaven. May we forever serve You, our Lord and Savior Jesus Christ. Amen.*

The prayer was a whole other language to me, separate from English, separate from Chinese, it was new grammar, new sounds, new forms. I wished to be fluent in prayer faster than it took me to become fluent in English but it was fucking difficult. It was like the time I decided I would look up every single word that I didn't know in *Bridge to Terabithia*, which meant looking up the words "copyright" "reserved" "registered" "trademark" and "dedication" before even cracking open the first numbered page. When an hour had gone by and I had only gotten through two of the assigned thirty pages, I was nearly inconsolable. I was bleary from going back and forth between the dictionary and the book and making things worse was when the definition for the word contained words that I had to look up. To understand the definition of the word "despise," I had to also look up "scorn" "contempt" "loathe" "disgust" "disdain" and "regard"—basically everything except the word "to" had to be looked up and then in looking up the definitions of the words used to define "despise" there were even more words that had to be looked up, and so on and so on until I finally looked up every foreign word nested inside a definition for another word, at which point, I still had to then retrace each word back to the previous definition where I had first encountered it. By the time I finally returned to "despise," I was so mixed up that I had to move on to the next word without ever figuring out what it meant. All was lost, all was impossible. I decided I would rather be successfully illiterate than fail over and over again at literacy.

It was no different praying with Fanpin. I tried to hold in my head all the words I didn't know to look up later while also remaining in the moment because I desperately wanted to talk to God and I desperately wanted God to speak to me. What was "benediction," what kind of "thanks" was both "insufficient" and contained "immensity"? Was there a kind of "draw" that didn't involve crayons, and a "will" that wasn't a name or an indicator of the future, what was "glory" and why "amen," why not "thank you," why not "bye"? Were the Heavenly Father, the Lord, our Father, our Savior, and Jesus Christ ever in competition with each other, and which was the most supreme God? How was I supposed to figure out the order of calling on my own the next time? I was left more uncertain than ever.

While I was mired in questions, Fanpin had moved on to snacks. Her mother only worked half-days selling ads for the *Shijie Ribao,* and was home every afternoon by two. Our school let out an hour later and by the time Fanpin and I got to her house there were sandwiches ready and juice boxes to choose from. It was perfect for someone with friends, only Fanpin didn't have any, which meant more sandwiches for me. She claimed that in third grade she had been friends with this girl Frangie, a weird raccoon-eyed girl who never spoke.

"What did her voice sound like?" I asked.

"Actually, really, really nice," Fanpin told me. "Kind of like the Pink Power Ranger. And she's got a dead mom."

"So how come she's not here now if you're such best friends?"

"Because I have a new best friend. The hell's with you? Stop being a bag of farts already."

It made me uncomfortable when Fanpin made it seem like we were in this together, when I was only there for the sandwiches on weekdays and to stay close to my mother on weekends. My mother liked going over to Fanpin's house to gossip with Fanpin's mom about the other moms they knew and the light chitchat always turned into a discussion of all the ways life had failed to live up to the promise of my mother's childhood dreams or whatever. It made me think my father was right: there was no satisfying her.

Our moms had a lot to say to each other because they both had married men who didn't know how to cook, who never brought them flowers on their birthdays, men so lacking in imagination and resources that they thought a good weekend was one when three Clint Eastwood Westerns aired on network television, men who came from families of much lower stature than their own and yet still insisted on being the "man" of the house, still insisted on a legacy named after them, as if, our mothers said, rolling their eyes, they would do anything of significance in their lifetimes.

While I was eavesdropping, Fanpin was usually in her room practicing karate, and I savored the precious few minutes I had between my mom no longer having any responsibility toward me and Fanpin realizing that I was hiding in the bathroom, listening in on our moms talking about all the things that oppressed them. I waited for my mom to reveal that, in fact, I was one of the things in her life that kept her from being happy, from realizing all of her dreams, from being the sort of full, brilliantly expansive, and interminably layered person she wanted to be, that I was the primary cause of her imprisonment. But they only ever spoke about the shortcomings of our fathers, or how this place was worse than anything they had ever experienced in China.

"After all," my mother said once, "I could have worked at the UN, I could have floated on the Dead Sea. I could have walked around the Arabian desert with Bedouins, but instead I married him. Then he had to go and immigrate to America. Look at me now. Have I even seen the Jersey shore? Will the northern lights ever appear above me?"

Sometimes, their conversations made my blood boil—all that ungratefulness they unleashed. It wasn't as if my father was a monster. And if America was so terrible, why the hell did they bring me here? Why did my mother, a grown woman, get to talk like all her hopes and dreams had been shat on, kicked, and set on fire, all the while pushing me, a mere girl, a child, to do better, to accomplish more, to face down all the odds and become a legend? Where was I supposed to go to complain the way they did? To be validated the way they validated each other?

"He puts his feet right on the coffee table," Fanpin's mom said once. "As if guests don't drink tea and eat guazi off of that table."

"Well, Jianjun might be a complete imbecile. He doesn't even bother taking a shower half the time. He takes the shower nozzle and sprays at his ass for a minute, then wipes it with the same color towel that my daughter uses to wash her face. What sort of grown man is stupid enough to pick a towel the same color as his kid's face towel to wipe his ass?"

"Your husband uses an ass towel?"

"Yeah. And who do you think gets the pleasure of washing it every week?"

"Us. You and me."

"Well, just me, actually."

"I know, I meant you and me in a metaphorical sense. I didn't mean I'm also literally washing your husband's ass towel."

"Our men are spoiled."

"When we're the ones who should be getting spoiled."

Our mothers weren't really friends. They just had to be because this was a lonely life. At night, my mom stuck cotton in my ears because those were the days when the Puerto Rican gangs shot at the black gangs who shot back at the Puerto Rican gangs who constantly fought over a corner with the Korean gangs who declared a truce with the Vietnamese gangs who together turned on the Puerto Rican gangs who temporarily teamed up with the black gangs who had a shoot-out with the Korean gangs over that same corner and lost, only to have the issue come back up again with a newly formed Cantonese gang who accidentally shot an old woman who was crossing the street too slowly. We clipped out photos of houses on Long Island that we were going to move into one day if we did everything right, if we lived long enough. We made secret and not-so-secret promises to ourselves that this current life was temporary. No one lived this way forever. We told ourselves we were going to escape one day or another, although I never figured out if dying counted as escape.

At least it was safe in Fanpin's house. At least she had a house. Even though she shared her two-story colonial row house with two other families, she still had her own room, she had a mom who made my favorite sandwiches—ham and cheese—and let me have as many as I wanted and never said anything like, "My, you are a hungry little girl. Do your parents not feed you enough? Do they not let you have seconds?" which was what the other, cattier parents always asked me because I was stick-thin and yawned all the time. At the Hong Kong Supermarket on Main Street on Saturdays, the other moms pushed their shopping carts close to ours and asked my mom if she ever let me eat meat, or was it all just rice and a few vegetables here and there? Fanpin's mom never bugged me about what I ate at home. She watched Taiwanese soap operas on a small portable TV in the kitchen while chopping vegetables and meat. She cleaned up after Fanpin and drove her to karate lessons and took us for Baskin-Robbins afterward. Her mom never yelled and always said yes to anything Fanpin wanted, or anything I wanted, for that matter. I liked asking her mom if I could have a second Juicy Juice juice box, mostly to test myself to see if I could say, "Can I have another Juicy Juice juice box?" without stumbling over the words because even though I had only learned English two years ago, that didn't stop the two white kids in my class from mocking me when I misspoke. There was the Irish kid whose skin was so white it blinded me on sunny days (and it wasn't just me because Minhee Kim and her posse called him "Albino Potato"), and there was the Italian girl who once stuck her foot out to trip me as I was going to put a box of crayons back into the art supply drawer and then laughed like a villain while pulling her eyes back to taunt me, "I knew you couldn't see with these!" It was doubly worse when they got the black and Spanish kids to join in, and even worse than that was when they got the Korean girls to participate, too, because most of them also spoke English with an accent, and there was something so undignified about having someone torment you for something they themselves were probably tormented for a year or two ago. It made me think the whole world was vicious. No one had it in them to have a heart for anyone, not even themselves, or at least, not the selves they once were that other people still had to be.

The Korean kids, who had all immigrated not too long before me (with the exception of Minhee, who, apparently, when she was one year old, was carried across a live minefield by a North Korean soldier who had defected, then smuggled through an underground railroad all the way to Thailand, where she was put into a refugee camp that sent her and her family on a plane to JFK airport, and when she told that story at show-and-tell, the part that none of us could believe was that of all the places her family could have ended up in, they chose . . . Flushing?), were the best at taunting me, knowing exactly how to push me over the edge by asking me if I needed another year of ESL, by asking me to pronounce P-e-n-e-l-o-p-e. "Do it, do it, do it," they said, "say her name." When I finally said, "Pen-ah-lope. Simple," everyone threw their heads back in delight and laughed, and I sheepishly laughed, too, even though what I wanted to say was:

Wet twat motherfucking cocksucking ass-opening reverse turd of a cocksucked smelly balls piece of shit shitfucker cuntpeeled fuck! I learned this language two years ago, does that mean anything at all to you? I don't come home and say, "Mom, I'm home!" I say, "Wo hui lai le ma ma." I say, "妈妈，我回来了." That's right, you mondo-clit. And while we're at it I'd like to say this to you: "你是一个臭王八蛋."* Yes, I mispronounced "stereo" last week but that's because we don't own a stereo, and even if we did, I wouldn't have an opportunity to say, "Mom, can you turn up the stereo?" I would say, "可不可以把音响关轻一点."†

My first year in America, no matter what language I used, I was always wrong. In English you can turn off the lights and close the door, but you can't close the lights and turn off the door, and in Chinese you can close down the lights, but you can't simply wear glasses and shirts and hats because each of those things had its own specific counting word for "wear," and every type of object in the world had to be counted differently. In English, some e's were soft, some g's were hard, some consonants sounded like others, every rule had an exception, no exceptions didn't have rules. I started to regret saying anything at all. I started to see how delusional I had been to believe that words could only lift me into the glorious upper stratosphere of possibility instead of pulling me down into the drowning waters of inarticulation. My bad tongue mocked me for ever thinking that language was miraculous,

---

* Literal translation in English: You piece of shit and also swollen bunghole of a waste of life.

† Sorry, no translation currently available.

like, for example, how did anyone ever come up with a hundred different ways of saying, "You have made this world a great one for me"?

For every single thing I gave two shits about, Fanpin gave none. She had this aura about her, like she could easily karate-chop a sixth grader into oblivion, and unlike the other girls, her long black hair made her look tough, like those men who wore beat-up jackets and swore while smoking and rode motorbikes on the highway, laughing all the way to the bank at all the other people on the road—the people with neat, trimmed hair, who drove dependable cars with the windows rolled up—and it intimidated and confused us, the way she could look like that while the rest of us idiots still heeded what we were told about being girls and boys who were supposed to grow up and become adult women and adult men.

Even if I did respect Fanpin a little bit, our so-called friendship was doomed. I knew it without even knowing God. Sure, I wanted to be loved and accepted, but why did it have to be by her? She embarrassed me when she insisted on holding my hand as we walked down the hallway, acting tough whenever a boy was around us. Once, she smacked Jason Lam in the face when he came up behind me and pinched the back of my shirt to see if I was wearing a bra. "Don't be touching my friend, Shrimpson," she said.

"What the hell," he said, recoiling. "Don't go around hitting people."

"Don't go around being sexist."

"Sex-what?" I said.

"Sexist, you idiot," Fanpin repeated. "Don't you know we live in a sexist society?"

"You don't need to tell me," I said. But she did. She needed to tell me and tell me and hover around me.

The day before Valentine's Day, Fanpin pulled me into the girls' bathroom and demanded that I touch her boob in the stall closest to the door. She pressed my hand to her breast like I was swearing on oath:

I do solemnly swear that I am not a lesbian, but you, Fanpin, my not-dear friend, are. And since you are also scary and practice karate (on your own and on me), and are already a purple belt (pretty gay color. Coincidence? Um, HIGHLY DOUBT IT), and because I have great hopes that you will scare my non-existent tits right out of me, I will do as you tell me to. Also, why are your breasts like two hard rocks? I do believe that is not normal. Amen.

Afterward, she said, "You better not wash your hands if you know what's good for you," when she saw me reaching for the faucet. She raised her hand as if to strike me. It was an all too familiar gesture and I winced. I was an autobot back then and certain expressions, certain ways that people lifted their arms made me flinch, made my skin prickle like it had been touched by an ice cube.

"I won't," I said. Her hand was still raised in the air. "Um, what if I just turn on the water? I won't use soap. It doesn't count if you don't use soap. My mom said."

"Oh, God, you little baby. You still call her Mommy? You're such a loser. You're so square. You're like a reject for life."

"I never said Mommy."

"I heard you."

"I didn't say it."

"Yeah, you did, liar."

"Did not."

"Bet you don't even know what a pussy is."

"Like hell I don't," I said, even though it was the first time

I had heard that word and knowing it could mean literally anything and knowing that I would never get another chance to encounter that word for the first time again frightened and elated me. Back then, I was always learning. I learned how to say everything and I would say it and say it and say it and say it until no one bothered me, and I would do the same with "pussy." I would walk home and say it until it was my only thought, until I could get to a point where every time I said the word I said it as perfectly and beautifully as any human being who ever existed ever could. And then, and only then, did I stand a chance at being free. Except I was so far from that point. Except everyone still bothered me.

There was no way to be free in this world.

There was no way to be free in this world.

There was just no way to be free in this world.

There was no way.

There was simply no way.

And to be safe? Forget it. No one on earth was safe.

"Okay, fine then. I think you're a pussy. You"—and she drew an equal sign in the air—"pussy. You glad you're a pussy? Or do you feel dissed?"

"Dissed. Duh," I said.

"Why?" she asked.

"Cause."

"Cause what?"

"Why should I tell you?" I had my hands on my hips and my head jutted out in her direction.

"Cause of this," she said and shook her fist at me again.

"So?"

"So, you're afraid of me."

"No, I'm not."

"Yeah, you are," Fanpin said. "You always do everything I tell you."

"No." I was shouting now. "Liar. Why would I be afraid of you? You don't even have your black belt yet."

"I'm going to get it this year. My sensei said so."

"Your senses said shit."

"Ha ha." Fanpin laughed. "You sound so dumb trying to talk like that."

"Not as dumb as you."

"You're going to get punched if you don't tell me what a pussy is."

"What are you going to punch me with?"

"What do you think? My fists. Now let me check your butt and make sure you wiped."

"Of course I wiped. Who wouldn't?"

"Well, I'm gonna be the one to decide that."

"Not this time, you won't," I said. I crossed my arms down low by my hips and grabbed the waistband of my sweatpants with my fingers.

"What are you doing?"

"Anything," I said. "I'm doing anything. It's a free country, remember?"

"Why're you talking like that? You make no sense." Fanpin reached her hand out and tried to pry my fingers away. She pushed me against the sink and tugged my pants down to my ankles. "Gosh, don't you know I'm doing you a favor? Your ass is disgusting. You don't even know how to wipe properly."

"Get away from there," I said, pulling my pants back up. "Who said you could look?"

"Who said you could tell me what to do?"

I didn't know why I was so weak all the time, why I had no grace or power to summon. Why was I so exposed? Was there no barrier separating me from the dangers of other people in this world? Before I left Shanghai for New York, my grandfather on my mother's side told me my great-great-grandfather had been a diplomat during the reign of the Qing dynasty. "He was the official ambassador to Britain, Belgium, Germany, and Italy. He spoke eight languages. Switched back and forth between them in conversation. The ladies went mad for him, especially when he spoke in Italian. There was a statue erected in his honor in a small public park in Wenzhou. Of course all those statues have since been destroyed but you can't destroy our pride. These are our origins. Our people traversed the globe. They lived for adventure. They were most at home when they were away. They could build a home anywhere. That's in our blood, you understand?" It was the only pep talk anyone had ever given that actually made me feel braver. I returned to it whenever I felt like nothing and needed to reconnect with the part of me, no matter how deeply buried away, that still felt immense and maybe even, one day, capable of brilliant things. But every day, my grandfather's speech dimmed from my memory. Yes, I had so much to say but nothing of what I felt inside ever came through—I was a follower and a coward and a mute and that was that. If I was descended from people who found a way to belong anywhere, it didn't show. If I came from adventurers and poets who lived for themselves and resisted captivity, those qualities must have skipped me. I was an embarrassment to my bloodline. I couldn't even stop Fanpin from forcing me to participate in the games she came up with, like when she made us pretend to be husband and wife so that we would know what it was like to be our parents. Playing that game embarrassed me but I did it anyway even though I didn't like how I had to lie on my side and how she had to lie down next to me and wrap herself around me like she was cellophane and I was a cookie, or she was foil and I was a cheeseburger. The truth was, I didn't even let my mom hold me that way in bed anymore, even though it made her cry the first time I told her not to wrap her legs around me on nights when she claimed she needed that to fall asleep, like after a bad fight with my dad, something she never explicitly referred to, but I knew that was why. I didn't like waking up in the middle of the night and seeing the moonlight reflected over her swollen eye or her busted lip. It sickened me. And worse was when I had to turn away. I sickened myself and that was the one thing I couldn't avoid. All there was to do was pray. For sleep, for loss of consciousness, for rest, for a few days of peace.

"Leave me alone, you sicko," I said to Fanpin. "You're disgusting and I'll be the one to punch you if you try to get me into the bathroom again." I inched sideways along the sink to get away from her. "And don't try to suck up to me later at your house, because last Sunday, I got all sickened looking at the posters on your wall, and don't think I haven't already told Minhee and Yun Hee about that one poster and what you did to it. Yeah, you know which one and you know what you did. It made me need to throw up and you knew it and you know that anyone who knows about it would throw up, too, and you can bet on anything I'm never going into your house again." I shot one fist straight out and punched her in the tit. It wasn't a remarkable punch or anything but I felt it: her fleshy boob smushing up against my bony knuckles.

I swear to God Fanpin met my eye with what looked almost like respect and then dropped down to the ground. As I ran out the door, I heard something—a low wail that chilled my heart and reminded me of a time when I had heard my father cry, the one and only time I ever heard him cry. It was after a fight with my mom. I had seen him through a crack in the door to his bedroom. He was slumped on the floor with his hands in his hair. I watched him pulling out strands of his hair and flinging them to the ground, and later, after several hours had passed, when it was all over, no one remembered me, no one remembered to explain to me what had happened; it was just quiet. At the end of the night, I took the vacuum out of the closet and I cleaned up my father's hair; I didn't want reminders like that to exist in our house.

I didn't look back after punching Fanpin in the tit, though it took me days, maybe longer, to forget the sound of her crying, which is why I still say, if anyone was traumatized, it was me, the innocent bunny who had to defend herself from the predatory wolf, and my red, wet eyes that afternoon after I punched her didn't mean I was sorry or that I regretted what I had done, it just meant my allergies were flaring up again . . . and what could I have done to prevent that?

Fanpin and I never spoke again, not even when Mrs. Silver paired us up to do a presentation on ancient Egypt. We worked on the project in separate corners of the room. She used a computer and I used my mind. She sneered the entire time I was making a life-sized model of King Tut out of toilet paper, and when Fanpin gave her part of the presentation, I yawned nonstop and slipped a few silent but deadly farts in her general direction and then, at recess, told everyone it was her. "Fanpin has a real farting problem. No, seriously. I used to go over to her house and it smelled like she had a turd machine in her closet." She was absent when I brought in a bag of puffy Cheetos for my in-class birthday celebration and I barfed during hers and got permission to leave school early.

I asked my mom to not bring me over to her house anymore because it was distracting me from my schoolwork. "And anyway, I'm old enough to stay home by myself."

"No, you aren't, but we can't very well have Fanpin's mom

babysit you for free just because your father"—and she looked over at him and raised her voice—"can't get it together to support this family on his own."

Whenever my mother insulted my father's ability to provide for the family, he would smile like he knew the world was going to end tomorrow. It was the ugliest smile I had ever seen on a face and he had the capacity to hold it and hold it. This time, he held the ugly smile for so long we had to look away while we waited for him to respond to my mother. Finally, he said, "Like you'd be happy staying home with 李微 all day." It meant something when my parents referred to me by my Chinese name. They had changed it to Mande because the first place my father ever took my mother shopping when they got to America was the Queens Center shopping mall and my mother was entranced by the sign for Mandee and went in, only to realize it was clothing for teenagers. She said to my father, We'll shop for 李薇 here one day, when she's grown. Before she goes to college, we'll come here.

You mean we'll shop for *Mandee* at Mandee. She'll go by Mandee here, my father said, and just like that, I was renamed. I would have two names, just like all the other Chinese people in America did, just like how my father went by Jerry and my mother went by Susan so that people didn't have to refer to them as 张建军 and 陆诗雨, which people inevitably pronounced *zang gee-ann juhn* and *loo she-yoo*. My father said they needed "American" names on their resumes when applying for jobs; they had to have names that were pronounceable to white American English speakers because they already had faces that were considered vile to look at and who was going to hire someone with their faces *and* their names? I thought my mother and my father had beautiful faces but my father corrected me, Not in America. We're ugly, and it's that simple. They look at us and think we're cretins. You think they like us going to their schools? You think they're okay with us working in their offices? Taking their jobs? You think they're happy to pick up laundry and takeout from businesses we've opened up? You think they want to go to the corner store and see our eyes and our teeth and our skin looking back at them from behind the counter? No! They don't want us here. They don't want to look at us and they sure as hell don't want to have to try to pronounce our Chinese names. X-U. Q-I-U. They don't want to see that! The more my father went on about how much they hated us, the more I started to suspect maybe he was the one who hated us. On the first day of school in America, I was so frazzled and fearful of everything that I accidentally left off the second *e* and I became Mande with one *e* and so I started my first day of school in America with a mistake. I was a failure right from the start.

My mother had agreed with my father on the name issue but on the issue of me wanting to come home to my own home instead of Fanpin's (which would require the luxury of being a single-income household where one parent could stay home and look after me, which already hadn't happened), she was indignant. "I wouldn't just be home with our daughter all day doing nothing. What do you think I am? I'd start writing poetry again. I'd go back to painting."

"I'm sorry," my father said. "Did I misunderstand? Are you a grown woman and a mother or are you a teenager now?"

"Please," I said in a rare instance when I didn't just slink away to hide in my bed. "I just want to go straight home after school to focus on my homework. It's hard at Fanpin's house. It's really loud over there and her mother is always watching TV, and the other family is sometimes there, too, and it's hard to concentrate. Please just let me come home and do my work here. I won't tell anyone at school. I'll wear the key on a string around my neck and hide it under my shirt. I won't *ever* make

eye contact with anyone. If anyone tries to talk to me, I'll refuse to speak. I'll go mute. I'll scream like a torture victim if
anyone comes near me. I'll be safer than I was with Fanpin.
Did you know Fanpin's always talking to strangers? Strange
men. She doesn't care. Not me. I'll get myself home at the
pace between a light jog and a brisk walk to signal how fast I
could run if I had to while also signaling that I'm totally un-
afraid, because I'll be *walking,* not *sprinting* home. When I get
to our block, I'll go around the secret way so no one sees me
going inside the building by myself and thinks there's no
adult waiting at home for me. I can do it. I know I can."

"Okay," my mother said. "You can come straight home
after school, honey. That sounds like a fine idea. Doesn't it,
Jianjun?"

My father relented. "Fine. But you will take every precau-
tion. We'll go over them again until it's memorized. And when
you come home, you leave—"

"—the blinds drawn, windows locked, door dead-bolted.
Never ever pick up the phone. Never ever take in the mail.
Stay completely invisible once inside the house. Never give
those crooks a chance to think there's someone to kidnap, as-
sault, beat, or worse. And yes, I know exactly what 'worse' is.
No one will ever know there's a child in here." I was excited to
be the one going on and on for once.

All that my father managed to follow up with was, "I want
to see nothing but 100s on your next report card."

For the rest of fourth grade, I went straight home. In fifth
grade, Fanpin and I were assigned to different classes. It
seemed like a chapter of my life had finally come to a close.
My father was busier than ever planning my future. He was
frequently in touch with this family we were friends with
back in Shanghai who now lived in Little Neck, and had struck
a deal with them to use their address on all of my school forms

and applications so I could attend the public school in their district. We had our credit card and telephone bills sent to them instead of our Flushing address to establish residency. "This," my father proudly said, "is what they call the long con. Do you know how long it goes for?"

"Till everyone's dead," I guessed.

"The whole world," my father corrected me. "Until human life itself ends."

We went over to their house in Little Neck quite often, and their daughter Peggy was two years younger than me and even shyer than I was. They lived in an attached townhouse in Little Neck, which was right by the Queens–Long Island border, and by attached, I mean they shared walls with their neighbors. We used to move with our ears along the walls, as if maybe we had been magnetized by the hand of God (we both used the same loose definition of God:

"God is definitely something."

"Yeah, I know. That's also what I think") and as if we were being pulled along by Him.

I loved Peggy's house and so I loved Little Neck, which was still in Queens, unlike its neighbor Great Neck, which was on the Long Island side, and it was easy to tell which side you were on; all you had to do was drive up Northern Boulevard. On the Queens side it was Korean barbecue restaurants and SAT and tutoring prep schools and Honda dealerships but as soon as you entered Great Neck (which my parents and all their friends pronounced "Green Neck" as if they were discussing someone who had been poisoned and had gangrene crawling up their neck) there were no more Korean restaurants, and it was all Italian places like Capobianco's Auto Repair and Pasquale's Pizzeria, and BMW dealerships where the cars were spaced out and not crammed in like on the Little Neck side. Sometimes when we were waiting at an intersection, we'd see a group of white girls in foamy black sandals with two thick white bands across their tanned feet, taking their sweet long-ass time crossing the street, and the sight of them made me curse God all over again for making them get to be them and making me have to be me.

My parents refused to resign themselves to the fate they thought I was inevitably headed toward: pregnancy, drug abuse, alcoholism, gangbanging, general ne'er-do-welling, etc., etc. They wanted to plop me in the land of kimchee clay-pots because going to middle school in Little Neck was the only thing—short of spending eighty grand on a down payment for a new house, short of having hundreds of thousands of dollars for private school tuition—that stood any chance of saving me from a life of misery, poverty, and pain.

Sixth grade passed in a haze and marked the end of my elementary school years. The most interesting thing I learned all year was in social studies class when we were assigned to write research papers on World War II and I found out from a library book that Wenzhou dialect had been used as a secret code during the war. When I went home to tell my parents that, my mother said, Of course it was. Your grandfather was a code talker. He was brought in to relay coded messages back and forth. He was responsible for sinking a Japanese warship that was about to set fire on our people. No wonder, I thought, being near him had felt as holy as kneeling before God.

Every now and then, my path crossed with Fanpin's, and sometimes, I would see her walking in front of me after school, her long black hair swishing back and forth. She had taken to wearing lace-up combat boots that hit mid-calf with black pants bunched up over the top of her boots and a long black trench. I could hardly believe I ever fought her and won. All of my friends wrote in my yearbook, "Why aren't you going to J.H.S. 181 for middle school? It's the best! (If you think prison is the best!) Miss u4ever, KIT." And I wrote in theirs, "Hell to the no-no. You think I want to get beat up by a buncha Spanish girls? Have fun getting kicked in the vagina and learning math from crack-ho teachers."

No one called me that summer. I ate Blimpie sandwiches every single day and watched *Let's Make a Deal* and waited for my mother to come home from work at eight so that I could tell her how much I loved the Blimpie sandwich she'd brought me the night before to eat for lunch while I watched game shows, and how much I was going to love the Blimpie sandwich she would surely bring home with her that night, and how much I loved her in general (and my father, too, when he was in a good mood), and that I believed in her, no matter what, I believed in her. I believed one day she wouldn't have to work six days a week, and one day she really could stay home with me and keep me company, not just because it was scary to be in the house alone after six P.M. but because I wanted her to be a poet like her granddaddy and I wanted her to see beautiful things like her granddaddy's granddaddy, and as for me? I wanted to be someone too. I was on the verge of telling her this the night she showed me some of the poems she had written when she was a young girl in Shanghai:

> *freed my heart*
> *lifting melting steel with old wings*
> *ancient pain wanders as free*
> *as a stream*

It's just a fragment, she said sheepishly. I was about to reassure her that it was the finest fragment I had ever read but my father came in, pissed that I wasn't asleep yet, so it had to be saved. All of it had to be saved, but it was okay—I was determined to take my time expressing myself. The rush and the urgency I felt before had calmed. I was eleven now, going on twelve, and I was going to take my time.

Seventh grade started after Labor Day, and it was all set that I would go to middle school at I.S. 25 in Little Neck. I had to take the bus from my house in Flushing to Little Neck, get off at the Western Union, and walk ten minutes up a hill to my new school. My parents thought that our lives were changing, that I was finally safe. They had gotten me out. I was still alive, still a virgin, still a child—even though I no longer felt like it was a good thing to be as small and protected as I had been.

My parents, who tried to account for everything, my parents who checked my coat pockets daily and checked my hair to make sure it didn't smell like it had been near a boy, who checked my math homework to make sure I had solved each problem at least two different ways, who clipped out articles from *The New York Times* and made me first copy each article in its entirety and then summarize it in three sentences, then five sentences, then two paragraphs, and then finally three sentences, which sometimes meant my summaries were longer than the original article depending on which section of the paper I chose (though eventually they limited my choices to the world news, U.S. news, and business sections), my parents, who truly believed I was going to go to Harvard and live the good life that they were willing not to have so I could have a stab at it, my sweet, well-intentioned parents, no matter how much they tried to see and anticipate and prevent all the things that could hurt me, in the end, had no idea what truly frightened me.

How was I going to be afraid of not going to Harvard when I was afraid to look people in the eye in the hallways at school because everyone in middle school was either in a gang or going to get beat up by someone in a gang, and guess which category I belonged to? Seventh grade was hard. I was lonely.

I wondered how Fanpin was faring in her middle school, if she ever got her black belt in karate, if the other kids gave her shit for dressing the way she did, if she found someone else to torture or if middle school had rendered her powerless. For the first time, I wondered if she was scared.

"You love your new school, don't you?" my parents asked me.

"It's the same."

"The *same*? You call a twenty-percent dropout rate versus forty percent the same? You call standardized testing scores in the eightieth-plus percentile for more than half the seventh-grade class the same as half the kids are dope fiends and the other half drug dealers? That's your idea of the same?"

"Jeez, Dad. I just mean it feels the same to me."

"Well, try to feel harder."

"Honey," my mother said to my father, "she's feeling as hard as she can."

"Sweetheart," my father said to my mother, "do you really think Mande is trying as hard as she can? Is she trying as hard as we tried to get her into this school? Is she trying as hard as spending the last two years filling out forty forms and making hundreds of phone calls and faxes and Xeroxes? As hard as conceiving this plan more than five years in advance?"

I thought I was trying, but what did I know? What did my parents know? They were home most nights for three, sometimes two, sometimes one, and occasionally zero of the hours that I was awake, and what did they actually have time for in those three or two or one or zero hours other than cooking dinner and refrigerating it in case the next day was one of the days when I saw them for one or zero hours? Or arguing over who had run down this month's savings to a measly sixty bucks when the goal was two-fifty, something that they had agreed on and very meticulously budgeted for? Or going over my homework to make me see how important it was to not just get a 99 in spelling, but a 100, and not just get a "Very good" on my English essay but a "This is perfect"? ("There's no such thing as this 'grade,' " I said, putting it in air quotes. "Perfection always exists," my father said. "Just look at your mother." "Ugh," I said. Maybe perfection did exist, maybe it was out there, but it only lasted as long as a sneeze. In a day or a week or in another few minutes, my father would lose that moony look in his eyes, my mother would fall from his esteem, and they would be estranged again, enemies once more. He would grab her by her throat or twist her arm or hit her in the face until she was quiet. She would grab a knife from the kitchen and say that she was going to stab him to death and then herself, wouldn't that be just great for everyone? I would hate him for hating her and then I would hate her for hating him. Then I would hate myself for not protecting my mother and then I would hate my mother for needing me to protect her, and then I would hate my father for causing my mother to need that protection, and finally, I would hate them both for insisting that the person who really needed protection was me, and if I had any chance of surviving, I would have to be better than perfect. What I wanted to know was if *my own parents* couldn't even be satisfactory to each other, then why I was expected to be *perfect*?)

So I was fed and I was looked after and I was encouraged to be perfect and I was told over and over that life would always improve, that this was how anyone at all was supposed to live, by striving, by being perfect when you were young and it was still easy to be perfect because just wait, my father would say, just wait until you're older, but I didn't need to wait. I was young now and I found it so fucking hard. In the three or two or one or zero hours I saw my parents every night, I kept waiting for them to ask me new questions, like how many friends did I have at school, and was it hard to be the new girl, and did I ever feel lonely when I came home from school and had to wait to see if this was a night of three or two or one or zero hours with them, and how was I coping with walking all the way to the Q12 bus stop on my own? Did strange men on the bus ever approach me and try to ask me if I wanted to make several babies with them, etc., etc., etc.?

At school, I crept around like a scared mouse, darting from one classroom to another when the bell rang, hoping not to accidentally be hit by a spitball or to open my locker to the smell of fresh dog shit or to look at someone I wasn't supposed to ever make eye contact with. Someone was always trying to beat on someone and the most notorious of the someones was this ninth grader Soo-Jin. She was the leader of a Korean gang and she was a true knockout, the kind of beautiful that was unapproachable and heightened by rumors of her sadism. You wanted to stare at her but you couldn't—it would get you jumped after school or worse. She made the word "feminine" look even more dangerous than it sounded. She wore a thick velvet choker with a little studded cross that dangled softly when she walked. Wherever she was, she was flanked by her two best friends, Eunsong and Eunice, who were only permitted to wear plain, thick, non-velvet chokers and never with a charm. They had stubby necks that reminded me of how my Barbies looked after I snapped their heads off and then screwed them tightly back in, whereas Soo-Jin's neck was long, white, and clean. She was the kind of creature who could have been painted and kept in a fine art gallery if only someone was allowed to look at her long enough to memorize the sharp angles of her cheekbones and her finely plucked eyebrows and her lippy, pouty scowl that was more alluring than any smile I had ever seen on anyone else. She was a gangster with the face of a heartbreaker.

Soo-Jin was never alone and that was how you knew she was powerful—she belonged to an order of teenage girls who would do anything for her without her even having to ask. She had adherents and the rest of us had friends we couldn't count on. Besides Eunsong and Eunice, there were a dozen or so girls in her posse, and plenty more who tried to join but weren't allowed in. I overhead in pre-calc that she "ate pussy like there was no tomorrow."

"Did you know," I told Peggy after school when I was over at her house waiting for my parents to come pick me up, "that you can eat pussy?" I mumbled the word, ashamed by the possibility that I had been the one to make Peggy aware of it, as I sure as hell didn't know that word when I was her age, and if she was anything like me then it meant I was her Fanpin. It was a horrifying thought.

"My dad says that's a racist thing people say to put down Chinese people."

"I'm not talking about cats. I'm talking about the hole you pee out of. You're supposed to let guys put their thing in there and that's what happens when you get a boyfriend."

"Disgusting."

"Yup," I agreed.

"Does God know about this?"

"He knows everything."

"Oh," she said. It was yet another thing my parents didn't know to warn me about and the more I thought about it, the more it excited me. That night, I got under the covers and tried to pray but couldn't stop laughing at the thought of my vagina as a lollipop, something sweet, something to desire. I wondered who, if anyone, would ever desire me in the way I desired to be desired. So far I had only ever fended off Fanpin, whose desire for me was a cancer and a stain, but maybe if I were truly desirable, if more people wanted me the way she had wanted me, I would have developed some real muscle, some real grit. Maybe it was all the better that I wasn't beautiful. After all, I hadn't even been decent-looking when I had to resort to violence to defend myself against Fanpin's advances. What would I have had to do if I had been a knockout like Soo-Jin?

My Lord and Savior Jesus Christ, grant me strength, I prayed in an attempt to resist the image of Fanpin's nine-year-old face appearing before me, asking me to pretend-sleep next to her with her crotch pressed up against my butt. Doesn't this feel nice? she used to ask me. *Watch over me in my hours of darkness. Protect me in spirit as well as in body when I sleep.* Stop moving around so much, she used to say every time I wiggled away to keep some distance between us. *I will forever honor you. I am wholly yours, your humble servant through whatever trials and tribulations that may test me.* This isn't right, I used to say. My mom says I can only do this with my future husband or with her. *Please help me to confront tomorrow with unwavering faith and without fear.* Whenever I mentioned a boy Fanpin would snap, even if it was an imaginary boy who was supposed to grow up and woo me into marriage one day. She'd say, Well, who told you to be such a little mommy's girl? And who says you have to get married to a man? She was wild and I was meek. Even in her total wrongness she would get a thing or two right, like how my parents were more naïve than I was if they thought what they had was something I would want one day. *Please,* I begged God, *show me the right way to live.* I didn't dare utter Fanpin's name though her presence was smeared all over my prayers—she had given me a structure and a vocabulary to speak to God all those years ago when I didn't know if I was doing it right, and now, speaking to God how she spoke to God, I felt simultaneously distant from Him and too close to her. She had wormed her way into my devotion. She had entered the part of me that was supposed to be only available to Him. *Dear God, I'm sorry . . . I have to say it the way I want to say it. Look, I need a sign. I know I'm not supposed to, but I need you to tap me on the shoulder when I'm walking to my first-period class. I need you to drop a leaf on my book bag when I'm waiting for the bus. I just need to know you're really there. I'm sorry, I know that's wrong. Only the faithless rely on signs and symbols. Only the selfish ask for their prayers to be answered directly. I know it's wrong to demand of you. I know, I know, I know. But I'm so lost. I'm afraid every night before I go to sleep and I'm afraid every morning when I wake. Is it normal to wake up disappointed I've survived another day? Sometimes I think it would be better not to wake up at all, never to have known what it was like to have lived a life. Is it too late? Will I always know this life? I can't imagine beyond this world there is another. I want to believe in your kingdom and your bounty but I can't imagine it. I want to move on, but to what? To where? Most days I can't imagine a tomorrow until it's already yesterday. Am I supposed to just keep waiting? Why did you create life? Is it so wrong to wish you had never made me or my mother or my father or their mothers and fathers and all the mothers and fathers who came before them? All I've ever known about any of them is how much pain they went through . . . and I'm just supposed to go through it too? Well, forgive me if I don't fucking feel like it. If I don't want to be a story my children rant about to their children when I'm dead. Forgive me. Fucking forgive me. Good night.*

I found out wearing yellow and black to school was like wearing a sign that said KICK MY ASS REALLY PLEASE DO IT when some kid in the hallway between eighth and last period made this motion like he was going to punch me right in the vagina but instead released his forefinger from his curled fist and pointed at my shirt—a garage sale gem I found one afternoon with Fanpin. It was fifty cents and she bought it for me because "that's what best friends do." I let her spoon me when we got back to her house without putting up much of a fight as thanks but never once wore the shirt in front of her—I didn't want her to think I was flirting back somehow. Now that I was in seventh grade and had the faintest contours of something resembling a pair of breasts, I wanted to be less timid, I wanted to be noticed by the right someone. If I was going to be truly delicious and succulent, I would have to expose myself a little, whether that meant showing a sliver of tummy or opening my mouth to speak. The plan was to dig up all my old elementary school shirts and wear them as shrunken baby tees, but I chickened out the first week of school and hid underneath big-ass sweaters that went down to my knees. I was so invisible kids walked right into me as if I were air. After enduring several days of a freakish September heat wave, I finally convinced myself to forgo the sweater and for whatever godforsaken reason, I chose to wear Fanpin's gift to me—a pale yellow ringer tee with black lettering that said, MY SUN IS A STAR!

"What?" I asked the kid who was pointing at me.

"You're just begging to get fucked up. It's almost funny."

I was one of the last to know but eventually I knew too—I was in colors verboten to everyone and anyone except Soo-Jin. Just about anything could make you the target of Soo-Jin's wrath, including: standing next to her, walking past her too quickly, walking past her too slowly, waving your hands near her, talking too loudly or too softly around her, looking at her, brazenly wearing a shirt that you thought was just you wanting to wear something so that you weren't naked, but, in fact, was something that deeply, deeply pissed the shit out of her and would be the reason for why you later had your ass beat.

There was a story that had been going around to scare in-coming sixth graders (which I, of course, was the last to know because I transferred in at the beginning of seventh) about how this one sixth grader was stupid enough to look at Soo-Jin the wrong way, and Soo-Jin grabbed her by the neck and said, "You think you can look at me like that and get away with it, you titless piece of shit?" The girl apologized and apolo-gized but Soo-Jin was still pissed, so after school she and her gang followed the sixth grader down the street and tied up her hands and feet with thick rope (and at this point of the story, whoever was hearing it for the first time was already spooked because what were ninth graders doing with ropes thick enough to be used as lassos?). They asked her, "Do you want to be untied, bitch? Do you think you're sorry enough that we should let you go?" And the girl said, "Yes, please. Please. I'm so sorry. I'm so so sorry. Please untie me." To that Soo-Jin said, "Okay, but first, there are a few things," and the girl said, "What things? What things? What things?" so des-perately and so many times that Soo-Jin had to shut her up by punching her in the mouth and knocking out her front teeth. Soo-Jin and her girls dragged this sixth grader into a Honda Accord that belonged to some high school senior who was so in love with Soo-Jin he gave her the keys to his car to try and win her over, not knowing she had something else in mind. They waited in the car, listening to the radio until it was dark. One of Soo-Jin's girls was instructed to go back to make sure the coast was clear, a task she took seriously, hiding out be-hind the dumpsters until all the lights in the building were shut off.

"I saw the janitor lock the main doors and drive off," she reported back to Soo-Jin, who turned to the sixth grader and asked, "Ever been over there after dark?" pointing at the empty asphalt-concrete parking lot surrounded by a barbed-wire fence, where the music teachers parked because it was closer to the band and chorus rooms. The sixth grader shook her head.

Soo-Jin kicked her out of the car and said, "You'll see." It was at this point of the story that the person listening wondered: What was the worst thing a ninth grader could do to a sixth grader? Was it a marker of adulthood to be able to imagine true horror? Then again, if the worst imaginable thing was something that had already happened to someone not so different from ourselves, then who among us was safe? What if there was something even worse that we could not imagine?

There was. There was much, much worse.

Soo-Jin walked over to the fence and scaled it in thick gardening gloves, uncoiled the barbed wire from the fence, climbed back down, and laid the barbed wire on the ground. She had her girls strip off the sixth grader's clothes and then she had them stand aside and watch as she slapped the sixth grader across the face with the barbed wire. Then Soo-Jin whistled through her teeth as she wrapped the barbed wire around the sixth grader as if she were decorating a Christmas tree. When she was done, she stood back and asked the sixth grader, "Do you still feel like looking at me?"

The other girls laughed with Soo-Jin as the girl fell to the ground. According to some accounts, one of the girls in the gang said, "All right, let's go home now, this bitch is done for," but Soo-Jin said, "No, not yet, there's one more thing we have to do." And that thing? Oh, the thing! We all secretly begged for a happy ending, the point in a movie when the impossible suddenly became possible, when the characters you felt sorry for were finally granted some mercy.

Here was the thing: while the sixth grader was writhing in pain, Soo-Jin had four of the girls hold her still and had another girl gag her with the T-shirt they had stripped off her earlier, and then, little by little, Soo-Jin yanked the barbed wire off this sixth-grade girl, tearing off strips of her flesh, which stuck to the razored edges like bitty flags flapping in the wind. When it was all over, the sixth grader was candy-cane swirled with her own blood and had already tried twice to bite off her tongue from the pain. Some of Soo-Jin's girls were shaking nervously, while others sneered but more out of performance than instinct, and Soo-Jin let out a very cute little giggle, as if she'd completed an adorable little prank, like slipping a banana peel in front of a walking cartoon character, or as if she had transgressed in the most insignificant of ways, like accidentally peeing on the toilet seat without wiping it clean. That was what made her such a brute—that, and how she somehow managed to pick up the girl-who-looked-at-her-wrong without any help and throw her right into the dumpster behind the rooms where band and chorus practiced.

Washington's birthday marked the first day of my midwinter break and when my parents came home from work the Friday before they talked about potentially going somewhere. Yes, yes, yes, yes, yes, yes, I said. Yes, yes, yes, yes, yes, yes, my mother said. Then yes, yes, yes, yes, yes, my father said. We had been getting along beautifully and my father announced that we had actually *exceeded* our savings goal this month. The next day, my parents loaded up the car while I was asleep and woke me up with a plate of fried eggs. The sun shone on every corner of our apartment.

"I smelled eggs in my dreams," I said to my mom, and I yanked her arm down farther so I could lick soy sauce from the egg.

"Use these," she said, handing me chopsticks. "But hurry, okay? Traffic is going to be bad unless we leave before eight, and I want to see the Lincoln Memorial. It never looks the same in the dark. I'll have to call my boss when we get to New Jersey and tell him I'm running a fever."

Every once in a rarest while, my parents would just suddenly drop everything to seek adventure. For a day or a weekend or a weekend and a day, they would undo those gnarly coils of fear that were tightly wrapped around all the flexible points of their bodies, and finally let loose. I had no way to predict when it would happen, but every now and then, my parents would show me how to be free. The scarcity of these moments made me see how precious this freedom was, that it would always have to be saved up for, that it would only happen in reaction to long periods of constant emergency. It wouldn't be long before I started to resist identifying as my parents' child, when I would no longer show the right kind of gratitude for everything they did to protect me and lead me and guide me, when I would fight them on almost everything and blame them for who I had become. But for now, I was still their child—it was all I knew to be—and I was only free when they let me and when they let themselves be, and so, when it happened, I basked in it.

My parents initially wanted to go south. The plan was to follow the Atlantic coastline all the way to Key West. But when we entered Pennsylvania, my mom said, "When are we going to see California?" and my dad said, "When are we going to give our daughter all the things we want to give her without sacrificing a single dream that she deserves to achieve and without needing to take out major loans from banks that will most likely deny us?" and I said, "Can we go to McDonald's? I want a fish sandwich so bad," and the whole car at times shook on the highway like the earthquakes we might never be witness to unless we drove farther and with more intention and unity. I threw my legs up in the air during traffic jams to entertain the cars behind us, and when we got to Maryland, I said, "Let's rename this state Mandeland," and my parents cheered me on, and we all got out at the welcome center and stretched like lions, big and lazy.

I stopped in front of a penny-flattening machine. "Mom," I shouted at her as she walked toward the restroom. "For a quarter, you can turn a penny into a historic souvenir."

"For nothing, you can use a penny as a penny and not waste a quarter."

"Please," I said, "please, please, please." I slipped my hands into her pockets, picked out four quarters, and said, "It's time we send some souvenirs home to yeye, nainai, haobu, gonggong." My mom smiled at me like I was the very girl she was meant to bring into this world, which meant I belonged to every single place I ever stepped foot on, but most of all, I was hers, and she was mine. "Be right back, Mom."

I squeezed out four flattened oval pennies with my mom's quarters and pulled a quarter from my own pocket and squeezed out one more. Back in the car, I asked my mom to fish out an envelope and stamp from the glove compartment because she kept everything there: pictures of me, pictures of herself, lipstick and maps of every city she wanted to drive to one day, newspaper clippings of food she wanted to try, laces for our shoes in case we tripped and broke them somehow, aspirin and diarrhea pills, moist towelettes, ketchup and hot sauce packets, secret letters that I would never know anything about—who wrote them and for what purpose and to whom? My mother was the only one allowed to access that compartment of wonders.

In the car it was 60 miles to Baltimore and 890 to Orlando,

a few more after that to the Gulf of Mexico and we all wanted to get there. We were intent on a southern destination and we were prepared for the long haul. My dad played tapes of old Communist chants and we turned up the volume and filled the car with the voices of young boys and girls who had pledged to be lifelong revolutionaries for their country. The first song on the tape was the Chinese national anthem. My parents sang along in the car, their voices so different from what I was used to—clear, booming, and deep. The way they were sitting in their car seats, it was as if they were standing at attention. I listened intently:

Rise up! Rise up! Rise up!
We are millions with one heart
We will take the oppressor's gunfire and march on!
We will take the oppressor's gunfire and march on!
Rise up! Rise up! Rise up!

Rise up! All you who refuse to be slaves!
By our blood and flesh, we'll build a new Great Wall
The Chinese people now face our greatest challenge
Everyone must let out their lion roar
Rise up! Rise up! Rise up!

I yelled, "Dad, did you sing these songs and wear the same uniforms these kids are wearing?"

"Of course we did. We were tiny soldiers."

The next song was an anti-imperialism song, a word I had finally learned in school and curiously, it was presented as a neutral thing, nothing to be ashamed of:

It's not the people who fear American imperialism
But American imperialism who fears the people!

A just cause enjoys great support, an unjust cause enjoys none!
The laws of history can't be broken, can't be broken!
American imperialism will certainly perish,
And the people of the world will surely be victorious
The people of the world will surely be victorious!

"Is this song basically bashing America?" I asked, but my mother had turned up the volume even more, and so my question went unanswered. When the tape ended, my father was in a strange mood; he glanced back at me in the rearview mirror and I swore one of his eyes was leaking. "The old days," he said simply, saying no more about them, and then he brightened. "Today is the day I want to experience. Why would anyone need friends when you have the world's best family in your car on an open highway on the warmest weekend in February? Huh? Tell me that, someone? Mande? Do you know why?"

"I have no idea, Dad. Do you know, Mom?"

"Nope," my mom said and put a handful of sunflower seeds in her mouth. "You and your daddy are my best friends." I had prayed for this kind of soft joy, this kind of contentment, a day like this followed by more days like this, and finally having it was like being born, only instead of not remembering what it was like to be born, I was fully cognizant and participating in my own creation and suddenly it was clear to me why we don't remember what it was like to be born—because it would give us too much insight into what it will be like to die. To be present for your own birth was suicide. To know the true wonder of suddenly existing was to know the true fear of suddenly ceasing to exist. They had to occur together and there was no prayer for what I knew in my flaky soul—that there was no way to escape the fear. It would always be there, amplifying joy and stealing from it. Still, it was tempting to sink into it, to roll around in its outer rings where occasionally the fear converted to a kind of happiness that turned an entire afternoon into an image that would stay forever, loom forever, return forever.

We flew over the slower cars on invisible ramps built for us to get down south. We were probably going to buy sombrero hats for a dollar apiece and let them fall apart in the ocean if and when we finally got there, and I contentedly waited for my parents to say, "We have to go back now."

In the car, my mother had taken off her shoes and socks and had her feet up by the dashboard, and I noticed the little bumps by the sides of her toes, how she said she was born the daughter of peasants because her feet were so hard and we all haw-hawed that joke right off our knees—her parents and her grandparents were college professors and poets and government officials. There had been violent breaks in the lineage, but there had also been restoration and there would be even more to come; we had been granted everything in life and it was funny to pretend we hadn't.

My mother asked my father again about California, and he said to drop it, but she asked again, and a few minutes later, asked again, and then again, and again, and finally she drew out a long and husky sigh from the back of her lungs and said, "The western part of any country is always the most beautiful, and everyone should get to see the most beautiful part of the country they live in."

My father swerved across the two lanes to his right, parked in the emergency shoulder lane, took his hands off the steering wheel, opened the passenger seat door, and pushed my mother out of the car.

"Get out," he said. "This isn't your car. You didn't pay for any part of it."

"建军," my mother said.

"Get out."

In the car, I watched her grow smaller and smaller as we drove down the highway in silence. I prayed my father would see it had all been harmless—her voluptuous desire, his momentary flare of rage, the mistakes we had already made in this lifetime—it was all far from deadly, far from finite, there were still choices we couldn't fathom yet, futures we hadn't stepped into. *WILL THIS WORLD SURVIVE?* Yes, it had already and it must and it will.

I didn't need to speak to God anymore. I just needed to speak. I gripped the door handle and let the impulse to open it and hurl myself out become just another fantasy. We were going so fast I felt as if we had crossed state lines again. There was so little anyone could count on in this life . . . still I permitted myself to fantasize about how I would breathe normally again when my father, at the last possible minute, decided to get off at the next exit and turn back on the other side of the highway, how I would not let myself linger on the question of how she had gotten herself over the median and past six lanes of speeding cars, first in one direction and then another, and how instead I would just anticipate the moment when her tiny dot of a figure grew larger and larger until she was exactly the size that she had always been, and the relief I would feel in knowing that was never going to change.

Why Were They Throwing Bricks?

66 I lost hearing in this ear when a horse jumped over a fence and collided against the side of my face," my grandmother told me when she arrived at Kennedy Airport. I was nine and hadn't seen her in four years. "In Shanghai you slept with me every single night. Every week we took you to your other grandmother's house. She called incessantly, asking for you. 'Can't I see my own granddaughter?' I said, 'Sure you can.' But—let's not spare any feelings—you didn't want to see her. Whenever you were at your waipo's house you cried and called my name and woke up the neighbors. You hated her face because it was round like the moon, and you thought mine was perfectly oval like an egg. You loved our house. It was your real home—and still is. Your waipo would frantically call a few minutes after I dropped you off asking me to come back, and I would sprint all the way there. Yes, my precious heart, your sixty-eight-year-old grandmother ran

through the streets for you. How could I let you suffer for even a second? You wouldn't stop crying until I arrived, and the minute I pulled you into my arms, you slept the deep happy sleep of a child who has come home to her true family."

"I sleep by myself now. I have my own bed with stickers on it," I told her in Chinese, without knowing the word for stickers. I hugged my body against my mother who was telling my father he would have to make two trips to the car because my grandmother had somehow persuaded the airline to let her bring three pieces of checked luggage *and* two carry-on items without any additional charges.

"And did you see that poor man dragging her suitcases off the plane for her? How does she always do that?" My mother shrugged me away and mouthed in English to me, Talk. To. Grandma.

My father threw his hands up. "You know exactly how," he said and went off with the first two bags.

"You remember how uncanny it was," my grandmother continued, tweaking her hearing aid until it made a small shrill sound and then a shriller sound and then another even shriller sound. "They called me a miracle worker and I said, 'No, no, I'm just her nainai,' but everyone said, 'You're a miracle worker. You're the only one who can make that child stop crying.' They said there was no need for me to be modest. 'This child prefers her grandmother to even her own mother and father! Why sugarcoat the truth?' I had to stop myself from stopping other people from saying it after a while. Was I supposed to keep insulting everyone's intelligence? Protesting endlessly? Your nainai isn't that type of person. And the truth is, people don't make things up out of nothing. There's truth in every widely believed saying, and that's just true."

"What?" I said. "I don't understand Chinese that good."

"I knew you wouldn't forget a moment of your real life,

your real home—the place you come from. Have you learned English yet?"

"That's all I speak. It's America."

"Your nainai is so proud of you. One day your English will catch up. It's such a gift to be here now with you. You don't know how many lonely nights I've spent dropping tears for you. It was wrong of me to let you go. Remember how you called for me when you let go of my hand and boarded the airplane with your mother? Remember how you howled that you wanted to take me with you? Four years ago, your father wrote to me, 'You can't keep my own wife and child away from me any longer. I'm sending for them immediately.' I wanted to know if he ever considered maybe you and your mother simply didn't want to go to America? In those days, you would've rather eaten a basement full of rats than be separated from your nainai. Your father's also stubborn, but I'm not the type to insult the spoonful of food nourishing me. You see what I mean? I won't say any more. I'm living in his house now and even though he has only made fatally wrong choices, we still have to listen to him. But remember how at the airport you cried and said, 'Nainai, I love you the most of everyone. I want to stay with you. I don't want to go to America.'"

"I don't remember that," I said to my grandmother. "Sorry."

"You remember everything, don't you? But it hurts too much to dredge up bad memories." Her hearing aid buzzed again and she twisted its tiny hidden knob with her thumb and index finger. "This thing works for a moment and then it goes dead for days. Your father said he would get me a proper hearing aid so I can hear your beautiful voice. You speak up now and let your grandmother look at you. She's only missed you every minute of every hour of every second of every single iota of a time unit that's elapsed since you last slept with your nainai every night, refusing to even close your eyes unless I was in the bed with you. You know what everyone's favorite joke was? 'Who's the mom? You?' Oh, I laughed."

"That's not a joke."

"That's right. It was the plain truth," she continued. "They all asked me, 'Doesn't your granddaughter ever want to sleep with her mother and father?' And I had to tell them—not in a bragging way, just in an informing way—'No. Her father is in America learning how to build computers and her mother works late at the factory and even if her mother didn't come home from work so late, my granddaughter has made it clear she can only sleep with me. I know it's not proper while her mother sleeps alone in another room under the same roof, but when a child wants something, how can you look her in the eye and deny her?'"

My grandmother lived with us in America for a year. She taught me how to knit and after school, I watched her make dinner and do dishes and sew curtains. At first, I wouldn't let her sleep with me in my bed. She cried and came every night to my bedroom and sat at the edge of the bed saying nothing. She had small red eyes and no teeth at night, except for four on the bottom row and a couple in the back. She ate daily bulbs of garlic so she'd live to be 117 and see me grow for another forty-five years, and the first few times she brought it up, I imagined myself running away from home just to get a few years to myself, but after a few weeks, the smell was comforting and I needed it near me before I could close my eyes, and just when I started to call for her more than she called for me, my parents announced that she had to move back to China to be with her dying husband. "Your grandfather," my grandmother said with disgust, "says the only proper way for a man to leave this world is in his own home with his wife by his side. Have you ever heard anything so spineless?"

My grandfather had been begging her to come back for six months. He had been diagnosed with lesions in his throat and he didn't want to die without her. For a year, I had slept in her bed, pressed up against her like she was my bedroom wall, and after she left, I stayed in her bed for two weeks, refusing to return to my own bed even after my mother threatened to push me off if I didn't get out.

"This room reeks," she said. "It smells like several people have died. You still want to sleep in here?"

I nodded.

"On sheets that haven't been washed for weeks?"

I nodded. "She said she's coming back after Grandpa dies."

"She also said you'd learn English in middle school. She said she learned to drive in her dreams and that's how she'll pass the driving test and take you to Mount Rushmore for your birthday. You believe everything she says? Have you gone back in time and lost all sense?"

I shook my head. Finally, she and my father dragged me out, my arms wrapped around the cheap white lacquered bed frame as my father held my legs and my mother pried my fingers free.

"You're going to sleep on your own," my mother said. "Like you did before she came around."

"You hear your mother?" my father said, wiping the tears from my face and blowing softly on my hot red cheeks. "Just a day at a time."

"Don't indulge this," my mother said.

"You want to beat the sadness out of her?" my father said. "Because that's what your mother wants. For us to be the bad guys and her to be the hero when she comes back."

"I'm not inviting her back," my mother said.

* * *

My grandmother came back two years later. I was in middle school, and my pathetic puberty struck like a flash of lightning in the middle of the night—I suddenly saw all my surroundings for what they were: hideous and threatening. I had no friends, social life, interests, talents, breasts, straight teeth, likability, normal clothes, or charm, and every day I came home weighed down with dread. I started to fake illnesses so I could stay home with my two-year-old brother. I followed him around everywhere, crawling when he crawled and walking on my knees when he learned to walk so that we were the same height.

When my grandmother moved in for the second time, she told us that this time she wasn't leaving. She was going to apply for a green card and raise my brother until he was old enough to be on his own—eighteen, maybe nineteen.

"We'll see about that," my father said in Chinese, and then to me and my mother in English, "Let Grandma believe what she wants to believe. My gut says we'll be back at the travel agency in March, or my name isn't Daddy, problem solver of this house."

I laughed at him. "But that isn't your name."

I made a point of telling my grandmother that I'd been sleeping by myself this whole time. "I also know how to cut my own toenails and braid my hair and make my own snacks." My mom was looking at me without pleasure. "Hi, Grandma. I missed you," I added.

Then she was babbling, hugging me up and down and side to side. "Nainai xiang ni le," she said. "Grandma missed you, oh, Grandma missed you, oh, Grandma missed you—"

"'Kay, got it," I said.

She stepped back and took my hand. "Baobei, you can sleep with your nainai if you want, but your brother will too. I don't know if three will fit, but I'm very happy to try. Does anything make your nainai happier than having her two grandchildren by her side? Your brother will sleep with me until he's old enough to sleep in his own bed. Most people say thirteen is the age when a child learns to sleep on their own but most people are selfish and looking out only for themselves. Not me. I say sixteen. I say seventeen. I say eighteen. And if he needs me to, I'll gladly sleep with your brother until he's twenty-one!"

I laughed. "Allen's not going to do that. It's different here. We wrote you about this."

My grandmother pulled me in so close I faked choking noises to make my point known. "Oh, baobei, I missed you. My hearing has gotten worse. In China doctors are crooks and charlatans. They take your money and make everything worse, or if you're lucky, exactly the same. I lost my hearing in this ear running away from boys who were throwing bricks. Why were they throwing bricks? Who knows. There was a violence back then no one can understand now. And where did those boys get the bricks? That's the real question. In those days no one had brick houses. Everyone lived like animals. You wouldn't have been able to tell your nainai had skin as white as a porcelain doll because she was covered in dirt. These rotten boys chased me until I tripped over a fence and a sharp spike of wood pierced my eardrum. I lay there for a night until the shepherd's daughter found me, curled up like a child."

"I thought you lost your hearing when a horse ran over a fence and trampled you."

"They took me to the village doctor and he grafted skin from my knee to my ear. I was bleeding so much I thought I would die. That was the worst I've ever experienced, and I've experienced awful things. Your nainai has lived through two wars and saw her own mother gunned down by Japanese soldiers. No child should see their mother die. But do you know what was worse than lying there in the mud with blood in my ears? Worse than seeing my own brother come back from war with only half a leg and no right arm? It was living in China with your grandfather, who didn't have the decency to die like he said he would, and being thousands of miles apart from you and your brother. I was hurting for your brother so much I told your lowlife grandfather that unless he died right this instant, he would have to learn to leave this world just as he came into it—without me. What could he do? Stop me from going to America? I said to him, 'Come with me if you need me around so badly.' 'But no,' he says. 'I'm comfortable here. This is our home. You should want to live in it with me. These are our golden years.' Blah blah blah. My home is where you and your brother are. Oh, I've missed him like I miss the skin from my knee."

"You just met him today."

"Speak louder, my heart, so your nainai can hear you."

"My mom says I can only call my grandmother on my dad's side nainai, and you're actually my waipo."

"Your father said he's going to replace this hearing aid. I might as well have kept that spike of wood in here. They wouldn't know technology from the inside of their asses in China. And it's filthy over there. Can you imagine some illiterate doctor with dirty hands touching your nainai's ear? This is why I couldn't stay in China. I missed your brother's birth because your grandfather said he was dying, and then I go back and guess who isn't dying? Guess who's walking around the garden and smoking? Every day he goes to the lao ganbu huodongshi to gamble. Does that seem like a man on his deathbed to you, my sweetheart, my baobei? Do you think your grandmother will forgive your grandfather for making her miss the birth of her one and only grandson? Will your grandmother fall for his bluff again? Not ever. I'll be here until I pass to another realm, my baobei."

"I'm not going to call you nainai."

"All of my grandchildren call me nainai because nainai is the dearest, closest name you can call a person in your family. You refused to call me waipo when you were little. You said to me, 'You're not my waipo, my waipo is that strange lady over there who feeds me food I don't like and has a cold bed.' Remember how you said that? Where's your brother now? I missed him so much. I pray hummingbirds peck my eyes and leave their droppings in my pecked-out sockets before I have to experience this heartbreak again. But I'm healing already. When I see your brother's precious face, I'll never know sadness again. My heart will be overrun with joy until my last dying breath. Where's your brother, baobei?"

The third time my grandmother came to live with us, I was fifteen and my brother was five. "Please don't let her get to you again like last time," I said to him. "You were obsessed with her."

"No, Stacey. Was not."

But soon he was sleeping in her bed again and talking back to my parents and getting mad when I wouldn't let him have the last Rice Krispies treat. Whenever he was upset with me, he ran to my grandmother, and she would come into my room and pretend to spank me in front of him, when really she was just clapping her hands near my ass.

"Your sister is crying so hard from my spanking," my grandmother said to my brother. "See? Nainai is punishing your sister for taking what's rightfully yours. You hear how hard I'm spanking her? Her tears are everywhere."

"I'm not crying," I said over my grandmother's clapping.

"I'm not crying," I repeated until I was so frustrated that I actually did start crying.

My brother cried on the weekends when my grandmother went to work at a factory where she folded dumplings for five cents apiece. Most of the other workers could only do fifty an hour, and when the owner noticed my grandmother typically clocked in at a hundred and was teaching her trade secrets to the other ladies during their fifteen-minute lunch break, he instituted "quality control" rules, mandating a certain amount of flour on each dumpling and folds at the edge between .4 and .6 centimeters. My grandmother pointed out that he was arbitrarily docking pay for "unfit dumplings" without any real inspection, and all the dumplings she folded, including the unacceptable ones, were thrown into the same freezer bags, and that was exploitative. She convinced the other workers to collectively demand back pay for all the rejected dumplings, and even organized a walkout one morning for higher wages. "Six cents a dumpling!" they chanted. The owner caved, and that day my grandmother came home pumping her fists like she was at a pep rally. Listening to her recount the day's victory, even I had to admit that she'd done a great thing.

"Don't you worry," she said, "you'll grow up to be just like your nainai one day."

"See, Grandma's a hero," Allen said. "She can do anything."

"Ugh," I said. "She just did it to get paid more. What's so great about that?"

I tried to save my brother, but my grandmother was too cunning. When we walked around the neighborhood at night, he hid inside her big, long nightgown. If I tried to ignore them my grandmother would tap me on the shoulder until I turned around and then she would ask, "Where did your brother go?" and I'd begin to say, "Oh God, no, please no," but it was always too late—by then, my grandmother had already flipped up her dress to expose my brother, tumbling out from under her and onto the grass.

"I'm alive," he shouted. "I'm born. I'm born. I'm zero years old. I'm suddenly born."

"That's how you were born," my grandmother cried out. "It was beautiful and majestic and everyone cried, and I cried the most. When you fell out of me, you awakened the gods and made them turn this world from an evil, corrupt world into one that is good and beneficent, eliminating poverty and hunger and violent death."

"You have to stop doing this with her," I said to him. "That's not how you were born and you know it."

"Grandma says it is."

"She's wrong," I said.

"And when your brother was little," my grandmother shouted with her hands in the air as if waiting to receive something promised to her, "he suckled on my breast because your mother's milk dried up, but my breasts have always produced milk whenever my grandchildren were born. Your cousin drank from my nipple, too, but no one drank as hungrily as your brother. He drank until it was all dried up. And when it hurt for me to produce any more, he would cry out in anguish for it. I had to pray to the gods for more milk so your brother could go on."

"This is disgusting. This never happened," I said, but as usual no one was listening, not the trees that bent away from me, not the road ahead that sloped up and curved into a C, not my grandmother who only heard what she wanted to hear, not my brother who was being slowly poisoned by her, not my parents who didn't listen when I said they'd lose my brother if they didn't start spending more time with us. What time?

my father demanded. Yes, what time? my mother asked. Should we stop working and paying our mortgage and saving for your college fund? Should we go back to sleeping ten people to a room where someone's kid was screaming all night about needing to scratch her legs? Should we stop eating and stop owning clothes and a car for this "time" you speak so highly of?

But I knew what I knew. One day, he'd be sixteen and still cowering underneath our grandmother's dress, clinging to her before she woke him up, waiting for her to make lunch or clear away dinner, curled up next to her like a pair of twisted vines in the living room. Don't you want more than this? I would ask him. Don't you want to make friends and kiss someone you aren't related to? And he would say, No, I just want nainai, and then I'd see her next to him, with her toothless nighttime smile and small, satisfied eyes, and the outrageous lies she inserted into our lives until they became the strange trivia to our family history, and there was nothing any of us could do to stop it from being that way.

One afternoon I came home to an empty house. An hour later, I saw my brother and my grandmother walking down the street, hand in hand. He was sweating even though it was still winter.

"Why are you sweating like that?"

"I was jumping."

"Jumping?"

"Grandma did it too."

"She was jumping with you?"

"Yeah. On that bouncing thing."

"What bouncing thing?"

"There's a purple bouncing thing and Grandma said it was okay to play on it."

"You mean a trampoline?"

"What's a trampoline?"

I drew him a picture of our grandmother in her nightgown suspended over a trampoline, and in the distance, five cops with their guns raised and pointed at her. Over their heads, I drew a collective dialogue bubble: "Kill her! It's the LAW!!!!!"

"Oh, yeah, that's the bounce thing," he said, ripping the police officers out of the picture. "It was at the purple house."

"Let me get this straight. There's a purple trampoline in that purple house down the street where no one lives?"

"Not *in* the house. In the backyard. Grandma said I could jump on it. She did first."

"She jumped on the trampoline?"

"Like thirty times."

"Did you tell her to?"

"No, she just did it on her own. Then she was like, Allen, come jump with nainai."

"My God. You two are criminals. How many times did you do it?"

"Jump on the thing?"

"How many times did Grandma take you there?"

"I don't know. Every day."

"Jesus," I said. "Didn't you see my picture? You're breaking the law."

"No, we're not."

"Yes, you are, and you're going to go to jail if someone finds out. I could call the police right now," I said, walking toward the kitchen phone.

"Stacey, don't. Please don't put Grandma in jail."

"Who cares if she goes to jail?"

"I don't want her to. Please, Stacey."

"Who would you rather go to jail, then? Someone has to go. Mom or Grandma?"

"Mom."

"I can't believe you just said that."

"I don't know."

"This is stupid," I said.

"Don't call the police, Stacey. Grandma didn't do any-thing."

"Grandma didn't do anything," I said, imitating him.

She left that year after a neighbor's dog knocked her down against the asphalt. She split her head open and had to get stitches, several CAT scans that turned up inconclusive, and an MRI. She had overstayed her visa and we didn't have in-surance for her so the hospital bills ended up burning through several months of my parents' savings. They were never able to diagnose her with anything but she complained of frequent headaches and started sleepwalking. Once, our neighbor down the street, a retired judge who'd fought in Vietnam and walked on crutches, returned her to us. "She knocked on my door. Now I'm knocking on yours."

"We have to send her home or we'll have to sell our house just to keep her alive," my father said to my mother later.

"I know," she said. "She won't go. But I know."

Things reached peak crisis mode when one night my grandmother sleepwalked her way to the main road and stepped out into oncoming traffic, causing a four-car pileup and several police to show up at our door.

"I won't send her back in a body bag," I overheard my mother say to my father.

"We'll have to tell her that she either leaves on her own accord or INS will have her deported and banned from ever coming back."

"I'm not going to lie to her."

"Do you think she agonizes like you do every time she tells a lie? Look, I know you want to be fair to her, but this isn't the time to be virtuous."

The night my grandmother left, I told my brother she was never coming back and he tried to hit himself in the face with closed fists.

"You have to get used to this," I said, holding his hands together. "I know how you feel. I felt this way once too. I thought I was going to die without her. But it's not so bad. You think it is now, but it's nothing. You just have to get used to it. Every day you'll miss her less. And then one day, you won't even think about her at all. I promise. And you can always talk to me if you feel sad."

He wasn't listening. His face was red all over like someone had slapped every part of it. The only time I had ever heard someone cry as violently as he was crying was in a documentary about the Vietnam War. This village woman had jumped into her dead husband's freshly dug grave. She wanted to be buried with him. The sight and sound of her crying, seized-up body being dragged out of her husband's grave haunted me for days.

"This is a good thing, Allen. It's not even the worst thing you'll ever experience. Honestly, I'm happy. I'm happy she's gone, and you know what? I won't let you ruin this moment for me," I said, my voice cracking a little.

The fourth and final time my grandmother came to live with us, I was seventeen. My brother had forgotten her in the two years that had elapsed. He and I were close again. He slept on my floor or in my bed whenever I let him and played computer games with headphones on while I did my homework. He asked me to sit with him when he practiced the violin, which he was terrible at, though it wounded him if I laughed. When my friends came over, he lurked in the corner pretending to check the doorframe for bugs. I told him he couldn't always attach himself to someone, even though I liked it. I liked his small body leaning on mine in restaurant booths, or the way he pulled his chair up close to me at home and sat with half his body on my chair, and how he often said he wished I didn't have homework or friends so I could spend all my time with him.

My grandmother tried to get him to sleep with her at night again, but he only wanted to sleep in my room. He taunted her sometimes, like when she asked if he would get under her dress like old times, and he did, but then punched her between her legs and scurried out and into my room. That was one of many days when she came and sat on the edge of my bed, waiting for my brother to come apologize and tell her that he loved her and never meant to hurt her, but he never did.

This time around she was deafer than ever and wore hearing aids in both ears. They were a new model my father purchased at Costco but worked just as poorly because she'd only use five-year-old batteries. Sometimes I saw her in her bedroom taking old batteries out and putting new old batteries in. She'd developed new interests and was teaching herself calligraphy and the history of American Indians. "America belongs to the Chinese," she said. "We were the first to settle North America."

"I thought the Native Americans were first."

"The Indians are the Chinese. Christopher Columbus saw Chinese faces and called them Indians. We invented spices and gum and paper, block painting on wood and then move-able type for paper, paper money, gunpowder, fireworks, tea, silk spinning, alchemy, which later became modern chemis-try, navigational tools for maritime exploration, weapons for war and machines for peace. That is why China sits in the center of the map."

"Not in American classrooms."

"You should be proud to be Chinese."

"Nainai, the Chinese aren't Indians."

"The first Africans were Chinese. The first South Ameri-cans were Chinese. No one lived in Australia for a long time. The civilization there was and is backward. Just think—all of North and South America, all of Africa, and most of eastern Europe, all of Russia, Siberia—all first settled by the Chi-nese."

All of her was laid bare now—I saw her. She was just a little old woman, raised in the country without education or any of the basic things she had given my mother and my mother's siblings, someone who'd been told as a young girl that women were put on this earth to give birth and rear children and not be a burden in any way but live as servants lived, produc-tively, without fatigue or requirements of their own, yet had been resourceful and clever enough to come up through the feminist movement that Mao had devised to get women out of the house and into fields and factories, someone who had been given more power than any of the women in her lineage, who alluded to all the people she "saved" but never men-tioned the people she turned in during the Cultural Revolu-tion, someone whose hearing loss fed right into her fears of becoming useless, becoming someone others no longer bothered to address, and to counter those fears, she had to adopt a confidence that was embarrassing to witness, she had to maintain an opinion of herself so excessively high that it bordered on delusional. She tried to circumvent her obsolescence by making her children believe they would perish without her, and when they knew better, attempting the same with her grandchildren. But we were growing up, too, and it would be years before we had our own children, and by then, she would be dead. Buried or incinerated unless her garlic really did let her live to 117. I was old enough to understand how one of trauma's many possible effects was to make the traumatized person insufferable, how my grandmother's unwillingness to be a victim was both pathetic and impressive and made her deserving of at least some compassion, but fuck, why did she have to be so greedy for it? Why did she demand so much of it? Why did she require total devotion? It repulsed me that she wanted my brother and me to love her more than we loved our own parents, more than we loved each other, more than we even loved ourselves.

So I taunted her. I ignored her. I told her that she spoke Chinese like a farmer, the deepest cut I could have made. "Here comes the Trail of Tears," my brother and I would say whenever we heard her whimper and sniffle. We sometimes bet on how long she could hold out, sitting on the edge of my bed while we ignored her, before she went downstairs to practice her calligraphy. She had only a third-grade education and was teaching herself characters so that she could write a book about her grandchildren.

"The world needs to know about you two," she said. For a moment, I was moved. But I knew if either of us had any chance of growing up into the kind of people that other people in this world would want to know about, we had to leave her behind.

"You should write about your own life, nainai," I said. "People should know about you too."

"You and your brother are my life," she insisted, and

though it was not the first time, I felt genuinely sad that not only did she know very little about us, but we knew even less about her.

After I graduated high school, my parents took my brother and me on a cruise to Canada with some other Chinese families. The night before we left, my brother started crying and wouldn't tell my parents why.

"Are you worried Grandma will be alone in the house crying a Trail of Tears?" I asked him when we were alone.

He nodded. "What if she's too scared to be by herself?"

"It's just a few days, Allen. She's been through much worse."

"What if she needs help?"

"Then she can call Dad's cellphone and we'll rush home right away."

"What if we're in the middle of the ocean?"

"Then she'll have to wait a few hours for us to land back on shore and get a flight home."

"What if she can't wait that long?"

"Then we call a neighbor and have them check on her."

"What if the neighbor doesn't pick up the phone?"

"Then she calls 911, just like Mom and Dad showed her, and don't ask me what if they don't understand her because I know *for a fact* they have Chinese-speaking 911 phone operators."

"But what if that day they don't?"

"Allen."

"What?"

"You know what," I said.

"Don't you feel bad for Grandma, Stacey?"

"I mean, yeah, it sucks to be alone in the house, but she

can handle it. I know she can. She has to. That's life, it just is. Not everyone can have everything they want."

"But Grandma doesn't have anything she wants."

"That's not true. She got to go to America four separate times and live with us each time. That's what she wanted. That's not bad. Some people don't get to come even once. Ever think about that?" Allen's lip was trembling again. "Look, why don't we find her something really cool to bring back from the cruise. Wanna?"

"Yeah."

"Remember when you gave her that toothbrush we got for free on the plane? She still holds it up every night like it's a rare diamond."

"Oh, yeah." Allen laughed. "She said she wanted to be buried with it when she dies."

"I bet she did."

The cruise was so much fun we completely forgot to get her a gift. On the car ride back, I rummaged through my backpack and found an empty mini Coke can with a bendy straw stuck in it. We tossed the straw and wrapped the can in a food-stained pamphlet about onboard ship safety.

"We got you a present, nainai," Allen said.

"It's a souvenir we brought from Ontario," I added.

"Sorry we drank it already."

"Oh, my two precious baobei. You have given me a gift fit for kings." She hugged Allen then hugged me then hugged both of us in an embrace so tight that all three of us started crying for different reasons. Our father interrupted us to ask if anyone rang the doorbell while we were gone and our grandmother said no one really except one afternoon a police officer had shown up and yes, it just so happened she opened the door a crack to talk to him while holding a knife behind her back.

"A knife?" our father repeated with horror. "You were hiding a *knife* while talking to an armed cop?"

"How was I to know if his uniform and badge were real or not? I had every right to keep a weapon on me."

"If that cop had seen the knife, he could have arrested you," our father said. "Then he would have found out about your expired visa, and there'd be trouble for us all."

"Could he have . . . killed her?" Allen asked our father in English.

He gave a curt nod and went back to chastising our grandmother. "And who knows with these cops. You piss the wrong one off at the wrong time and who knows. You could be sitting in a detention center right now, awaiting deportation. This is why I told you not to answer the door for *any* reason."

"Well, no, he couldn't have, because I would have pummeled him without mercy if he so much as *tried* to step one foot through the door."

Our father shook his head and went downstairs to tell our mother what had happened. We figured out the next day that the cop had actually come to tell my grandmother not to turn on the sprinklers on Tuesdays and Thursdays because of new neighborhood ordinances. She had been turning on the sprinklers every day thinking our lawn was in dire need of extra watering, and some particularly meddlesome neighbor must have called the cops to complain.

"Someone complained about you, you know," I said to my grandmother. "They didn't like that you were using up more water than is permitted."

"Your nainai knows martial arts. If a bad guy came into this house, your grandmother would only need to look at him and he'd be done for. I could fling him through all the corners of the house and out the back door and that's just with my eyes alone. Now picture how it would be if your grandmother used her hands. Dead within five minutes. That's why I have to fight with my eyes. More humane."

"That's cool, nainai," I said. "You're very talented."

"I am. That's why I'll stay with you two forever and you'll never have to be scared as long as your nainai is in the house."

She left that summer. Her head injury from three years ago hadn't completely healed. She got headaches and started sleepwalking again. My grandfather wrote to her once more and told her that he was about to be diagnosed with lymphatic cancer. It was real this time, he wrote, and she had to go home and be with him.

"He's a liar, you know," she told me and my brother.

"We know, nainai."

"He's jealous that it's my fourth time in America when he's too chickenshit and complacent to come even once. He wants to take me away from everything I love. Why should I leave my grandchildren and my real home for that worthless sack of bones? I won't let you two grow up without the one person who matters the most to you."

She returned to Shanghai shortly before I went to college. My mother had to ask Allen several times if he was sure he wanted to stay behind at home with me instead of coming along to the airport. At the last minute, as my father was dragging the last of my grandmother's suitcases to the car, I said that I wanted to go with them.

"There's no room for both of you," my father said.

"Who said I wanted to go?" Allen said.

"Well, you can't stay alone," my mother said. "I suppose Daddy can stay with Allen."

"Forget it," I said. "It's too complicated and she"—my grandmother was kneeling down next to Allen, who was on the couch playing *Super Smash Bros.*, and she was trying to turn his body toward her but he kept shrugging away from her grasp, annoyed every time she caused him to mess up—"won't be happy if I'm the one who comes. We all know who her cherished angel grandchild is. She'd rip her ear canal out before she'd have me take his spot."

She wouldn't let go of Allen, and it was getting so late that finally we told her Allen was coming, which made him so mad he refused to look her in the eye.

"My own grandson won't even look at me because I've let him down so completely," she said. "I'm so ashamed. I'd rather die by his side than live a long life in China without him."

"He doesn't even give a shit," I mumbled in English.

When we got my grandmother in the backseat of the car, she kept motioning for Allen to sit on her lap while my father started the engine.

"I said I didn't want to go," Allen said, starting to cry next to the open car door.

"Oh," my grandmother wailed. "And now he's crying for me."

She tugged on Allen's arm until his elbow was resting on her knee, while the rest of him was angled as far away from her as possible. My father nodded at me, and I stepped in between them, prying her fingers off his arm with all my strength.

"It'll be too sad for him, nainai," I said quickly. "We love you, have a good trip, see you next time." Once Allen got loose, he ran into the house without looking back or waving. I slammed the car door and saw my father engage the child-safety locks. My grandmother was trying to open the door, banging on the window with her fists like an animal who had been feral and free her whole life. My father backed the car out of the driveway and drove up the C-shaped hill, away from view. I heard a familiar low whine by my feet and looked down to see one of her hearing aids on the ground.

"It's like you just won't go," I said, kicking it away from me, then running to pick it up, cradling it in my hand and tenderly brushing the sediment away from its face like I had done when I found my grandmother three years ago, fallen on the asphalt, bleeding from her head.

The night my grandmother told me she was leaving for the third time, I felt strange inside. My father reassured me she would have the very best doctors back home, who would figure out what was going on with her headaches and sleepwalking, and once she was healed she could come back again. I wanted her to get better but I didn't necessarily want her to come back. I lay in bed until everyone was asleep and then crept downstairs and snuck out of the house as I often did back then. I circled the neighborhood under a sliver of moon and imagined being born to a different family. On the walk back, I stopped in front of the purple house, then followed the stepping stones to the backyard.

I had a feeling she would be there and she was, crouched by the chain-link fence, facing the purple trampoline. "Nainai," I called out, even though I knew she could not hear me. I wanted to jump with her. Though I would forget in a few days, though my resistance to her would rise again the next and last time she came to visit, in that moment, I felt her loneliness and it scared me.

She stepped forward and then she was running so fast that she looked like a young girl, no longer saggy and round in the middle. She was a straight line—something I could understand, something I could relate to. I closed my eyes, afraid she would trip. When I opened them again she was high in the air, her dress flying up. I knew there might come a time in my life when I would want to sleep next to her again, return to her after the uncertain, shapeless part of my life was over, when no one would mistake me for a child except for her. Her children and her children's children were children forever—that was how she planned on becoming God and dragging us into her eternity.

I was about to run to her, to reveal myself, when I realized she wasn't awake.

"Mother," she said, jumping on the trampoline. "Mother, I didn't want to leave you, but I had to go with Father into the mountains. Mother, you told me to take care of my brother and I let him fight and he lost his legs. Mother, I let you down. Mother, you said you wanted to die in my arms and instead I watched our house burn with you inside as I fled to the mountains. I told Father I wanted to get off the horse and die with you and he gripped me to his chest and would not let me get down. Mother, I would have died with you, but you told me to go. I should not have gone."

I took a step toward her. Her eyes were open but they did not see me. In the dark, I thought I would always remember that night and be profoundly affected by having seen her this way, but it was like one of those dreams where you think to yourself while the dream is happening that you must remember the dream when you wake. That if you remember this dream, it will change you, unlock secrets from your life that would otherwise be permanently closed. But when you wake up, the only thing you can remember is telling yourself to remember it. After trying to conjure up details and images and coming up blank, you think, Oh well, it was probably stupid anyway, and you go on with your life, and you learn nothing, and you don't change at all.

You Fell into the River
and I Saved You!

Reunion #1

I
t was my fault our families had to play with watermelon
seeds instead of real poker chips because, earlier that day,
I had flung all the chips at the birch tree that shaded our living room, and I only regretted it later when my aunt mentioned she saw a bird choking on something.

"A poker chip?" I asked her.

"Possibly," she said.

My uncle Shawn had brought his deluxe poker set from his
house in North Carolina, which I had visited once when I was
nine. On the car ride back I wrote an essay, "My Favorite Place
and Yeeeahhh It's a Real Place!" where I described each of the
rooms in his house and the various Monet watercolors and
framed photographs of the old American West that I had been
enamored with—they were a sign of patronage, a sign of having so much money that it had to be squandered on objects
with no purpose except to be beautiful or interesting. (Only

later did I realize that they were also a sign of having unre-
fined taste, that there was another whole class of people who
would have found my uncle's art collection garish.) It was a
real house with long corridors and real Oriental-with-a-
capital-*O* rugs, though later I found out some were Persian
rugs from Iran, a connection that confused and delighted me,
even if the connection was made up by white people who
would never consider moving the continent of Asia to the
center of the map or redrawing the continents to scale so that
South America became the emaciated drumstick dangling off
the shriveled forefinger of the withered arthritic hand of
North America that it really was. No one who believed in the
"discovery" of America could stand to see Europe as anything
but centered or America as anything but inflated.

But even more amazing than the artwork and the four bed-
rooms and the two and a half bathrooms and the finished
basement with a minibar and entertainment center and the
Oriental rugs that were steamed clean every six months was
that my uncle lived in a *gated* community. When my father
drove our sputtering maroon Oldsmobile up to the booth by
the gate to tell the attendant we were here to see the Qiu family on 14 Willow Creek Drive, we felt like the wretched and
the needy, a couple of peasants crawling up to the gates of the
royal palace, asking to be let in, to see what we had only heard
about, to confirm that not only anything we had ever dreamed
of was real but things that we had not yet been able to dream
existed too.

Wrought iron with gold fleur-de-lis tips, my uncle told me
on a walk around his gated community.

Whatta whatta golda? I said, making him laugh and repeat
himself more slowly.

Let's move here, I begged my parents each time the gates
opened up for us, and my father said, Why wait? We're al-

ready here! But five days later, we were back home in our tiny apartment in Bushwick that collapsed only a few weeks later. I submitted my essay to a writing contest and won a ribbon from my teacher, the first time I had ever been commended in school, and I kept it clean and unwrinkled and pinned permanently to my special-occasions crushed velvet dress. My mother had taken a set of photos with me holding up my essay in my velvet dress and ribbon and sent them to my uncle, who in return took a set of photos of him holding up a sign that read CONGRATULATIONS! over his mouth, which was so big and wide that even behind the white construction paper I could make out the faint contours of his smile.

Those days were long past. My uncle and my aunt had driven fourteen hours to see us before moving to Thailand for my uncle's new job developing face creams for men.

"I don't understand," my mother said to my uncle the first night they arrived. "What do men need face creams for? They're *supposed* to have terrible, rough-looking faces."

"So did women before face creams were invented," I said.

"She's got a great point," my uncle said, putting his arms around me. I shrugged them off and longed to be somewhere where I could say anything I wanted and still be left alone.

My cousins Maddy and Tony were seven and six. They were going to go to boarding school in Massachusetts next year, and my parents had promised to visit every month to make sure they were settling in okay. I was fourteen and didn't want to be involved in any of this, but I was a part of it as always, and as always, everyone kept asking me, What's wrong? Are you okay? Is something bothering you? At night I flung my pillow against my mattress and prayed to my fake jade statue of the Guanyin goddess to give me a different face so that people would stop looking at my current one and asking me what was the matter.

On our last night together as two families we decided to play poker. We had been playing for an hour, and Aunt Janet was beating everyone, and no one was good except her, and none of the betting was fun because of it, and between each play she turned to my sister, Emily, and cooed at her like she was a little baby hamster.

"She's three years old, you know," I said to Aunt Janet, slurring a little from sneaking sips from my father's glass of Rémy Martin all night long.

"Three is still a baby," she said and turned to my sister again. "Now, isn't it? A goo goo goo goo. Isn't your auntie right, you big baby? Ga ga goo goo coo coo." I looked at her with disgust and she returned my gaze with a kind of simple sweetness, like I could hate her but I couldn't cut her, I could never destroy the fullness and the aggressiveness of her joy. She tried to shame me into conspiring with her, but I could not. I wanted to feel tenderness, I wanted to be more generous, but I could not. I was sure I had always been sour. Our sour girl, my parents used to say back when we all woke up in the same bed.

Am I still the sourest girl you know? I asked my mom when I came back from China and saw that her eight-months-pregnant belly prevented her from seeing the tops of her feet, her distorted, callused feet that I had spent so many evenings rubbing and clipping and sanding down and soaking, evenings when I would literally lie by her feet and massage them and run a warm towel over them—they were hidden now, they were the least of her concerns, she had a baby on the way. I was going to be a sister. I was no longer going to be her only child.

Always, she said.

Will she be sour too? I pointed at her belly. Will she become one of us?

That's the dream, sourheart.

The next day I woke up thinking I was born angry.

Is it too late to abort, I said to my mother, knowing that it was already too late for so much. The day they decided to send me away, I already knew this, but still, I could not accept it.

Oh, sours, she said,

No, I said. I don't eat sour things anymore. Grandma taught me to eat sweet peaches and scoop out sweet watermelon with a spoon. I'm a sweet girl. She said so. And you, I said, hesitating before continuing, you're here just giving me bullshit after bullshit. Even as I said those words, I knew it sounded like I was testing them out. My mom had tiny little tears trickling down her face, but I lowered my eyes and turned away from her then.

I know change is difficult, but I promise—

You know shit about me, I said, interrupting, changing into someone I knew I wouldn't be able to stop becoming.

"I don't want to play anymore," I said to my aunt. "I'm done with this game."

"C'mon, Chrissie," my uncle said, reaching over to rub my shoulders. "Let's just have some harmless fun tonight." I stared icily at my aunt who was laying out the flop. Her darty eyes rankled my heart, made it sour like the last pickle in a decade-old jar of brine, and I knew there was nothing wrong with her eyes, darty or not, and I knew there was nothing anyone could do about the way their eyes darted just like how I couldn't do anything about the resting frown on my face, and how I didn't mean to start ninth grade with a face that looked like it wanted to spit on anyone who asked me a question. I had vowed to find it within myself to see what I didn't understand as adventure rather than a particular kind of hell, to be someone who was moved by other people's attempts to be good and had the ability to sense the love in a room before anything else, but it was too hard. I could not.

"Nah," I said, getting up and then stumbling back into my chair. "I was defending Emily. Why does she talk to her like that? Is everyone here against me?" I climbed onto the table, scattering the watermelon seeds.

"Zang si diao le," my mother said.

"I can't understand what you're saying, Christina," my father said, his face looking old and exhausted.

"Come down and join us, sweetheart," Aunt Janet said, as if I could have been teetering on the ledge of a hundred-story building or on the second step of a staircase—it was all not to be panicked over. "It's fine. We can pause the game and get some snacks. How does that sound?"

"I wanna shoot you with this gun," my cousin Tony said, pointing his Lego gun at my face. "Boom, boom, boom, boom, boom—"

"Tony," my cousin Maddy interrupted. "You done yet? You've killed her. Are ya happy now? You've killed our favorite cousin."

"You see?" I shouted, the Rémy Martin gurgling through my gut. Was I standing anywhere significant? No, just standing on the table my father built when he was thirty-seven and I was nine and my mother was thirty-six, a time when the three of us would spend entire afternoons walking down Fifth Avenue, stopping at every pay phone to check for change. My father used to lift me up and let me push my sticky, candy-coated fingers into the change slot. Ka-ching, I said when I felt Washington's raised, chiseled face, or the copper-nickel of the American eagle. "See, some people still love me," I said, swallowing my vomity burp back down.

"Xia lai before you hurt yourself," my mother said.

"There's no need for this, Christina," my father said.

"Why don't you come down, Chrissie? Maddy and Tony really want to get some playing time in with their favorite cousin," my uncle said.

"We all want to," my aunt said.

"Don't listen to them," my cousin Maddy said. "Christina can do anything she wants."

"Boom, boom, boom, boom, boom, boom," my cousin Tony said.

"Is Chrissie going to throw up?" my sister asked our mother.

"She'll be fine," my mother said, extending her hand to me. I took it though I didn't want to be touched and fell into her arms. "I would slap you if your aunt and uncle weren't here right now," she hissed in my ear before pushing me away.

"Go ahead," I dared her. "Hit me and get it over with. I know you want to."

"I don't like you this way," she said and I said, "Well, neither do I," and ran up the stairs.

In my room, I grabbed a half-drunk two-liter bottle of soda and poured it over my carpet. I pretended it was gasoline and that I was setting the whole house on fire. I considered going back down to repent, to proclaim that I was sorry for it all and sorry for having been born, that I believed in God now and not just the five-dollar plastic Guanyin goddess that sat high on my shelf, but as soon as the sour bile of preserved duck eggs and lake shrimp and chicken and tomato and scallion and rice and string beans and ground pork rolled up through my stomach and into my throat and out my mouth in an upward-curving trajectory through the air before plopping down by my feet, I knew that nothing was going to change. I would spend the next hour tearing things off my wall—embarrassing lyrics from a Sunny Day Real Estate song ("forward on/to the place we sail") that I had scribbled on construction paper, a poster I bought at a tourist shop in Little Italy of construction workers eating lunch while sitting unharnessed on a girder suspended high above the city that I later found out was really just a staged photo to promote a skyscraper that had been built during the Great Depression, flyers for basement shows and anarchist rallies that I never went to but felt were somehow my destiny, and cheesy pictures of JTT and Devon Sawa and Rider Strong and Leonardo DiCaprio that I tore out of the *Tiger Beat* magazines I stole from 7-Eleven, doing the unimaginative thing of drawing penises and breasts over their faces when what I really wanted was to mush my breasts into their faces, sincerely and without malice. When there was nothing left to rip off the walls, I would go back downstairs, where everyone was still sitting around, eating and chatting, and pretend not to regret anything. I would remain angry. I would grab food off the table and go back into my room to eat by myself, and in the morning, I would be angry still and angry the next day, and even when I no longer had the strength for it, even when I was sure that I no longer wanted to feel like I was being balled up into a fist, I would only become angrier when I realized that I was incapable of unclenching.

Reunion #2

"In the golden days," my mother told me when I was twenty-two and about to leave her and our home for the third time, "our family would gather around the dinner table to listen to your grandfather—your father's father—tell stories."

"Your mom means the old days," my father said, explaining the only part of my mother's reminiscence that was in English. I didn't blame my mother for her verbal mishaps—

she only learned English when she was thirty, and my father liked to say she wouldn't have learned it at all if she wasn't born beautiful and meant to stay that way for the rest of her life. Not long after we immigrated to New York a man approached her while she was waiting to check out Chinese books from the public library and offered to tutor her in English for free. He scared her during their first lesson, the way he kept inching closer to her when talking so that she had to back up her chair until it was against the wall. He kept offering more and more things to get her to come back: a can of soda, a deli sandwich which was later upgraded to a *gourmet* deli sandwich, which was then upgraded to a *gourmet* deli sandwich *and* soup. Despite my mother's misgivings, she kept going back because no one in my family has ever been known to refuse free services.

"The shining days," my mother said in English before continuing in Chinese. "I often think about those days. There was so much food on the table that we worried about it collapsing. We ate fast, like a bunch of deprived animals after the winter thaw. Your father always had to loosen his belt after the first round of eating. You think it looks like he's carrying a watermelon in there now? Try going back in time and he could really show you a watermelon baby."

"I thought there was no food back then."

"Mo wo de arm."

I touched her shoulder even though I already knew what her skin felt like—smooth and cold, my greatest source of comfort on warm summer nights.

"Mei you hair. Do you know why?"

"Because you were born into a famine?"

She nodded. "I didn't get my lao peng you until I was seventeen either."

"I thought that was because you were so tiny. And that's

268

why I was so tiny? Dad, remember how Darling pretended she couldn't see me because I was so small and she'd pick up a Cheeto from the floor and be like, Crispy, is that you?"

"What a clown," my father said.

"What's wrong with clowns?" We had been getting into it a lot lately but my mother wasn't interested.

"I do come from a family of small women, but my body needed nutrients it wasn't getting. Too much stress on a girl's body can keep her from becoming a woman."

"Doesn't that happen to those creepy little gymnasts? You think they're ten and then you find out they're like twenty-two."

"Yeah, but we didn't do it to win medals. It was done to us." My mother went and got some plums from the refrigerator.

"Please tell me these are sour," I said to my father, who did the shopping this week and was notoriously bad at picking out fruit sour enough for me and my mom.

"I think you'll be pleased," he said.

My mom bit into one and gave me the thumbs-up. "I used to steal grapes from our neighbor. He kept this really nice grapevine after the worst of the famine passed."

"It wasn't like, boom, famine's over," my father clarified. "We were still hungry all the time. It wasn't starvation exactly either. Let's just say I don't remember ever going to bed on a full stomach as a kid."

"That's right. But I did have this neighbor with a grape-vine. Poor guy, he never figured out how to keep me and my friends away. We'd steal the grapes before they ripened. We thought they were delicious. Or I did. The other kids ate them out of desperation, but for me they were the finest grapes I had ever tasted. Even till this day."

"Lucky," I said.

"The food situation did get better after you were born.

And your father's family had more access than most because your yeye nainai fought in both wars."

"The civil war and the war against Japan," my father explained. "So they were ranked pretty high up."

"They'd get extra rations and little privileges like that. It's even better for them now. They're considered lao ganbu. When they die, they'll be buried in a locker room full of the ashes of martyrs. It has the best feng shui in all of Shanghai."

"Fung shway?" I pronounced it the way my white freshman-year roommate had pronounced it when she informed me that her white Buddhist boyfriend was going to perform a Tibetan blessing on our room and clear it of bad energy. Not that I have to explain it to you, she had added, trying so hard to respect me that it became disrespectful. Right, I had said. I don't need to know more. "I thought that stuff was bullshit. Like something celebrities get into to cover up the emptiness of their lives."

"No, it's real," my mother said. "That's why we didn't buy that house with the pool. It was at the bottom of the hill. It's really bad feng shui to let everyone else's shit roll down into your house."

"Your mother takes that stuff very seriously."

"And it's a good thing I do! Tell me, is our house cold in the winters?"

I shook my head.

"Is it hot in the summers?"

I shook my head again.

"It's because the entrance to our house sits north and faces south. That's no small detail. The spot where your grandparents' ashes will one day rest is the most peaceful in all of Shanghai. Your father and I took a tour of the place in March. You can't hear the traffic outside at all. It's very still."

"Weird. I don't get how feng shui works."

"Common sense," my father said. "It's just paying attention to your surroundings. It's like how Americans have a knack for laziness. No one taught them how to slack off at their jobs. No one taught them to get away with doing the least amount of work possible, and yet they're the best at it in the whole world. They're born with it. It's the same thing with feng shui for us. It's innate."

"Not for me," I said.

My mom reached out and stroked my hair. "Well, you're a rare breed." I beamed at her touch, though it stung to know I was leaving the next day. The three of us had stayed up after Emily went to bed to finish packing and go through some of the boxes I had shipped home after graduating from college. Months prior, I had accepted a job teaching English at a French high school outside of Paris. Doing what your daddy couldn't, my mother had remarked when I told her my plans.

It's even worse over there, my father had said. It's all reversed because their suburbs are our Brooklyn. Dou shi hei ren he a la bo ren. You won't have many French kids in your classes, I'm guessing.

I had been offended by his insinuation. They're all French over there. It's *France*. And anyway you really have to catch up. Brooklyn is the land of art galleries and trust-fund anarchists who dumpster dive as a lifestyle choice. I'm sure in five years Emily will end up dating, like, a terrible performance artist living in a loft in Bushwick.

At the time, France had seemed so incredibly far away, and the overwhelming number of things I had to do to get ready for my move had kept the immensity of my decision from sinking in, but now that all there was left to do was get on a plane, it was starting to hit me—I was moving to another continent, this time of my own volition.

"So yeye nainai are veterans?" I asked, looping back to an unfinished strand.

"Sort of," my father said. "Though they didn't see much action."

"They were extremely fortunate," my mother added. "Plenty of cadres survived both wars and ended up purged anyway. My father wasn't so lucky. His father had been a land-owner and his mother a schoolteacher. So he was stripped of his ranking even though he joined the Party early on. He vol-unteered because he believed in the Communist credo. Your grandfather was a man of ideals."

"And we all know how well that works out," my father said.

"My father's younger brother was jealous that my grand-father had willed his property to my father so he tried to stir up trouble. This was before anyone understood what the con-sequences were."

"What were the consequences?"

"A public hearing for anyone accused of being a counter-revolutionary," my mother replied.

"Well, that's putting it mildly," my father said. "It was a public humiliation."

"What did that entail exactly?"

My mother shook her head. "No reason to relive those days. Anyway, they never had a chance because my father went up to the top floor of my elementary school and jumped out the window."

"Oh my God. He committed suicide?"

"He tried, but he survived. He broke both his legs and was sent to the hospital. The Party leaders said that was proof of his guilt. Thankfully my mother was an extremely resourceful woman. Her sister—my aunt—was a nurse at the hospital and my mother instructed her to give him a lethal shot of potassium chloride. He died before they could smear his reputation. That was what he wanted."

"Damn," I said. "That's a rough way to go."

"That wasn't even the end of it," my father said. "People talked and the plan was found out. Your great-auntie was sentenced to hard labor at prison camp up north for twenty years. And your grandmother was never the same. She blamed herself for not wanting to divide the estate with your grandfather's brother."

"Originally my father had been planning on sharing it with his brother. But my mother convinced him that was foolish."

"It wasn't her fault," my father said. "She did the best she could. It was chaos in those days. People were poor like you wouldn't believe."

"It wasn't all bad. There was a kind of freedom back then. Kids could do anything. Really anything. You could say, Mom, Dad, I'm going to travel the country for three months. And take off. Just like that."

"There was no adult supervision. Kids were out on the street. No one gave a damn if you skipped school and fucked around all day."

"And then schools were closed for a few years," my mother said. "We thought we were so lucky."

"Really?"

"Well, yeah," she said. "Weren't you glad any time you got to skip school?"

"I was fucking ecstatic. I hated school."

"So imagine that lasting for years. It was like a permanent vacation."

"You can't give young people that much freedom and not expect chaos. Kids were wilding in the streets," my father said.

"Sounds crazy."

"It was," he said.

"I kind of miss it. Every single day you could go downstairs and find your friends playing outside. It was nice. I remember being nine and thinking, Just let me stay this age forever." I waited for my mother to continue. She was gone from us for a second and then she was back. "Did you know your father went all around China by train and on foot?"

"You Jack Kerouac-ed, Dad?"

"I was young and foolish." Now it was my father's turn to slip away from us and then come back. "Your mother was with me for part of it. We were how old?"

"It would have been chu er for you and chu yi for me."

"So basically middle school," my father calculated.

"Yes," my mom said.

"I tried to flirt with your mom but she was immune."

"There was no flirting back then!" she said.

"They opened the trains for 'revolutionary youth.' That's what they called us. That's how they justified it. We were encouraged to leave home and see our country. Broaden our vision and really see how the people lived. We got free passes to travel anywhere, stay anywhere. We thought, No parental supervision? Hell, yeah!"

"The trains were unbelievably crowded. In some cars, people were literally piled on top of each other. You had to crawl over hundreds of bodies just to get out. After the first day, I thought for sure I was going to suffocate to death from being so tightly packed in."

"So I spot your mom at one point—we had gone to the same school but were in different grades—and I always thought she was pretty, but that day on the train, she was glowing."

"I was miserable," my mother clarified.

"I decided to work up the nerve to approach her."

"You didn't really consort with people who weren't in your class, especially if they were of the opposite gender."

"Finally as the train is about to enter this village outside of Pingxiang, I approach your mom and I'm like, Hey, let's get off here. I've got an uncle who lives three kilometers away from the station. He can put us up."

"Did you go, Mom?" My mother looked at my father and my father looked at my mother. "Okay, if Emily was up, she'd be so grossed out right now."

"Your mom can't resist me."

"I keep falling for him, is what it is. There was no uncle. It would have been romantic if it hadn't been a total setup."

"Now, wait a minute, my uncle *was* there but then he got reassigned to Sichuan. I had no idea! It wasn't like you could just email someone back then. So we ended up in this village. Didn't know a soul, but it turned out my uncle was beloved there. He made a really good impression on the villagers and when they found out I was his nephew, they welcomed us like we were family. We partied our asses off. Your mother was *wasted* the first night. They had this secret stash of alcohol. It was *foul*. They insisted we drink with them. Help us drain the evidence! they said. So we did. I tried to kiss your mom but even six drinks deep, she still rejected me."

I laughed. "Good move, Mom."

"You see how your father's always been this way?"

"It was a great time," my father concluded. "It was *better* than I promised."

"Okay," my mother said, getting up to throw away our plum pits. "We have to wrap this up and get you packed for Paris."

"Montreuil," I corrected.

My father glanced up to the clock. "It's already two in the morning? Let's get the scale out and weigh your suitcases."

"Don't you want to stay up all night with your firstborn before she goes off to a scary new country?"

"And crash the car taking you to the airport? I'm not about to chance that."

"I guess we are overdue for that kind of thing," I said fearfully.

My mother gazed at me with amazement. "Our baby's going to France."

"Our baby's no longer a baby," my father said.

"Let's stay up all night!" my mother said, suddenly exuberant.

"Okay!" My father perked up, too, we all did. "Car crash on the way to the airport it is!"

It was everything I wanted before I had to go.

Reunion #3

More and more, I no longer remembered my days in Shanghai. I was only one and two and three and three and a half when I lived there, and ten when my parents sent me away to live with my grandparents for six months, and twelve when I visited for four weeks, and thirteen when I visited for three weeks, and fifteen when I visited for ten days, and nineteen when I visited for four days, and twenty-one when I visited for ten.

When I was twenty-one and visited for ten days, my cousin Fang, who worked for a German pharmaceutical company where she corresponded with her boss in the form of handwritten letters in English that she faxed throughout the day and worked weekends as a voice-dubbing actress for American cartoons that flopped in the U.S. but were big in Asia, explained some things to me about our grandfather. "Grandpa's side of the family was dirt-poor. No one in the generation above him lived past the age of forty. When he was fourteen they sent him to this village to work for a rich family who was looking to basically purchase a full-time laborer."

"Like an indentured servant?"

"Yes, exactly. He hated it so he ran back home but his family wouldn't take him back. They were like, Oh you're a loser, you're a failure, you're a good-for-nothing—that kind of stuff."

"Why?"

"You're not supposed to come back empty-handed. You come back when you've made it. And he lasted . . . two weeks? A month? He was an embarrassment. So his family kicked him out and told him to go back to the village and fulfill his duties."

"That sucks. I probably would have lasted one day."

"Me too. So our grandpa's hometown is right at the base of Lao shan. It's really beautiful. Clear springs, stunning waterfalls. It's like a painting."

"Oooh."

"I'll take you there next time you come."

"Can't wait."

"So he's got nowhere to go and he runs up into the mountains and falls asleep against a tree. He *loved* to sleep."

"Hee hee," I said. "Now I know where I get my good genes from."

"Right?" she said. "It's the Zhang family curse. Anyway, all he wanted to do was sleep. He was exhausted. When he was working for the family, they only let him sleep four or five hours a day. So he slept in his clothes, freezing all night. When he woke up in the morning he thought he was going to die up on that mountain, but thankfully a high-up army commander was out doing some kind of reconnaissance and found him."

"And then?"

"And then he was conscripted into the army."

"Wow, so his laziness got him a job."

"Exactly. The funny thing is, his unwillingness to work saved him a bunch of times. But you know how it is. This family has always been lucky. We've always had fortune on our side."

"This family," I repeated. "I never realized it, but you're right."

Reunion #4

When I was ten, my mother took me to Shanghai. It was supposed to be a good thing but I didn't see it that way. When you come back, you'll see. Everything will be different. We'll live like fat little princes, she promised me. I don't believe anything you say anymore, I replied. She was six weeks pregnant at the time and I was the last to know. All I knew was that she had been appointed by my dad's mother to bring me to Shanghai to live with my grandparents while my parents got back on their feet. They paid for our plane tickets and even sent along a pair of hand-knit socks with twenty dollars stuffed in each sock so we could buy snacks at the terminal before boarding. Later, when I was an adult, my mother admitted that she had begged my father's mother to let her be the one to take me, even though it would have made more sense for my father to go so he could see his own parents.

"Is this, like, your way of telling me that you couldn't bear to be separated from me?"

She smiled in that way she'd let herself smile ever since I was grown, ever since I wasn't so wounded by every instance when she acted not just as my mother, but as her own person with her own needs and her own fears and her own dreams.

"Is that why you stayed with me in Shanghai for a whole month? Because you wanted to make the transition easier for me?"

She smiled again.

"Wait," I pressed her, "what's the real reason why?"

"That was one of the reasons."

"But what else?"

"What do you think?"

"Because you wanted to get away from Dad?"

"Ding ding ding ding ding."

In the weeks leading up to the trip, I had started scratching my skin raw again and my itchiness was exacerbated further when I got to China and found that everything, including the bedsheets and couch cushions, was rough and uncomfortable and smelled faintly of mold, piss, and shit. I was sullen from the shock of not knowing the place where I was from. Everyone stared at me when I went outside. Waiters and shopkeepers asked my mom if I was deaf or dumb or mute or just plain stupid when I took too long to answer their questions.

In the evenings, I sat around at my grandmother's house and waited and ate oranges and grapes while the adults cooked food I never wanted to eat and then apologized for not having a hamburger or fried chicken or hot dog on hand. I wanted to say that I didn't even like hamburgers or fried chicken or hot dogs all that much, and that actually my favorite food was Chinese food, just not the Chinese food in China. After dinner, everyone talked at each other and over each other as if there were not enough hours left in the day to get everything out and so it all had to happen at the same time—the listening and the expressing and the laughing could not happen one after the other but instead had to coalesce on top of each other into a massive cloud of noise. My silence was conspicuous, it signaled something, and everyone wanted to dissect it and make an emergency out of it. I was quiet not because I didn't have anything to say, but because I was overwhelmed by it all, and I didn't want anyone to pity me or laugh at me or throw their hands up in the air at the absurdity of a Chinese person who couldn't speak Chinese. I didn't want to promise to learn Chinese perfectly because I still needed people in America to look at me and know instantly that I spoke perfect English instead of looking at me and assuming that I didn't know how just because I was quiet. I took my parents at their word when they said my time in China was temporary, and if it was temporary, then I wasn't going to commit to being a Chinese person in China when I already had so much trouble being a Chinese person back home.

My relatives in Shanghai took my silence to mean that I was lonely or sad, or that I didn't like it in Shanghai, or I didn't like the food, or I was bored with the television shows, or I was unhappy with the bathrooms, all of which was basically true, especially my displeasure with the bathrooms since the one in my grandmother's house really did smell of fecal matter. The smell was so repulsive, I couldn't stand to be in the bathroom long enough to expel shit from my own body, and by the end of my first week in Shanghai, I was so constipated and backed up that I had to be hospitalized, which would have been embarrassing if I hadn't already embarrassed myself by sobbing on the toilet the night before when I thought I was finally going to drop a turd, but it turned out to be nothing more than a massive fart. Other than that incident, though, I was all right. In fact, I was doing much better than I had been in the weeks leading up to leaving New York. I was coping like a goddamn champ, as Darling used to say to me whenever I showed up to my father's class. "The goddamn champ of the world is here," she would say, pretending to rub the top of my head like she was shining a trophy to put on display.

After I came back from the hospital, having expelled all the shit that had been backed up inside me, I decided to try to do the thing my parents had been pushing for all along: be less attached to them. For years, when they encouraged me to go off on my own, I would think: So you do it too. Be less devoted to me, then. Don't love me so much that it becomes all I know.

How was I supposed to know that they would follow through on my dare? That they would actually push me away? You'll have to harden your heart against us, my mother used to say to me. Whether you like it or not, there'll come a time when you'll just have to do it. We deluded ourselves into thinking that there was some way to prepare for it, like twisting your baby tooth a little bit each day until it was loose and then you only had to touch it with as much pressure as a feather against a rock to make it fall out painlessly and beautifully.

After months of crying and begging and arguing and bargaining and planning and delaying, it suddenly happened. We got two plane tickets and a pair of socks in the mail one week, and the next week I was at the airport with my mother, clutching her hand and then letting it go and then clutching it and then letting it go again and then finally just clutching my own two hands like I was about to bump a volleyball. I didn't even wave goodbye to my father as we turned the corner through the security gate. I had no idea he would spend the summer painting houses and becoming the man we not only deserved but dreamed of. Everyone I knew agreed. It was never too late to change. So we did. The family I hadn't known long enough to care about would be my family once I got to Shanghai and the family I never wanted to be separated from, the one that I had based my entire identity on, whose love was the only thing I was sure of, would have to become something else.

I was three and a half when my parents and I moved to New

York. My mom ordered a phone line right away even though in the winters we could only afford heat a few hours at a time. In the beginning, she called Shanghai every other week. My mom would put me up on a stool so I could reach the phone that was mounted on the wall and say into the receiver in Chinese, "I love you grandpa, I love you grandma, I love you big auntie, I love you middle auntie, I love you small auntie, I love you uncle, I love you cousin, I love you favorite uncle, I love you auntie who just married my uncle, I love you cousin who I never met, I love you grandma on my mom's side, I love you great-grandma and the spots of dirt on your head that look green in photos, I love you great-auntie, I love you great-uncle, I love you nephew who is older than me and who I never met and who is visiting us soon, I love you all and wish you good health in the coming year." My mom would rehearse the speech with me over and over before calling, and even though I knew exactly what I was supposed to say into the phone, I never said a single word. My mother would take the phone from me and sheepishly say, "Did you hear her? She speaks very softly." I knew that I had failed somehow, even though I didn't understand at the time what was so dire about telling someone on the phone that you loved them. What made that more significant and profound than knowing you felt it—a warm and settling love that heated your insides and worked its way into your dreams at night? I revisited that question every time my relatives pressed into me, waiting for me to say something to relieve them of their fear that I would always be distant, that I would always keep myself hidden.

A week after we arrived in Shanghai, my mother went out to see her high school classmates and as soon as she left, my relatives cornered me and asked me questions like, "All these houses you lived in—wasn't it tiring after a while?"

"Yes," I said solemnly. "It was a hardship," I thought I was saying to them in Chinese, but I was really saying, "It was a man."

"A man? I thought she was a woman," they said, referring to my father's girlfriend at the time. "A man, you say?"

"Yes, a man," I said.

A few days after I went to the hospital and took so many laxatives that I couldn't sit down without tricking my butt into opening and thinking that I was going to take a shit, my cousin Fang sat down next to me after dinner (which I ate ravenously, to the satisfaction of my aunts and uncles and grandparents) and asked me what sort of music I liked. She was four years older than me; we had grown up together in my grandparents' house before I moved to New York. I didn't know her very well anymore. She talked with me about a popular boy band whose sixth member was a real live monkey, and as she was talking, I could tell that she thought I thought she was boring, and I could tell she wanted me to feel an alliance with her, and I could tell that she could tell that I didn't remember growing up with her and needing her all the time when I was a baby, and I could tell that she thought need was the basis of any familial relationship, and I could tell that it pained her whenever our grandmother mentioned the time my cousin drew my face in the dirt after I left for America with my parents, because when our grandmother told that story it never moved me the way it moved our grandmother, which was always to tears because it reminded her of all the times people in her life had left her, whereas for me, none of it impacted me much, at least not in a way that was easily read by others, and I knew that my indifference disturbed my cousin greatly.

"You know," she said to me after a long silence during

which we ate watermelon with seeds (I swallowed all the seeds and she picked them out, even the white ones, which were soft and nice to chew), "when you were three, right before you and your parents moved to America, the whole family took the train to the country and had a picnic. You wanted to go into this cave very badly. For some reason, that day your parents gave me permission to take you. It was pretty small, but still—can you imagine? The two of us, three and seven years old, alone in a cave. You were overjoyed. I was really happy too. It was nice to go exploring on our own for a while. At some point, we found a small river running through the inside of the cave. You wanted to hop over it like Sun Wukong. Remember those comics about the monkey who has all these magical powers and hangs out with a really uptight monk? You were obsessed. I told you never to copy him. I said, You know Sun Wukong isn't real, right? You know that real people can't fly and part trees with their fingers, right? You asked me why not, and then suddenly, there was a big splash and you were in the water. I knew you'd panic once you realized where you were so I jumped in and pulled you out."

"There are rivers in caves?"

"Yes. There was one in this cave."

"And I fell in?"

"Yes."

"And you saved me?"

"That's exactly what I did."

"You did?"

"I really did."

"Are you sure?"

"Yes."

"Did you just remember this?"

"No, I've always remembered."

"You never forgot?"

"No," she said. "How could I forget it?"

"I can't believe you saved me."

"I really did. You fell into the river and I saved you!"

We both laughed at how something like this could have happened, and after that I no longer looked at her and wondered what it would have been like to know her instead of just knowing that she was my cousin and I was hers because our mothers told us so. We had endured something together. We were family now.

"I think I might be obsessed with jumping into rivers," I told my cousin.

"Oh, yeah?"

"I jumped into this river back in New York a couple of weeks ago. It was really gross. There were solid human dumps floating everywhere. I might have even swallowed some."

"No!" my cousin yelled, the two of us almost screaming with laughter at the thought of me guzzling human turds as I breaststroked my way across the river. I didn't tell her my family had been trying to sink our maroon Oldsmobile, that I had felt a kind of nebulous fear I had never experienced before, this fear that I could never go back, and I didn't know if it meant I couldn't go back to dry land or back to my parents or back to our home or something even worse, like from this point on, I could never go back to the person I had been—whatever it was, I felt like it was closing in on me and I had to swim far and fast to escape it. I didn't tell my cousin any of this and instead I just bragged that I parted that sea of decaying stools and almost got myself halfway to New Jersey.

"You crazy girl! You still think you're a magical monkey who can fly and do the impossible," my cousin said, barely able to get out the words in between laughing.

"That's me. Crazy monkey girl reporting for duty." I made a mental note to reread my old Sun Wukong comics so I could keep up with my cousin's references.

Later that night, I told my mother while we were getting ready to brush our teeth, "I actually don't mind it here," to which my mother replied, "I'm so relieved to hear that, sours. Oh, you have no idea how happy it makes me to hear you say that. I knew you'd come around."

From that moment on, my cousin and I were together every minute of every day for the next six months until my mother surprised me by calling in the middle of the night, giddy as anything. "Oh, sours, this is the greatest news I've ever gotten to deliver," she said over the phone. "Your father, your brilliant, brilliant father has finally done it."

"What?" I said with disinterest. "What has he done now?" What he had done was the noble thing of actually saving up money and finding us a proper apartment that we could live in until he saved up even more money for an even more proper house. He was a hero, finally. He had done what he couldn't do the night I jumped into the Harlem River. He finally figured out how to take care of us. Later, I found out that my grandparents had gifted my family five thousand dollars from their life savings because my father had written several times, pleading with them to consider some solution that didn't involve me living on the other side of the world, especially now that there was another baby on the way.

The next time I went back to Shanghai with my parents and my baby sister, my cousin and I were strangers again—I felt as warm toward her as a fish toward a frozen pond, and I tried to remember how it all felt two summers ago when we rediscovered each other, and I tried to remember how she saved me from drowning and how that meant we would always be close, but it was futile. My cousin and I were beginning to understand why our grandmother cried so often, and how there were so few options for coping with the reappearances and disappearances that we would both continue to make in each other's lives.

Reunion #5

"You really lucked out, Emmy," I said to my sister after she showed me and our parents around her new Brooklyn apartment.

"Right," she said, scrolling through her phone. "I'm *sooo* lucky I get to pay thirteen hundred dollars a month to live in a glorified closet in Williamsburg."

"It's not"—my mother paused to choose her words—"what I would have picked. But I'm not you."

"Remember that apartment we had in Williamsburg, Mom?" I asked.

"I'll always remember that apartment. It had a bathtub!"

"And that teddy bear that was taller than me. I used to hug it every day after school." I pretended to cry. "Because no one was home to hug me, waaahhh."

My parents laughed.

"Was it as dinky as this place?" Emily asked.

"Oh, it was the king's palace," my father said.

I took Emily's phone from her hand. "No, you wayward twat, it was ten thousand times worse. Our whole apartment was the size of your room."

She snatched her phone back. "I'm sending snaps."

"Your sister is being a sourpuss," my mother said. "It was a great apartment. One of the best we ever had."

"Let me guess," Emily said, trying to record us on her phone but my mother and I covered our faces right away. "You paid like five hundred bucks for it?"

"Less," my father said.

"Less?"

"Less."

"I'm seriously going to cry if you say four hundred."

"I think it was about two hundred bucks a month," my mom said.

"How's that even possible?" Emily said. I didn't know either how any of it had been possible. It was one thing to live through it, it was another to remember.

"We paid even less when we were in East Flatbush," my father said.

"I love how you guys lived in all these places and never made friends with a single black person," Emily said.

"Why would you assume that?" I said.

"I have eyes that work?"

"Let's go for a walk around the neighborhood," my mother suggested. "I haven't been back here in over twenty years."

We went outside and walked past a cold-press juice bar, a coffee shop run by Australian surfers, a cocktail lounge that specialized in absinthe cocktails, and a fusion tapas–dim sum restaurant.

"Is this how you remember it?" Emily asked.

"Not at all," my father said. "We used to step over drunk Polish men passed out in the streets and Puerto Rican kids who dealt drugs on the corner."

"You think all Latinos are drug dealers, Dad," Emily said.

"He really does," I agreed.

Our mother walked ahead of us, turning the corner onto Driggs. "This is it," she said. "That's where we used to live."

We caught up with her and stood across the street from a construction site.

"Oh my God," Emily said. "Is that an *apod*ment?"

"It was a two-family house when we lived here," my mother said.

"That's one way of putting it," my father said.

"Not *apart*ment. *Apod*ment. They're like teeny tiny luxury apartments for tech bros who can't give up dorm life."

My mother gave no indication she'd heard my sister. "Do you remember?" she asked me. "It was a shabby little red house with vinyl siding. I thought it was adorable. Your dad thought it was hideous."

"It was very nice for a flophouse," my father conceded.

I nodded, trying to remember. "How the hell did we ever get that place?"

"The landlord felt bad for us."

"Cause we were—" I searched for the right word.

"—because you guys were so raggedy back then?" Emily guessed.

"We were pretty raggedy," I agreed.

"No," my mother said. "Actually it was because of Tiananmen."

"When we went to see the place the owner started grilling us about life in China," my father said. "Your mom barely spoke."

"My English wasn't very good then."

"The guy was like, Are you afraid to speak? You're afraid the government's tracking you, aren't you? You think they're listening, don't you? Once he realized we were from China, he started speaking at a whisper."

My mom laughed. "He actually thought we were dissidents or something."

"Which was stupid because if we were leaders of the student movement, how the hell could we already be in the U.S.? Tiananmen had only happened two days before."

"He must have thought of himself as some kind of defender of American democracy. He kept saying, You're safe here. I'll make sure of it."

"Which was bullshit," my father said, "because the guy was a slumlord."

"Fuck," Emily said. "I love it when you can get stuff out of low-key racists."

My father seemed offended by the idea. "He wasn't a racist. He was just extremely ignorant."

"Your father's talent is benefiting from other people's ignorance," my mother added.

"Wow," I said. "I don't remember this at all."

"I mean, he did have some reason to believe we were dissidents, I suppose. We had come straight from the demonstration. You were still carrying the sign your mother made. You wouldn't let me take it from you. So, in a strange way, the timing worked to our advantage."

"We went to a protest?" I was really shocked now.

"You don't remember?" Emily asked. "There's video footage."

"There is? How do you even know that?"

"I watched it. Mom and Dad kind of looked like some far-out radicals back then."

"Emily took all our old videos and photographs and got them digitalized," my mother explained.

"I told Mom and Dad it was time to stop living in the Paleolithic Age."

"How did we even afford a video camera?"

"Oh." My mother smiled. "Your dad stole one."

"I literally do not remember that."

"Yeah, your mom was mad at me so I drove to The Wiz, thinking I'd get her something." I knew he meant scam her something but I didn't want to correct him. "I had just parked and for whatever reason, I looked down and noticed a receipt on the ground and picked it up. It was for this really nice camcorder. So naturally, I went inside and found the same make and model and tried to return it. It was a lot of money! I told the woman at customer service that my credit card had been stolen and she was really nice about it. She said she couldn't do a return since I didn't have the original form of payment but I could exchange it for something else. I couldn't think of what else to get so I got a slightly crappier model and convinced the woman to refund me the difference."

"Of course you did," my mother said.

"Okay, this is too much," Emily said. "I literally go back into the store when they accidentally *undercharge* me."

My dad was horrified by the idea. "Why would you ever do that?"

"These places dock their employees' pay if the till is off. I'm a law-abiding citizen, Dad."

"We only had the camera for a year or so," my mom said.

"We had to pawn it to buy your mom a plane ticket back to China when your grandmother died."

"The footage is pretty cool," Emily said. "I was thinking of making a video with it."

"You want to make a video of a video?" my father asked.

"It's for her"—and I curled my fingers into air quotes—"*art.*"

"Mom and Dad had on white headbands with, like, fake blood on them."

"We cut up one of your dad's old white undershirts and tied them around our foreheads. I think we drew on them with red marker to represent the blood of the slain students."

"You begged your mom to let you wear one because all the adults had them but your mom said no, it was too morbid."

"I was not about to let my child wear a bloody rag around her head."

"It was symbolic," my father said.

"It was real life."

"Damn," Emily said. "You guys went hard."

My mom started walking again. "Let's keep going."

"You don't want a picture?" Emily asked.

"Of what?" my father countered and pointed at the building under construction. "That?"

My mother shook her head. "I don't feel very photogenic today." We walked in silence for a bit, passing another juice shop and a cheese shop.

"And I thought this whole time we had just gotten lucky for once," I finally said.

"We did get lucky," Dad said. "We were lucky to encounter someone who was gullible and suffering from whatever guilty conscience led him to approve our application even though we had no savings or credit."

We were approaching North Sixth now and my mother stopped in front of a junk shop. "Heping. It's still here."

"Did you used to shop here?" Emily asked.

My mother nodded.

"Life really is a circle," my father said.

"I can't tell if that's totally depressing or totally comforting," Emily said.

"Me either," I said, feeling a fraction of what my parents must have felt—old and plump with the familiarity of how we had once been.

Reunion #6

The day my father quit his job and swore off teaching forever after finding out his school was being shut down by the Department of Education and all the teachers were going to be reassigned to even worse districts, he came home with a map of the world and a tin of silvery thumbtacks.

"Of all the things you could have taken, you chose that?"

my mother asked him, looking up from chopping vegetables in the kitchen.

"First of all, I'd much rather take back my sanity than any material object and second of all, I want to show our sourpuss something important." He laid the map down on the floor and beckoned me over. "Right here is where your mommy was born." He set a thumbtack down next to a unnamed part of the map near the East China Sea. "She moved to Shanghai when she was three."

I was into it right away. "Like me but opposite."

"Exactly. And here is where your grandfather—Mommy's daddy—was born and this is the town where he discovered oil and started his own business. Your first auntie was assigned to work in this village when she was fourteen and ended up staying for ten years. Your second auntie lived on this island for a few years. It was considered a good assignment. It was only a half-day journey by boat to Shanghai, so I saw her more frequently than your first auntie. She was supposed to help build windmills but ended up marrying the mayor of the village after his wife died."

"That's why she's so fat," my mother added. "She never had to work."

"Your little auntie lived here for two years."

"In Russia?"

"No, but it was right by the Siberian border. She delivered babies. She hated it. She told me she used to retch before, during, and after. There wasn't much to eat so she really messed up her stomach and throat."

"Poor thing," my mother said. "She refused to marry when she came back. Rejected every guy we tried to set her up with. She said none of them were suitable but I think it's because she was too traumatized to want children of her own."

"Could be," my father said, putting two thumbtacks on a thin lizard-shaped island. "Now we actually have some family in Malaysia—here and here—and a very distant uncle in Pakistan. They escaped during the civil war."

"How did they escape?"

"They went by foot through the mountains."

"They climbed mountains?"

"It was pretty rough. You had to have a lot of stamina. Some people went by boat to Hong Kong if they were lucky. A lot of desperate people tried to swim. Speaking of Hong Kong, your mother has two cousins there."

"Never met them," my mother said.

"Did they swim or take a boat?" I asked.

"Probably boat," my mother answered.

"This right here is where your uncle first landed," my father continued.

"Atlanta?"

"Atlanta, Georgia. He was a prodigy in China. Ranked number one in all of Shanghai and number three in the entire country for his particular field."

My mother came over and stood next to us. "We were so proud of him. He was part of the very first wave of students. He got accepted everywhere. Colleges were competing for him."

"Is that why he lives in such a nice house?"

"Could be," my father said. "It was great for us because then he was able to sponsor us."

"We got really lucky," my mother said. "It was really rare for a sibling sponsorship to go through."

"How come we don't live in Atlanta?"

My mother stood up. "It's a tragic story," she said and went back into the kitchen to finish dinner.

"He got a temporary job in New York after he graduated,"

my father explained. "I think he got along well here but then his first wife was hit by a truck on Canal Street on her way to work and died instantly. He met your aunt Janet the year our visas were approved. She was about to start school at UNC so he moved down there with her."

"I don't want anyone to get hit by a truck and die," I said.

"No one's going to die, sourheart," my father reassured me. "Daddy's here to make sure of that."

"What if you or Mommy gets hit by a car?"

"We won't. Because we always look both ways, isn't that right?"

"Sometimes you just walk without looking," I said, draping my body across his lap.

"I'll never do that again. Okay. This is our final destination. Here is the town where your grandmother was born and right next to it is where your grandfather was born. My mom and my dad. That's where it all started."

I sat up and studied the map. "So many places."

"I think it's time we take a road trip. What do you think sours?"

"How about tomorrow?"

My father laughed. "Maybe, if your mom agrees. Wanna ask her?"

I called my mother over and she sat down next to us to look at what we'd made. "Wouldn't it be nice if instead of all this"— and she traced the thumbtacks we had set over all the places where we had family—"being scaled to the whole world, wouldn't it be nice if this were our own private continent?"

My father considered it and came up with a better solution. "Maybe we can think of this as a blueprint for our future home with a big backyard and—"

"—a pool!" I suggested.

"And a pool for sours, naturally," my father said.

My mother sighed. "It would be so much easier."

I wiped a tear from her cheek. "What's wrong, Mommy?"

"I'm okay," she said, pressing her wet cheek against mine. "I just miss my family." It was jarring to hear her refer to someone other than me and my father as her family.

My father tried to console her. "We'll just have to get rich and rent a big house and fly everyone to us."

"Sure," she said, suddenly switching to anger. "I'm sure that'll happen. And when it does, we can build a special wing for whoever your mistress is too."

"No way," I said immediately and then mushing my words together, "No cunts," but my parents were only hearing themselves now. They went into the kitchen and left me alone with the map for a while. They argued back and forth, my father vowing to get rich and my mother countervowing to get richer so she wouldn't have to be dependent on his extravagant promises, which were more and more becoming lies. My father kept saying he would take care of this family and why didn't she ever believe him and my mother kept saying she'd believe it when she saw it, which, she added, would certainly be after she was dead so unless ghosts really did haunt this earth she would never ever see it or believe it. After a long while, they finally came out of the kitchen and told me we were going to McDonald's for dinner.

As we were putting on our shoes, my father said, "Okay, here's a promise I *know* I can keep. I vow that if my father lives to be a hundred years old, I will plan the most epic reunion. I'm talking every single person who is related to us. Whatever it takes. I will make it happen. And then we can all go to our graves satisfied. How's that?"

"That's ridiculous, Heping. I told you to drop it."

"Can we just make up?" I said, tugging on my mother's jacket sleeve. "Please?"

"Okay," my mother relented. "Okay, let's make up."

The next morning, I was the first to wake and saw that someone had hung our map on the wall with all the thumbtacks pushed in, and a big circle drawn around New York City with the number "2024" written next to it in black marker.

I crawled back into bed and woke up my parents. "What's 2024?" My father's eyes were still closed and my mother was nestled into the crook of his shoulder. They tried to pull me in between them but I resisted. "Why did you write 2024 on the map?" I asked again.

"Oh," my father said, slowly taking me in, still heavy with sleep. "That's when we'll have our reunion."

"That's ridiculous." My mother's stance hadn't changed since yesterday, though this time I swore her voice was weak with hope.

"Something to look forward to," my father said, and it was, and I did, even after our apartment collapsed and we had to be concerned with what would happen the next day and the day after that and the day after that until we were living hour to hour, minute to minute, and even then, I still believed in my father, who insisted there had to be something—anything—to look forward to.

Reunion #7

Tomorrow is my grandfather's one hundredth birthday and so I decide to grow what some people might think of as wings, but what I think of as a natural desire to collect my family, which I do, sweeping down into cities and towns and villages I've never been in before and pulling each person close to me for a brief moment before throwing them into a sack.

Hello, I say to each member of my family as I pick them up from their homes or their place of work or the restaurants where they are having their lunches or the recreation centers where they are shooting the shit about old times, and I say: hello, hello! hello there, hello remember me, I'm your cousin, remember me, I'm your niece, do you know me, I'm your second cousin, remember me, I'm your twice-removed cousin, have you heard of me, I'm your littlest aunt and I held you when you were born, I'm your great-grandniece, I'm your granddaughter, it's really me, your daughter, your sister.

The answers I get are: no hi yes yes yeah yup dang ran ji de sour angel I've missed you ning ning baobei is it really you you can fly piao liang gu niang it looks like your eczema's flared up again do you still speak Chinese you look old.

When I was three, I asked my aunts where humans came from and they started to talk about a woman opening up like a blossom for a man who loves her, and I said, No! The first human, where did they come from? My first aunt said, No one can really say, but I think, and my second aunt interrupted her and said, God created all of us, and my third aunt interrupted and said, The first humans came from monkeys. She then hunched her shoulders and lowered her arms and started to hoot like a monkey, and I jumped into her arms like she was my mom and these were our normal bedtime games. When I scoop up my third aunt from the hospital in Tianjin where she works, she says to me, But do you even remember how I was with you? I used to wipe your butt when you were a child, and I taught you about God and where humans came from.

Monkeys, I say, we came from monkeys.

Yes, and also God, my aunt reminds me.

I pick up my grandfather last. He's wearing a collar with no shirt attached. Looking good, Grandpa, I say. Xiao ning ning, he says, calling me by my first name, the one my parents dropped when we got to the States, the name I didn't think about again until I went back to China and my idea of home became a problem once more. Ning ning's home, my grandfather called out with unrestrained glee to the rest of my family as soon as my mother and I pulled up to his house in a taxi. He had been waiting outside for us all morning. Never forget, he had said to me on the first day, when my body was shaking all over, unable to accept that it had to remain still in the country where I was born. Your first three years were here. I already forgot, I responded, panicked, in bad Chinese, meaning to say the opposite, that I *wouldn't* forget.

Of all the voices speaking to me, it is my grandfather's voice that I hear the clearest. Where is my little world-traveling granddaughter coming from now? he asks. Weren't you in St. Petersburg last year? Or was it Berlin? Or Budapest? Or Buenos Aires? Mexico City? Manila? Bangkok? Seoul? All of those places, Grandpa, I say, tightening the bag.

Is there a home for us somewhere? I ask the bag of my family, and immediately, I hear muffled votes for New York! Shanghai! Beijing! Shandong! Wenzhou! Heilongjiang! Tianjin! San Francisco! Williamsburg! Los Angeles! London! Bushwick! Paris! Sichuan! Hunan! Hong Kong! Washington Heights! E Flat!

I try to take in all their suggestions but there's too many and still more coming in. Without knowing exactly where I am, I begin to descend. We will all live to see this moment, I say into the bag of my family. We will land wherever there is solid ground, I promise. Everyone cheers and tells me they will go wherever I take them. There are so many voices talking at once to each other and to me and over me and over each other that I am suddenly flooded with an old, familiar anxiety from when I was younger and my life was filled with people who were my family for one minute and strangers the next, when we shared our home with other families who were close enough to hear our secrets but not close enough to understand them, when I would get so overwhelmed by the people around me that I would wish everyone, even my parents, could disappear, and when they did, when they left me alone for a few hours at night, I'd blame myself for letting the thought of living without them cross my mind, certain that of all the things I had ever wished for, this would be the one to come true and the more I thought about it the more I froze until I was gripped in a loneliness so stunning I could only stand still, surrendering myself to it and replaying every moment of the last few hours, reenacting all the conversations adults had around me, all the conversations I should have joined, all the phone calls back to Shanghai I should have participated in, only this time, I responded with the words that I thought were expected of me, and I said them, exactly as gracefully and graciously as they were meant to be said, sounding them out in my head and whispering just the beginnings of each response out loud: I am so grateful for . . . I know you tried your best . . . May you have . . . I wish I could offer . . . I don't need . . . When I grow up . . . I hope one day . . . I do miss . . . yeye nainai I . . . I'm sorry I didn't . . . Well, my favorite . . . I'm very fond of . . . I remember . . . It was wonderful to . . . Funny because . . . I plan on visiting . . . Ha ha ha . . . I don't want to be so . . . You know what I miss . . . Studying has to be a priority . . . You're right . . . I'd like to try . . . I shouldn't have been so . . . I know what you . . . No one is more beautiful . . . If you don't want me to I won't . . . Yes, I will come and see you . . . and it went on like that until my parents came looking for me, and without me having to ask, they would lie down next to me, sensing exactly the kind of exhaustion I was trying to outlive, and pet me and ask me questions that required no answer. How did we end up with such a sour girl? How did we get so lucky? they'd say, clearing away the frantic voices of who I thought I was supposed to be, and though I knew it wouldn't last forever, I stayed between them until I remembered who I was again and no longer felt lonely.

Acknowledgments

Thank you, Kaela Myers, for guiding these stories into adulthood and seeing the true creature inside each one. To Samantha Shea for bestowing so much faith onto this book that I eventually had it too. To Andy Ward, who right away welcomed these stories with warmth and generosity. To Lena Dunham, for offering this book a home—thank you for reviving what I was ready to give up.

And to the whole team at Random House & Lenny who worked on this book, often without me knowing—the rarest and most undeserved of privileges to possess and I did—thank you.

I am grateful to Linda Swanson-Davies for being the first to accept a short story of mine and rooting for me to keep going. And to Tavi Gevinson for plucking me out of a slush pile a year later and offering a space for me to roam free.

Heartfelt thanks to my teachers and classmates at Stanford and the Iowa Writers' workshop who read me, wrote me, and fought for me, especially Rick Barot, Edward Carey, and Marilynne Robinson. My deepest gratitude to Samantha Chang and Connie Brothers for supporting me without exception.

To Adrian for exceeding my dreams.

To my friends: Durga Chew-Bose, Harry Chiu, Leopoldine

Core, Anthony Ha, Benjamin Hale, Sarah Heyward, Leslie Jamison, Alice Sola Kim, Tom Macher, Karan Mahajan, Monica McClure, Anna North, and Vauhini Vara, who went through it with me and cared for me through all my whining and spiraling.

To my chosen brother, Tony Tulathimutte, who read these stories at their limpest and nurtured them till they were stronger, and because of it, they are, and I am too.

Finally, eternal love to my family in Shanghai and New York. To my nainai, yeye, haobu, gonggong—I am always trying to reach you in my baby tongue. And to my mother, father, and brother, who made this book with me, who speak to me in the finest, most private of tongues, who have loved me without stipulation and protected me from what I want—thank you. You are my only home that is constant.

JENNY ZHANG is a writer and poet
based in New York.

jennybagel.com

About the Type

The text of this book was set in Filosofia, a typeface designed in 1996 by Zuzana Licko, who created it for digital typesetting as an interpretation of the eighteenth-century typeface Bodoni, designed by Giambattista Bodoni (1740–1813). Filosofia, an example of Licko's unusual font designs, has classical proportions with a strong vertical feeling, softened by rounded droplike serifs. She has designed many typefaces and is the cofounder of *Emigre* magazine, where many of them first appeared. Born in Bratislava, Czechoslovakia, in 1961, Licko came to the United States in 1968. She studied graphic communications at the University of California, Berkeley, graduating in 1984.